SECOND-HAND STIFF

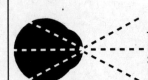

This Large Print Book carries the
Seal of Approval of N.A.V.H.

AN ODELIA GREY MYSTERY

SECOND-HAND STIFF

SUE ANN JAFFARIAN

THORNDIKE PRESS
A part of Gale, Cengage Learning

GALE
CENGAGE Learning·

Farmington Hills, Mich • San Francisco • New York • Waterville, Maine
Meriden, Conn • Mason, Ohio • Chicago

GALE
CENGAGE Learning®

LIBRARY OF CONGRESS CATALOGING-IN-PUBLICATION DATA

Jaffarian, Sue Ann, 1952–
  Second-hand stiff : an Odelia Grey mystery / by Sue Ann Jaffarian. — Large print edition.
    pages ; cm. — (Thorndike Press large print mystery)
    ISBN 978-1-4104-6662-4 (hardcover) — ISBN 1-4104-6662-0 (hardcover)
  1. Grey, Odelia (Fictitious character)—Fiction. 2. Legal assistants—California—Fiction. 3. Overweight women—Fiction. 4. Large type books. I. Title.
PS3610.A359S43 2014
813'.6—dc23   2013047277

Published in 2014 by arrangement with Midnight Ink, an imprint of Llewellyn Publications, Woodbury MN 55125-2989 USA

Printed in Mexico
1 2 3 4 5 6 7 18 17 16 15 14

For Cyn Reilley.

I can't thank you enough for all the great friendship and support you have given me and my work. Who knew when you started the Sue Ann Jaffarian Fan Club that it would become as large and as fun as it is today.

ACKNOWLEDGMENTS

To the usual suspects: my agent, Whitney Lee; my editor at Midnight Ink, Terri Bischoff; and everyone else at Midnight Ink/ Llewellyn Worldwide who had a hand in making this book, and all those before it, a reality. Number eight — who'da thunk it!

ONE

"Harpy bitch!" the woman with the bad bleach job shouted.

"Excuse me?" Horrified, I leaned away from her, a hand cupped over my fast-beating heart. The words had come with heat, like a furnace blast with extra garlic.

It wasn't uncommon for me to piss people off, but usually they got to know me first. Without getting too close, I peered at the woman, wondering if we had met before. I took in her low-slung jeans and a no-longer-white tank top that showed off buffed arms and shoulders along with a plethora of tattoos. I scanned her face, more than once. She could have been in her late twenties or her forties; the hardness of her face made it difficult to tell. No bells of familiarity went off, though I was sorely tempted to give her some laundry tips and a breath mint.

Ina Bruce put a hand on my shoulder and pushed me aside a few inches. "Relax,

9

Odelia. The nasty skank is talking to me."

Ina stepped forward, going almost boob to boob with Ms. Skank.

My mother and mother-in-law moved up behind me. "What's going on, Odelia?" Renee Stevens asked.

"Some sort of Neanderthal welcome wagon, I think."

"Humph," my mother, Grace Littlejohn, snorted. "Ina's no debutante, but next to that one, she's a Catholic schoolgirl."

"Mom," I scolded. "Ina's family."

"Grace is right," added Renee. "Ina's a tough cookie — always has been — but that other one looks like she just escaped from prison."

While the three of us watched, Ina and the other woman glared at each other, slowly circling, both looking ready to throw a punch should the other blink an insult.

We were standing in the parking lot of Elite Storage in Long Beach, which looked anything but elite. Not that it was a dump, but when I think of the word *elite,* rows of utilitarian storage lockers painted the color of dry clay do not pop into my mind. The four of us were on a field trip of sorts. Really, the three of us — Mom, Renee, and I — were on an excursion; Ina was working. Ina and her husband, Tom, owned a secondhand and consignment shop in Culver City and attended storage auctions regularly, on the hunt for merchandise to fill their store.

And that's why our little posse was here today. Not that Ina needed help doing her job, but when my mother found out that Ina went to storage auctions, wild horses couldn't keep her from begging Ina to take her along. It had been embarrassing to watch my eighty-something mom act like a kid hoping to win a ticket to Disneyland, and even more embarrassing watching her nearly wet herself with glee when Ina agreed to let Mom accompany her to an auction being held in Long Beach the Monday after Thanksgiving.

"That's very nice of you," I'd said to Ina as we were all gathered around Renee's holiday table, "but Mom's going home on Monday."

My mother looked at me like I'd just farted. "No, I'm not," she corrected. She turned to my half brother, who was sitting to my left. He continued chewing a mouthful of turkey and oyster dressing, pretending not to hear the exchange. "Isn't that what you said, Clark?" my mother asked. "That I'm staying longer?"

Clark ignored Mom and started shoveling food into his mouth like a starving orphan.

I half expected him to start stuffing it into his ears so he could block out Mom's question entirely.

All day I had been waiting for the turkey to hit the fan, giblet gravy and all. Not literally, of course, but figuratively — though literally might be amusing and would certainly liven up this annual clambake or, more to the point, rather tense Thanksgiving gathering. I had expected my mother to be the perpetrator of the chaos, but not in this way.

My husband accuses me of being a glass-half-empty kind of gal. I prefer to think of myself as a realist and a firm believer in whatever can go wrong, will go wrong. You'd think, after all the dead bodies I've found — through no effort on my own part, I can assure you — my husband would have the same jaded eye, but he doesn't. Bodies keep turning up, and he keeps hoping they won't and that the last one was just that — the last one. Like my being a corpse magnet, a nickname given to me by our friend Seth Washington, is just some pesky wart that shows up suddenly on the top of your foot, then disappears a few years later with no warning or goodbye.

On this Thanksgiving I not only saw the glass half empty, I saw it full of cracks and ready to explode into sharp, deadly shards. All it needed was a little misguided pressure in the wrong spot by the wrong person.

Every Thanksgiving since I married Greg, I have spent the holiday at my in-laws' beautiful home in Pacific Palisades. Usually it's just the Stevens family and me, with the occasional friend or stray family member tossed in. Earlier this year, Greg's sister and her husband and their two boys had moved to Northern California. Greg's brother and his wife had flown to Florida to visit her parents for the holidays. This would be the first Thanksgiving in years without them, and I could see that my mother-in-law was grieving. Many of the chairs around the large dining table would have been empty if not for three of the seats being filled by guests — one from Greg's family and two from mine. Enter the candidates most likely to shatter the half-empty glass.

Looking around the table, I wasn't sure which family add-on would receive the Turkey of the Year award. The candidates were Ina Bruce, Greg's second cousin, and my mother, Grace Littlejohn, who was visiting us from New Hampshire. The third family stray was Clark Littlejohn, my half brother. He was keeping a tight rein on our mother and looked like he could use a stiff drink, even though he'd stopped drinking years ago.

Having Mom and Clark visit us over Thanksgiving had been my bright idea, so I have no one else to blame, except that Greg could have raised concerns. But he didn't, and Mom had been hinting that she'd like to come for a visit "before I croak." When I suggested the Littlejohns travel to California for the holiday, Greg had been behind the idea with full-throttle enthusiasm, even though he knew my mother could be a pill. His family had already met Clark on several occasions and seemed to like him a great deal, but Grace Littlejohn was a different drumstick on the same bird.

What can I say about my mother that doesn't come off as snarky or ungrateful or bitter? Not much, I can tell you that, though I have been making progress in sorting out my feelings ever since I located her a couple of years ago. Greg thought having her as a guest in our home might help me along in that endeavor. Maybe, maybe not; it could also end up with me drowning her in the whirlpool tub in the guest bathroom. The installation of the large, multi-jetted tub had been a gift to me from Greg last Christmas, and it was certainly big enough to be a convenient murder scene. Since I outweighed my elderly mother by at least seventy pounds, the odds were in my favor.

When I was sixteen, my mother disappeared — *poof!* — like magic. One day I came home from high school to find that her personal things had been cleared out of our apartment. There was no note or explanation of any kind, nor had she given any indication that this might happen. One day she was there; the next day she was G-O-N-E. I had to go live with my father, who is now deceased, and his crazy-ass wife, Gigi. I'm still not sure which I resented more, Mom leaving in general or that her disappearance forced me to live with Gigi until I turned eighteen. When I finally located my mother over thirty years later, she was living in Massachusetts. I also discovered she had two other children. Clark was older than me by a few years. Grady, our half brother, was younger than me by sixteen years. All of us were fathered by different men. Grady is now dead. Soon after Grady's death, Mom moved to a retirement home in New Hampshire. Clark divides his time between his childhood home in Massachusetts and Phoenix, where he is head of security for a company belonging to our friend Willie Proctor. Well, publicly the company doesn't belong to Willie, who is wanted by the feds, but we all know who's behind it.

See? Life is complicated. It's giblet gravy ready to go airborne.

As if Renee's depression and my mother's crotchety attitude weren't enough to make the day memorable, there was always Ina to spice things up. She is the only grandchild of Renee Stevens's brother, Stuart, who passed away about the time Greg and I got engaged. Stu was Greg's favorite uncle and his sudden death had hit the family hard. Ina's father had died when she was not much more than a baby. Her mother had remarried a few years later and had more children, making Ina the odd child out, whether by her mother's hand or by her own emotions. According to Greg, Ina was a troubled teen who eventually went to live with Stu and his wife until she hooked up with Tom Bruce, a slick-talking low-life, right out of high school. Shortly after Stu's death and against her family's wishes, she and Tom had married and moved to California. She'd been only nineteen at the time. We've seen Ina and Tom a dozen times at most since they moved here, usually at family functions or the occasional holiday. Renee tries to keep in touch with Ina as much as possible and has helped her out financially from time to time. When they first arrived, Greg offered Tom a job in his graphic arts and print shop, Ocean Breeze Graphics. Tom was a surly, lazy worker who quit after a month, claiming he had bigger fish to fry. Greg was relieved, since it saved him the trouble of firing the guy.

Ina had arrived for Thanksgiving dinner alone.

"Where's Tom?" Greg had asked his cousin, not at all unhappy by her single status at dinner.

"Not sure. Don't care," Ina had replied as she shrugged off her leather jacket.

Ina was of average height and thin. The last time we'd seen her, her mousy, straight brown hair had been halfway down her back. Now it was dyed dark purple and worn close to her head. The severity of her hair made her look waifish and cute in a wood nymph-gone-goth sort of way. It brought out her high cheekbones and highlighted her brown eyes, which were heavy with black eyeliner and mascara. Her Aunt Renee took one disapproving look at Ina's raggedy jeans and snug long-sleeved tee shirt and went back into the kitchen. Renee Stevens didn't care for sloppiness at her holiday tables. She didn't require jackets, ties, hose, or high heels, but jeans were definitely a no-no. We all knew that, including Ina. Something told me any lumps in the gravy didn't stand a chance.

My own mother took one look at Ina and sized her up, her lips pursed in disapproval, which didn't surprise me since my mother disapproves of everything and everyone except Greg. She adores my husband. She probably loves him more than me and Clark combined, something I once brought up to Clark when we were alone.

"Be glad, sis," my big bro had said upon hearing my complaint. "In the long run, the more attention Mom gives Greg, the less fault she can find with us." It was an excellent point.

After making introductions, Greg's father asked Ina, "You and Tom have a fight?" Without waiting for a reply, Ronald Stevens went to the wet bar in the corner of the family's den and lifted a bottle of white wine from an ice bucket. "White or red, Ina? Or something else?"

"Red, please, Uncle Ron." In spite of her surliness and sloppy appearance, at least Ina hadn't forgotten her manners. Ron put down the white wine, picked up an open bottle of red wine, and poured her a glass. Ina casually pushed the sleeves of her shirt up, revealing a tattoo of a decaying rose on her right forearm. "As for Tom," she answered with a shrug, "we had a difference of opinion about the business, and he's off sulking somewhere."

"What kind of business are you in?" Clark asked before taking a sip of his sparkling water.

"Resale," Ina answered, viewing Clark through narrowed eyes. In spite of Clark's frequent visits, it was the first time he and Ina had met. "And I'll bet you're a cop."

"Retired," Clark responded.

Ina offered him a tight-lipped smile. "I can always tell a cop — or should I say, smell one."

My brother didn't seem to take offense, but he did study Ina closer. "Just like I can smell a girl in trouble." He indicated her tattoo. I leaned forward for a closer look and noticed for the first time that near the rose, just above Ina's wrist, her skin appeared bruised. Not fresh black and blue, but the pukey green-yellow color of healing. There were marks on her other arm, too. "Is that why your husband isn't here?" Clark persisted.

"None of your freaking business," Ina shot back, pulling the sleeves of her shirt down to cover her wrists. "I was moving something in the store a few days ago, and it fell across my arms. Hurt like a bitch. Or is being clumsy against the law?"

"Behave yourself, Ina," Ron admonished, handing her the wine. "Clark's a guest, and your Aunt Renee has gone to a lot of trouble today. She's kind of blue because the other kids aren't here. Let's make the day as nice as possible for her, shall we?"

At that point, I thought about going into the kitchen to see if I could help Renee but didn't for two reasons: one, I'd offered earlier and had been gently rebuffed, which didn't bother me since I knew my mother-in-law was a control freak in the kitchen. And two, I didn't want to miss anything. Ina had a particularly big and nervous chip on her shoulder today and was just itching for someone to knock it off. I only hoped it wouldn't be someone in my family who took the swing, so I was relieved to see Clark back down on the subject of the bruises.

"What do you mean by resale?" my mother asked, moving the chat along. She still wore a veil of disapproval, as if she were spotless in the sin department.

Ina swallowed a mouthful of the expensive wine like it was lemonade on a hot day. "We buy stuff at auctions, clean it up, and sell it in our store."

Mom perked up. "You mean like on those shows on TV where they buy abandoned

20

stuff without knowing what they're getting?"

"Sometimes we buy storage lockers. Other times we go to estate sales or yard sales."

My mother loved those shows where they auctioned off storage units. Since she'd been in town, she'd been glued to our TV watching reruns. Some episodes she'd seen a few times. She'd even asked if we could visit the store owned by one of the buyers featured on the show. Like a rocket, Ina went from disrespectful slob to rock star in my mother's eyes. By the time we'd started dinner, Mom had wrangled the invitation from Ina and I was questioning Mom's travel schedule.

"What does Mom mean, Clark?" I turned in my chair to face my brother, my body language challenging him to ignore me. "I thought her flight left Monday."

When Clark didn't stop eating, I reached my left hand over and placed it on his right arm, stopping the progression of his fork. The table fell as silent as a box of cotton. Across the table from me, Greg's fork was suspended halfway to his mouth. From it dripped homemade cranberry sauce seasoned with orange peel.

Clark put down his fork and turned to me. "I was going to talk to you and Greg about that after we got home tonight." He glanced over at Greg, who had lowered his fork and was listening — waiting, no doubt, to see if I would start slinging yams. "I got a call earlier today from work," Clark continued. "I have to fly out first thing in the morning directly to a job and won't be back in time to escort Mom home on Monday." His head swung between me and Greg as if on a loose hinge. "I was hoping you two would let her stay until I come back. I don't think it's a good idea for her to travel alone. Do you?"

There it was: the real choice. We could let Mom stay until Clark finished his job or I could fly back with Mom, get her settled in her retirement home, and then fly home myself. Hmm, fly the unfriendly skies after Thanksgiving, the busiest time to hit the air, or have Mom stay a few days longer. For most, it would be an easy choice; for me, it was a tough call.

I looked to my husband, trying to pick up on his vibes. Mom and Clark had already been here for two days, and while Clark was great to have around, Mom's constant presence and negativity had been trying, even for Greg. Even our animals stayed out of her way most of the time. But what could we say? *No! Heave her interfering, selfish ass out on the tarmac and let her take her chances.* I'd be tempted to say that if we'd been alone, but around a Thanksgiving table with my delightful in-laws, I was compelled to behave.

In silence, I counted my blessings. I had Greg and his family. I'd found my mother and my brother. We were all healthy and relatively happy. What would a few more days matter? I would have preferred not to have been blind-sided over a holiday meal.

"Maybe Clark will be back before the auction," I said, trying to keep hope out of my voice. I looked to Ina. "When is it again?"

Ina seemed oblivious to the tension her invitation had caused. "Monday morning in Long Beach."

I turned back to Clark. "Will you be back before then? I'd hate to have Mom all excited for the trip, then you come in and swoop her away."

Clark wiped his mouth with a creamy linen napkin edged with lace. They were Renee's special linens, used for all holidays except Christmas. For that meal the table-cloth and napkins would be embroidered with poinsettias. "Tell you what, sis. Even if my job is done, why don't we plan on Mom staying with you and Greg through next week. That way you can plan other outings without worrying about all that *swooping.*" His face and voice were blank, but his eyes looked at me with mischief. I was tempted to stomp on his foot under the table.

"Maybe Mom doesn't want to be away from home that long. Did you ask her?"

Clark turned to Mom. "What about it, Mom? Instead of a few days, would you like to stay a little longer here in *sunny* California with Odelia and Greg?"

Without hesitation, Mom responded, "According to the news, it was twenty-seven degrees in New Hampshire this morning. What do you think?"

Everyone at the table turned to me. I caught my father-in-law trying to suppress a grin. Not wanting to display the panic bubbling up in side of me, I shrugged instead. "It's okay by me," I said with a forced smile. "Although I'm not sure how much time I can get off work next week."

"I'll be fine on my own at your house," Mom assured me. "I can walk down to the beach. Can't do that in November back home, not that I'm even near the beach."

"Renee and I can take her out sightseeing a day or two," Ron added. "So don't you worry a bit about Grace."

I looked to Greg, hoping he'd find some excuse and take the pressure off me. "What about you, honey?"

"Why not?" Greg answered with his own

24

smile, although I trusted his to be more genuine than mine. "Glad to have you aboard, Grace."

"Wonderful," said Mom, clasping her hands together with joy. "It will be fun, and I can't wait to see one of those auctions in person."

"Can I come, too?" We all turned toward the end of the table. The question had come from Renee, who'd been quiet since placing the green bean casserole on the table and sitting down. "I'd like to see one of those," she added with enthusiasm. "We can make it a fun girls' day out."

It was the first time all day my mother-in-law had appeared chipper, though I did not share her optimism at spending a day with her and Mom together. It's not that they didn't get along. They'd met the day Mom and Clark arrived, and, while they were cordial enough with each other, it was clear Renee had immediately tagged Grace Little-john as a blight on motherhood — something that was sacred to Greg's mother. As for my mother, I think she would have liked Renee better if she were the sort of med-dling, overbearing mother-in-law I might bitch about. As it was, I got along famously with Renee, and Mom had picked up on that immediately. In Renee's presence,

Mom tended to bristle like a displaced hedgehog. She might have abandoned me over thirty years ago, but now she was claiming ownership rights.

I picked up my wine glass and drained it, wishing I could follow-up with a face-first plunge into Renee's amazing pecan pie. If I was lucky, it would rain on Monday and I'd be slammed next week at work. I was only working part-time these days and knew the office would be fairly quiet through the end of the year. Getting extra time off would not be a problem, even though Steele would give me grief just for show.

I looked at Mom. She seemed thrilled. I glanced at Renee. She also looked pleased and excited. Ina was oblivious, but the men all appeared amused by the turn of events and entertained by my obvious attempts to wiggle out of them.

Bottom line: Mom was staying with us an extra week. I'd just have to pull on my big-girl panties and deal with it.

Two

While Ina and the bleached blond continued to hiss and throw colorful insults at each other, a crowd gathered, circling them as if watching a cockfight. Slung over one of Ina's shoulders was a backpack. I half expected her to slough it off and turn it into a weapon.

"Do something, Odelia," Renee whispered, still standing behind me. I moved over a few inches, putting myself squarely in front of both mothers, using my bulk as a shield should the conflict expand.

I eyed the people watching the spectacle. There were about a dozen, with the group swelling quickly as more cars, vans, and trucks parked and people spilled out into the November sunshine. The crowd was diverse in ethnicity, with both men and women favoring jeans or cargo pants worn with tee shirts or work shirts. Some wore muscle shirts and shorts. A few middle-aged women in nubby polyester and loud prints were sprinkled in the crowd like wildflowers. The group also contained a few couples — possibly husbands and wives running a family business like Ina and Tom. Ages covered every decade from twenty-something to Medicare-eligible. Almost everyone wore sunglasses, except for one short, squat black woman who wore a visor sporting an Indian casino logo. Ina and the blond were the only two young women present.

"What do you expect me to do?" I whispered back to Renee. "Turn a fire hose on them?"

For the first time, I noticed our own appearances. Renee was dressed in an aqua twin sweater set and pressed khakis, her golden hair meticulously coiffed. My mother wore a prim blue belted shirt dress with a sweater draped over her shoulders. I did have on jeans, but they were loose "mom" jeans paired with a sunny yellow sweater, both clean and without blemish. With our handbags, comfortable walking shoes, and discreet and tasteful jewelry, the three of us looked like we had gotten lost on our way to a ladies' lunch or a day of shopping at an upscale mall and had stopped to ask for directions in the wrong part of town. Out-of-town tourists, ripe for a scam, might have blended in better. If the crowd hadn't been so entertained by Ina and her angry little friend, we would have garnered a lot of unwanted curiosity. Ina, in her basic uniform of jeans and snug long-sleeved tee, didn't look like she knew us, let alone was with us.

"Okay, break it up," ordered a bald, portly man of mixed race. He lumbered out of the office of Elite Storage with authority and purpose and approached the crowd. With him was a young woman holding a clipboard. At first blush she could have been taken for an adolescent boy, but it was a woman, slight and wiry, with short-cropped hair and glasses that gave her a Harry Potterish appearance.

"Ina. Linda," the man said, addressing the combatants. "You know I don't tolerate scuffles at my auctions."

"Aw, come on, Red," said one of bystanders, "let 'em go at it. A good cat fight might bring in more business." Everyone in the crowd laughed but us.

The man named Red scowled at the crowd and began his pitch. "I'm Redmond Stokes, the auctioneer," he announced without further ado. He jerked a thumb at his androgynous assistant. "This is Kim

Pawlak. When the auction is over, you'll be paying her." Red gave us a rundown of the rules. We could not go into any of the storage units up for sale and only had minutes to view it from the opening before the bidding began. Sales were final and cash only.

"Just like on TV," gushed my mother. She was tittering like a excited bird seeing its first worm.

"The first unit up today is number fourteen," continued Red after a glance at Kim's clipboard. "A 5×10." He turned and started walking through the open gate and down the main road through the compound.

I glanced at Renee, but she seemed more interested in what was going on with Ina. The crowd started after Red like a slow-moving herd, going around the two angry women like a patch of nasty cactus in its way. Ina broke away from her fight and rejoined us to follow the crowd to the first auction, but not before launching one last verbal attack: "Stay away from me or you'll regret you were ever born."

Linda took two aggressive steps forward and gestured like Rocky Balboa urging on his opponent. "Bring it on, you skinny, stupid bitch."

With fire in her eyes and clenched fists, Ina studied her adversary, then turned away.

I sighed with relief, knowing she was capable of pulverizing the other woman.

"Who is that?" Renee asked, indicating the blond.

"Her name is Linda McIntyre, Aunt Renee," Ina replied through tight lips. "She's the ho sleeping with my husband." She got in step behind the crowd, not looking back to see if we were following.

I don't think my mother heard Ina because she was moving with the crowd on Red's heels, anxious not to miss a moment of the auction activity. Renee and I were rooted to the concrete, staring at the woman named Linda. As she passed by us, she gifted us with a snarl.

"Did you know Tom and Ina were having problems?" I asked Renee.

She slowly shook her head. "She did say at Thanksgiving that they'd had a fight, but I didn't know it was this serious."

"Did you see the bruises on her arms that day?"

"No, but Ron told me about them after you all left. He said Ina claimed they were from an accident at the store, but we're quite concerned."

I took my mother-in-law's arm and guided her after the group. "Maybe when this is over, we can talk to her about it."

"Ina's not the sharing type," Renee reminded me. "But it might do the girl good to know her family is here for her."

The Elite Storage compound was clean and orderly, with rows of storage lockers lined up like a battalion of garages without attached houses. As we left the parking and office area, I noted several small roads leading off in different directions like streets in a planned community. The buildings were stucco, with the doors to each locker made of sturdy metal secured by padlocks.

The group walked down the main road and turned left, then took another left. Red came to a halt in front of a unit. A man with *Elite Storage* printed across the back of his work shirt materialized with a small power saw. With a short, high-pitched buzz, he easily cut the padlock from the unit and rolled the door up. The crowd surged forward for a better look. Renee and I joined Ina and Mom up near the front.

To my untrained eye, the large storage locker appeared to be stuffed with household junk, including a well-worn box spring and mattress set. Some of it was neatly stacked and wedged into the space in an orderly fashion, while much of the small stuff looked heaved in at the last moment. Several individuals in the crowd moved forward, flashlights in hand. Standing at the doorway, they shined their limited lights on various items in the locker, poking their beams here and there, over and under the furniture and boxes, going where their hands could not pry. All were hoping to spot some treasure no one else would see. Satisfied, they moved back, and several others moved forward. Ina followed suit. There was general low-key chat among the buyers as to individual items and worth. Next to me, the two Latinos in baseball caps held a hushed conference in Spanish. Across from us, two separate pairs of couples had their heads together, plotting strategy. Everyone eyed their competition with jumpy peripheral vision.

"You going to bid on this one?" my mother asked Ina.

"Maybe," she whispered just loud enough for the three of us to hear. "It looks like the contents of a small house. See," she said, pointing the large flashlight she'd produced from her backpack to a spot beyond the mattress. It hit upon a corner of some white enamel. "Behind there might be a washer and dryer or a refrigerator." She moved her light. "And there's a table and chairs in the back. You can just make out the legs, and next to it is possibly a sofa. And those plastic bins off to the side are marked *kitchen*." She turned off her light. "There might be some good stuff here for the shop if the bidding isn't too high."

I bent closer. "If you win, how are you going to move it all?"

"We have a couple of guys who work for us part-time," Ina explained. "If I win any of these lockers, I'll call them and they'll come with a truck and move it to the shop for sorting. If I find anything small of value right off, I'll take it back with me."

"What about Tom?" I asked, being the first to verbalize his absence. "Why isn't he here to help?"

Ina turned and looked from me to Renee, ready to identify the elephant in the room and dispatch it quickly with a high-powered hunting rifle. "I have no idea where Tom is." She glanced over at Linda McIntyre, then raised her eyebrows at us, challenging us to press further. Neither of us did. Mom, thankfully, had inched closer to the auctioneer and missed the exchange. I didn't need her nosing about in Ina's touchy business.

The auctioneer asked for an opening bid, and the auction was off and running. I don't know how Red kept everything and everyone straight. Words flew out of his mouth like sparrows spooked from a tree. Around us people offered grunts and yips — some loud, others quiet — signaling bids. Other bidders merely moved a hand or a few fingers. Ina's bids were indicated by a sharp nod of her head. Across from us stood Linda McIntyre. Her bids were noted with a guttural "yeah" reminiscent of a dry smoker's cough. She bid higher every time Ina was in the lead. Redmond Stokes saw and heard it all and kept the bids climbing.

"That locker ain't gonna be yours," Linda sneered across the few yards that divided her from Ina. "Any more than Tom is yours."

Next to me I felt Ina tense, ready to spring forward and pummel her adversary. Instead, she volleyed, "Who says I want the loser back?" Around us people laughed, enjoying the free entertainment.

Even with the sideshow, the bidding was over in a fast-paced two minutes, with the two chatty Latinos winning the locker. Ina had pulled out of the race just several bids before, and Linda had pulled out shortly after.

"Wow," Mom said, fanning herself, "that was exciting." She turned to Ina. "Why'd you stop?"

"Because the bidding passed my limit," she explained to us. "Auctions are a lot like gambling. You have to set a limit and stop when it's reached, otherwise you overspend and lose your shirt. Some people," she said, shooting her chin in Linda McIntyre's direction, "even drive the bidding up on purpose, just to stick an overly competitive bidder or someone they don't like with a higher price. She had no intention of buying that locker."

I was beginning to have a whole new appreciation for Ina and her business sense. Even cloaked in anger, she was displaying an impressive level head.

The crowd moved on to another unit about the same size. Once the lock was cut and the door raised, we could see it was a room containing office furniture and equipment. It was full but not jammed to the roof like the locker before it, and the contents were better packed. I noted several basic desks and swivel chairs, along with what appeared to be computer equipment, fax machines, and bookshelves. Off to the side, banker's boxes were neatly stacked and labeled to indicate they contained receipts and invoices from specific years. While my mother and Ina stepped forward to take their turn viewing the contents, I noted that Renee was having a difficult time keeping her eyes off Linda.

"You okay?" I asked her.

Renee gave me a weak nod. "I'm wondering what Tom sees in that tramp."

Besides huge boobs and loose morals? But I kept that to myself and instead replied, "Who knows? He's always been kind of a jerk, hasn't he?"

"True, but I still hate to see Ina hurt like this. She's had a rough life and deserves better."

"You going to bid on this one?" Mom asked Ina like a coconspirator as the two of them rejoined us in the crowd.

"Yes," Ina said quietly. "Office furniture and equipment have good resale value if they're in decent condition."

A few minutes later, Red was off and running with the auction. A lot of other bidders felt the same as Ina, and the bids were flying around like angry bees. Once again Linda dogged Ina's bids, outbidding her at every turn. I lifted my arm to readjust a falling bra strap and was shocked to find the auctioneer pointing in my direction.

"Is that a bid, princess?" Red asked me.

"Huh?"

Everyone stared at me. Some were giggling. Most were annoyed by the stop in the action.

"Um, no, it wasn't," I clarified. "Sorry."

Next to me, a grizzled old guy groused,

"Amateurs."

"This ain't no fancy reality show," Red admonished. "People are working here. Next time, the bid sticks."

"Sorry," I said again, putting my arm down straight. I left it there, afraid to move a muscle.

The bidding resumed, ending with everyone being outbid by a burly guy in a blue wife-beater shirt.

Once again we moved *en masse* through the storage complex on our way to the next auction. According to Red, there were five lockers up for auction today. The third one was a bit larger than the last two and located almost at the far end of the property. I was glad I'd worn sturdy shoes. Both Mom and Renee were holding up great, though I'm sure Mom's energy was fueled by the excitement and the stories she planned to tell back at her retirement home.

When we were all gathered around the third unit, Linda snarled at Ina, "Don't even bother." Ina ignored her.

Like kids at Christmas, we anxiously awaited for the padlock to be cut and door number three to be flung open to show us its secrets.

THREE

One of my least favorable attributes is that dead bodies crop up like persistent acne whenever I'm around. Upon seeing the latest corpse, my first thoughts were purely selfish: *Why me?* How come I've become a middle-aged, two-hundred-plus-pound divining rod who ferrets out stiffs instead of water — a human edition of one of those cadaver-sniffing dogs?

My pity party was short-lived as I quickly remembered the people standing with me and stood ready to catch anyone about to faint. My mother-in-law had a hand clasped over her mouth, her blue eyes as large and bright with shock as a full moon, but she seemed steady enough. My own mother appeared less shocked and more curious. Mom leaned forward, squinted through her glasses, and muttered, "Is that thing real?"

Ina was the most shaken by the sight of the body. As soon as the door to the storage

locker had been unlocked and rolled up-
ward, she had let out a blood-curdling
scream that had vibrated the pavement
under us like a mild quake.

The others let out varying degrees of
gasps and cries. A short, wet scream of
anguish had come out of tough-girl Linda.

Before us was another storage locker of
household goods. In the center, just behind
the door, was a beat-up lounger covered in
ugly plaid fabric. It looked like the chair my
father had had for years and adored. The
lounge chair had been tilted back, its foot-
rest up. In the chair was a man, his head
back, his arms slack and draped over the
sides of the chair. He looked like he'd dozed
off during halftime while watching football.
All he needed was a half-empty beer bottle
dangling from one hand and a bag of chips
in his lap.

The worst part was I knew the corpse.
And so did three out of four in my party, as
well as many in the crowd. Sitting in the
lounge chair with a bloody hole in the left
side of his head, taking a final forever nap,
was Tom Bruce, Ina's philandering husband.

Red quickly shook off his own shocked
stupor. Seeing half the crowd snapping off
photos with their phones, he waved his arms
at them like an unbalanced windmill, but it

only resulted in more phones being produced. Ina lunged forward but was restrained by Red before she could enter the locker.

"That's my husband!" Ina cried, beating her fists against the sturdy auctioneer.

"Get that damn door down," Red yelled at the fellow with the saw. Overcoming his own surprise, the guy grabbed the door and rolled it down. People were still snapping off photos, bending to get the last shot as the door came crashing down. Dollars to donuts, photos and videos of Tom's final pose would be posted to the Internet in the next sixty seconds and would go viral within five to ten minutes.

Kim Pawlak had whipped out her own cell phone, but instead of taking macabre photos, she was talking into it, giving hurried orders and details to someone on the other end. Finished, she turned to Red. "I called the front office. They're calling the police."

"Let me go," Ina pleaded. "He might still be alive!"

Pretty much everyone standing there believed that ship had sailed, but stranger things have happened. And I think that idea crossed Red's mind the same time it did mine. He turned to the crowd. "Everyone back up, way up, and put away those damn phones. Don't you have a shred of decency?"

The gawkers backed up until they were against the row of units facing the locker. One of the Latino guys who'd won the earlier auction still had his phone aimed at the chaos.

"Put that damn thing away," Red roared at him.

The guy's friend said something to him in Spanish, causing him to pocket his phone quick as a bunny.

Glancing at the guy by the door, Red signaled for it to be raised. He let loose of Ina. "You stay put," he ordered and moved her back several feet.

Renee, Mom, and I gathered around Ina. Renee put an arm around her. Ina clung to her but never took her frightened eyes from the door of the storage locker. If Ina decided to make a break for Tom's body, there was no chance my mother-in-law would ever be able to stop her, so I stayed close. I understood Ina's desire and need to be with her husband. If that had been Greg in there, I would have crashed through the closed metal door like a charging bull. If by some miracle Tom Bruce was still alive, someone with a clear head would have to do the checking. If he wasn't, a grieving widow wouldn't do the crime scene any good.

The door raised, displaying Tom in the same place where we'd last seen him. I had half hoped it had been some sick prank staged by Tom to scare the crap out of his wife and auction-seeking colleagues. You know, a little stage blood and the right timing. That when the door was raised again, the lounger would be empty and Tom would be standing off to the side, tall and lanky, healthy and whole, ready to jump out at everyone. But it wasn't a joke. The body was there just as we'd last seen it, and so was the large hole in his head and the massive bloodstain on the back of the headrest. Everyone stared in silence; the only sound this time was the faint buzzing of flies.

Ina stared through her tears as Red checked the body for life. Finding none, he slowly shook his head in our direction. Ina struggled against her aunt. I grabbed her by both arms. "You can't help Tom, Ina," I told her, infusing as much comfort as I could into my voice.

Ina reared back from me, nearly toppling Renee. When I reached out to stop Renee's fall, hoping to avoid a broken hip, Ina broke free and ran into the storage locker. I didn't have the heart to stop her, nor did Red. No matter how much of a jerk Tom Bruce had been, he was Ina's husband. She reached to touch the gaping wound but stopped herself at the last minute. From where we stood, we could hear stifled whimpers. Assured Renee was stable on her feet, I moved forward to stand with Ina, who had fallen to her knees by the lounger in a sobbing mess. I placing a hand gently on her shoulder.

Red started to object to my presence in the locker. "We're her family," I told him, indicating myself, Mom, and Renee. He nodded and backed off.

Through her weeping I thought Ina was saying something to me. I bent closer, but it wasn't me she was speaking to, it was Tom. She raised her head, stared at the corpse of her husband, and whispered, "You stupid, stupid bastard."

Before I could delicately ask Ina what she meant, we heard sirens. They were still off in the distance but approaching quickly, like a sandstorm. Kim took off at a trot in the direction of the front gate, probably with the intent of guiding them to the crime scene.

I looked back at the crowd, scanning it for Linda McIntyre, to see how she was taking Tom's death. After her initial screech of horror, I half expected her to fight Ina for grieving rights, but she was otherwise occupied. Off by the end of the building, out of earshot, she was having words with the short African American woman with the visor. Their words were animated, but the volume was contained. The woman with the visor was pointing at the storage unit, her face scrunched into red-hot anger. Linda looked pasty and distraught. When she started to leave, the woman grabbed her arm, but Linda easily shook it off and made a beeline for the exit. A few others had quietly drifted away, too, making me wonder if they were avoiding the snarl of time it would take to go through questioning or if they were simply avoiding the police altogether. My experience told me that as soon as the police arrived, the storage facility would be under lockdown, with no one going in or out without clearance from the authorities.

And I was right. Just after Linda disappeared, I spotted the two Latinos slinking off, only to be stopped by a pair of uniformed police heading our way. They said something to the men. The English-speaking one put up a small argument. I couldn't hear the words, but the pleading tone and gestures spoke volumes about the need to be somewhere — anywhere — but here. In the end, the men were forced to turn around and rejoin the group. I wondered if Linda had made it out. When I didn't see her being herded back to the crowd, I was pretty sure she'd managed to slip out in the nick of time.

Renee came up to me. In her hands was her phone. "It's Greg. I hope you don't mind, but I called him."

I smiled at my mother-in-law. Greg needed to know about Tom, and hearing it first from his mother was certainly better than hearing it from me. I'm sure his first reaction was about why we had to be the ones to find him, even if we were in a crowd when it happened.

I took the phone and turned Ina over to Renee. Leaving the locker, I moved off to the side to take the call, but first I checked on Mom, making sure she was okay. Next to my mother stood the man in the wife-beater shirt holding his phone low, pointing it at the locker. I was about to say something when my mother noticed it. Using her bulky handbag, she knocked the phone out of his hands. "Didn't your mother teach you any manners?" she snapped at him. Had Mom not been old enough to be his grandma, I'm sure the guy would have thrown a punch or at least given her a powerful shove. Instead, he growled in her direction, then stooped to retrieve his phone from the pavement and promptly pocketed it. He also moved away from Mom and her deadly purse.

I put Renee's phone to my left ear and stuck an index finger into my right ear to block out noise. "Hi, honey. How's your day going?"

"My day's going just fine; busy but good. It's yours I'm worried about."

"Yeah, I was going to call you in a bit to let you know what's going on."

"My mother said Tom showed up. Did he cause trouble for Ina?"

I glanced over at the storage locker. More police had arrived and were taking charge. Kim was helping them corral the crowd to a new area away from the crime scene while still keeping them together. Soon the investigators would cut them off from the herd, one by one, for questioning. Now that the shock of seeing Tom's body was wearing off, they were getting restless and starting to voice complaints about delays. I'm sure most were wishing they had disappeared earlier like some of the others — as Linda McIntyre had.

"Yes," I said into the phone, realizing Renee had not filled Greg in on Tom's death, leaving me with the unsavory task.

I glanced over at the locker. Renee was standing with Ina just outside of it, comforting her while a police officer talked to her. My own mother had been rounded up with the crowd and was watching nervously from the sidelines. I could see her fidgeting with the handles of her purse, fussing with the leather on the strap like a string of worry beads. Cut from the comfort of people she knew, she appeared frail and vulnerable — a bird fallen from the security of its nest, hoping a cat didn't wander by while it waited to be rescued. She spotted me and raised a thin arm to catch my attention. I signaled back, indicating for her to hold on, I'd be there to help shortly. At least if she was in the makeshift holding pen, I knew she wouldn't be getting into mischief while I brought Greg up to speed.

"Tom did show up, and his presence has caused trouble," I said into the phone, keeping half an eye on Mom, "but not in the way you might think." I paused. It didn't matter how many times I had to tell Greg about a dead body in my orbit, it didn't get any easier. "Did you know he was cheating on Ina?"

"No, but it doesn't surprise me." My husband paused before voicing his next thought. "Please tell me Tom did not bring his mistress to the auction and flaunt her in front of Ina."

"Um, no, not exactly, though said mistress was here and faced off with Ina with some pretty colorful language."

"And Tom just stood by and watched?"

"Not exactly, Greg." I drew out the words, giving them more weight, then just let them sit there like clues in a board game. I was unsure of where to go next and hoped Greg could somehow read my mind and save me the trouble of painting him a whole picture. It was a childish and cowardly way out, but now wasn't the time to get clever and creative.

"What are you *not* telling me, Odelia?" Through the phone, I heard Greg deliberately inhale, then exhale, giving his breath similar emphasis to my drawn-out wordplay. I could tell he was just as concerned about asking me as I was of telling him.

"We have a *big* problem here, honey."

"Someone's dead, right?" He asked the question with a bluntness usually reserved for phone solicitors. This was followed by a few seconds of cursing that came through the phone line like stage whispers.

"Yes," I answered without any further dancing. I glanced back at my mother. Somehow she'd caught Renee's attention, who'd convinced a uniformed cop to spring Mom from the corral. The two elderly women were walking back to rejoin Ina, their heads close together as they chatted.

After the swearing subsided, Greg said, "Don't tell me: Tom's accused of murder, and you want to help him. But why should you if he cheated on my cousin? Let him hang."

"Um, that's not the problem. The dead body *is* Tom Bruce, and it could be Ina we'll be needing to help."

"Tom's dead?" Greg's voice got high, as it always did when he was surprised.

"As a doornail. He was found in one of the storage lockers up for auction." I stopped to rethink, then amended my comment. "Well, the locker was up for auction, not Tom. The door of the unit went up right in front of both his wife and his mistress, and at least twenty others."

A long pause, then, "How did the moms take it?"

"Both were shocked, but they seem okay now. Your mother is giving Ina a lot of support. Mine seems along for the ride, like it's part of her vacation adventure. Ina is being questioned right now, but I'm sure she'll have to go to the station at some point."

"You think she'll be considered a suspect?"

"Yes, I do. She and Linda — that's Tom's side squeeze — got into it pretty good, leaving no doubt in anyone's mind about Ina knowing about her husband's affair."

"Motive."

"Yep. Not to mention, Ina threatened Linda right in front of the crowd."

"I'll be right there. Tell me exactly where you are."

"That's okay, Greg. We'll be fine. There's really nothing you can do."

"I can get my mother and yours the hell out of there, and you can stay with Ina. Or you can drive the moms and I'll stay with Ina. Either way, we need to get the old girls home."

What he said made sense. The police would take Renee and Mom's statements, then release them. They might take Ina in or release her. It was difficult to say, but her questioning would take longer.

"Should we call Seth?" I asked. "He helped me through questioning last time."

"I'm going to call Seth, but for a referral for an experienced criminal lawyer. Something tells me this might need more legal muscle. Find out if Ina has a lawyer. If not, we can use the referral."

51

"Oh, crap!" I said into the phone, remembering something. "Seth and Zee are still out of town." Their daughter, Hannah, had recently moved with her husband to Chicago. Seth and Zee had taken off for a couple of weeks to spend Thanksgiving with them and then see friends who lived in the Midwest.

"I can still call him," said Greg. "If I don't reach him, I'll call Steele."

I groaned. Mike Steele was my obnoxious boss. He had a sick love for my stumbling in and out of trouble, but he was a kick-ass attorney, though not in the field of criminal law. "But call Seth first," I insisted. "We could even call Clark, who could ask Willie. I'm sure Willie knows lots of experienced criminal attorneys. Or even Dev, though I'm not sure I want Dev knowing I stumbled upon another body."

"All good ideas, sweetheart. One way or another, we'll find Ina an excellent lawyer."

I held the phone like a lifeline, worried about my next question. "Greg, do you think Ina might have had something to do with Tom's death? She did seem genuinely shocked when she saw the body, but you never know."

"Ina's no angel, and she and Tom have always had problems, but I can't imagine her killing anyone."

I'm sure the families of most killers thought that. I did not voice my thoughts to Greg.

"But either way," he continued, "she'll need competent legal help to get through this. If she and Tom were having problems and Tom was cheating, the cops will see it as motive. I sure hope she has a good alibi." There was a pause, but it wasn't followed by swearing. "For once, I'm glad you were there when a body was found. I'd hate to think of Ina going through this on her own."

I tapped the phone to make sure I'd heard correctly. "So you're not going to tell me to keep my nose out of it?"

"I think this is the perfect time for both of us to stick our noses into something." He cleared his throat. "Of course, only if Ina is implicated."

Yeah, right. I know my husband. Even if Ina is totally cleared as a suspect, Greg will want to get to the bottom of who killed Tom Bruce. He may not have liked Tom, but the killing was too close to home for him to stay out of it.

I glanced back at the locker to find the police moving everyone out of the area. The group of bystanders, including Ina, Renee, and Mom, was being herded once again, but this time toward the front of the storage compound.

"Honey, I have to go. They're clearing the area."

"I'll be there as soon as I can. Stick close to Ina. The moms will probably be okay, but who knows what might come out of Ina's mouth under the circumstances."

"Aye, aye, captain." I love it when my hubby exerts his take-charge personality — well, I love it when it doesn't collide with my own pig-headed streak.

FOUR

When I caught up to the crowd, they were being held in an area just inside the front gate of Elite Storage. The police were methodically working through everyone, taking names, contact information, and short statements. It looked like we might be here a good long time. Kim Pawlak sensed the same thing and disappeared into the office, returning with two folding chairs for Renee and Mom, for which I thanked her.

Ina was off to the side. With her was the big guy in the wife-beater shirt, the guy Mom had attacked with her purse. He was holding Ina while she sobbed. Seeing that Mom and Renee appeared cool and collected, at least for the moment, I scooted over to Ina, curious about her comforter. He had ruthlessly outbid her for a locker earlier and now was providing a shoulder to cry on.

"Ina, how are you doing?" I asked as I approached.

She pulled away from the man and sniffled. "How do you think I'm doing?" she snapped. "My husband is dead."

The man looked me over, his face not nearly as hard as his overall appearance. I placed him in his early forties. When he held out a hand to me in introduction, I took it. "Name's Clarence Goodwin, but everyone calls me Buck. I'm a colleague of Tom and Ina's — and their friend."

"Odelia Grey. I'm married to one of Ina's cousins."

Buck gave me a small smile of recognition. "That would be the guy in the wheelchair, right? Ina's told me a lot about him."

I nodded. It didn't surprise me that Ina had mentioned Greg. In spite of her gruff exterior, I knew she adored him. That was also the reason Greg was jumping in to help her. He considered Ina a wayward younger sister more than a second cousin.

I turned to face Ina. "In fact, that was Greg on the phone. He's on his way here." She looked up with surprise, so I explained. "One of us will take Renee and my mother home, and one of us will stay with you. Greg's also finding an attorney to help you through the questioning. Or do you have your own lawyer?"

"I don't need a damn lawyer," Ina hissed through her tears. "I didn't kill Tom!"

"I'm sure you didn't," I told her. "But it's best to have an attorney present during questioning like this. As the spouse, you'll be scrutinized."

"She's right, Ina," Buck added. "Cops can twist your words all around if you don't have a good mouthpiece."

Ina took a deep breath, and the three of us looked back in the direction of the locker, which, thankfully, we could not see from where we stood.

"Have they questioned you?" I asked.

Ina didn't respond, but Buck did. "I don't think they've done anything except take her statement of what happened just now, like they're doing to all of us."

"They might take her to the station for her questioning." I looked at Ina again. Her heavy eye makeup was dripping like melting licorice. "Do you have an attorney you can call?" I asked again. Ina shook her head.

"Greg and I know several attorneys. We'll find someone to help you."

"But I can't afford an attorney," she whined.

"Don't worry about that right now," I said. "We'll deal with that later."

I looked around at the people being

questioned and those waiting to be questioned. "What happened to Linda McIntyre?" Even though I knew she'd disappeared shortly after Tom was discovered, there was always the possibility she hadn't gone far.

Buck surveyed the parking lot just beyond the front gate. "Her SUV's gone," he reported. "It was parked right next to my truck. She drives a red Chevy Tahoe." He pointed toward a silver Ford pickup. The space next to it was empty.

I checked out the parking lot, looking for a red SUV. Nothing. "The police are going to want to talk to her for sure."

"Why?" whined Ina. "Can't I even be a widow without her coming between me and Tom?"

It was Buck who answered her. "For starters, the police will want to talk to Linda because she was here when Tom was found. And considering her personal relationship with him, she could be a suspect."

The last part of his comment struck a chord with Ina. "You think maybe *she* killed him?" Her ink-rimmed eyes went wide — but not with surprise, more with satisfaction. "If she did kill Tom, it serves him right."

"Shh," I cautioned, looking around to see

if anyone had heard her. "You might not want to seem so pleased about the prospect."

Buck also surveyed the area to see if anyone had their ears tuned to us, but it appeared we were pretty much alone. "Odelia's right. The police will push you to the wall on this; there's no need to give them fuel for the fire. Keep comments like that to yourself and your lawyer."

"Tell me," I said to Ina, "can you think of anyone who might have had reason to kill Tom?"

Instead of answering, Ina wiped the back of her hand across her face, dragging it over her runny nose and streaks of black makeup. Before I could dig a tissue from my purse, Buck handed her a clean blue cotton handkerchief produced from a pocket of his cargo shorts. While Ina mopped herself up, I checked Buck out, taking in the bulky tat-covered arms, the stubble on his face, and his thinning blond hair.

He noticed my unabashed curiosity and gave me a small grin. "In spite of what that old bag with the big purse said about my upbringing, my mother taught me never to leave the house without a clean hankie."

"That old bag is my mother," I informed him.

"Oh. Sorry." He looked away with embarrassment.

Maybe Buck Goodwin didn't get mad at my mother's attack because of her age. Maybe it was just years of good upbringing that had kept him from ripping her offending purse from her arm and stomping on it, as I might have done.

I turned my attention back to the conversation. "We'll have to make sure the police know that Linda was here and took off." I looked around. "I think several others took off, too."

"Yeah," Buck agreed. "Ted Hudsinger and Pedro Serrano are both gone. No surprise there; both have had run-ins with the law over the years."

"Any problems between them and Tom?" I asked.

Ina remained mute, but Buck shook his head and answered, "Not that I know of. They both have their issues but pretty much get along with the other buyers. Most of the regulars know each other, even if they're not drinking buddies."

"I saw the two guys in the baseball hats try to make a break for it, but the police stopped them. What do you know about them?"

Buck surveyed the crowd until his eyes

settled on the two men I'd mentioned. "The tall one is Roberto Vasquez. He seems to be a cool enough guy — a family man. Sometimes his wife comes to the auctions with him. The guy with him today is his nephew Guillermo. He's been coming around more lately."

Ina came out of her silent haze to also check out those who were left in the crowd. "Mazie Moore is also gone." Ina wiped her nose again, this time using Buck's handkerchief. "I'll bet she left with Linda. Those two are thick as thieves."

I thought about Linda and the woman with the visor. "I didn't notice Linda with anyone until after, when she was having words with a short black woman."

Ina nodded. "That would be Mazie. They always come separately, but often partner up in the bidding. They like to think the rest of us don't know they work together, but they do."

"Mazie owns two secondhand shops. One in Inglewood and another in Pico Rivera," Buck explained.

"Where is Linda's shop?" I asked.

"She doesn't have one," snorted Ina. "She mostly buys for people who can't make the auctions. She thinks she's so high and mighty, strutting around with that Bluetooth in her ear like she's some high-paid rep at a fancy art auction house."

From the way Buck chuckled, I got the feeling he agreed with Ina about Linda. "The scuttlebutt is," he added, "Mazie and Linda are looking to partner up and expand Mazie's stores into a good-size chain."

"And Mazie is the short African American woman with the visor?" I asked to confirm.

Ina sneered. "Yeah, Mazie's the gnarled little gnome. The tall black woman was Dionne Hudsinger, Ted's wife. She's pretty nice most of the time. Mazie's the dumpy mailbox without legs."

Being short and stout myself, I bristled inside at the comment, but kept my personal feelings under wraps. "I remember her. She was bidding on the first locker right along with everyone else, even in competition with Linda. Why would she do that if she's supposed to be in partnership with Linda?"

Ina looked away while Buck answered, "Linda was probably bidding today for one of her clients. As I said, their partnership is rumor, not necessarily fact."

Ina nudged Buck with an elbow. "Guess Mazie didn't leave. There she is now."

Our eyes turned to watch Mazie Moore coming out of the Elite Storage office. She'd removed her visor and was slowly making her way down the few short steps to the pavement.

Okay, I'm short and fat, but even without standing next to her I could tell Mazie Moore's mahogany head was several inches below mine, putting her well under five feet. Ina's mailbox comment wasn't too far off the mark. Mazie wasn't just short; she was as wide as she was tall, almost literally, reminding me of a brown mini-fridge.

As soon as Mazie descended the stairs, I saw Kim Pawlak signal to Renee, who left her seat and climbed the stairs. I also noted that Kim had brought out a few other folding chairs. Mazie moved one of them off to the side by itself and plunked down in it to await her turn for questioning. After making sure Buck could stay with Ina, I scooted over to where my mother sat on the folding chair.

"Where did Renee go?"

"Bathroom breaks," Mom answered. "Seems they only have one on the premises, and it's unisex. I'm next in line."

I sat down on Renee's chair and leaned toward my mother. "Have the police spoken to you yet?"

"They took my name and Renee's and our information. I gave them your home phone. I hope you don't mind? Couldn't see what good it would be giving them my number in New Hampshire when I'm out here."

"Of course that's fine, but they will also want your home number in case they have questions after you leave. Murder investigations can take a long time."

"I also gave them my cell phone number."

Feeling more settled, I noticed Mom watching the crowd like a hawk. I discreetly pointed to Mazie. "Have you had a chance to chat with that woman yet?"

Mom tore her eyes away from the crowd and looked at me funny. "Why would I?"

"I don't know." I shrugged. "Maybe out of curiosity. You know, chitchat to pass the time."

After consideration, Mom shook an index finger in my direction. "You don't fool me, missy. Those cogs in that head of yours are already working this as if it's a case to be solved."

"It *is* a case to be solved, and it involves someone we know. What would have happened if I hadn't stuck my nose into things back in Massachusetts?"

Mom turned away from me. "I would have been fine," she sniffed. "They knew I didn't kill that man." Mom went back to watching the crowd, and we slipped into a loud silence until she said, "That woman — the one you pointed out. Ina doesn't like her much."

"Did she tell you that?"

"Didn't need to," Mom explained. "I could tell by the way they eyed each other during the auctions. It's not the same hatred she has for that other woman — you know, the cheap blond." I nodded to let her know I knew who she meant. "But Ina doesn't like her, and that woman doesn't like Ina. Maybe it's just a competitive thing, but I don't think so. Ina's in competition with a lot of these people, but I didn't get the same feeling between her and the others."

"What about that man over there?" I tried to indicate Buck Goodwin without being obvious. He was still standing guard over Ina.

Mom squinted at Buck almost a full minute before answering. I watched her profile as she concentrated. Although I had my dad's eyes and short, stocky build, I clearly had my mother's other features. If I lost weight and my face became less roly-poly, it would almost be like looking in the mirror, minus the silver hair. Greg had pointed this out when Mom first arrived, but I had failed to see it until now, or maybe I didn't want to admit it. He had also claimed Mom and I were a lot alike in other ways — he almost ended up sleeping on the sofa for that remark.

"Could be he's making an advance on her," Mom said, making her diagnosis. "A young widow might be easy pickings for a guy like him. If he provides a shoulder to cry on now, it might pay off later."

I looked at my mother with unabashed surprise.

"What?" she snorted. "When you're retired, you read and watch a lot of TV. Wouldn't be the first time a man showed a grieving woman support to get into her panties. It's a common theme." She looked back over at Ina and Buck. "Or maybe he's just being a comforting friend. Hard to tell." Mom turned to me. "He was taking pictures of the body. I made him stop."

"I saw you. Good job."

My mother gave me a small smile. My mother didn't smile often. Usually her lips were set in a concrete slash of disappointment and disapproval, but here she was, giving me a small, tight-lipped ooze of happiness. I was suddenly ashamed of my reluctance in having her extend her stay.

"So." The word came out of Mom's mouth alone and without any indication if it was a question or a declaration. The hint of smile was gone as she eyed me with expectation.

"So, what?"

Mom peered at me over the top of her glasses and remained silent. I squirmed in my seat. It didn't matter that until recently we hadn't seen each other for over three decades or that she was getting up in years; she was still my mother, and, as such, she had some sort of magical bullshit detector. It made me wonder if she had the same power over Clark. I was relieved when Renee joined us. It not only diluted some of Mom's voodoo spell, but I wouldn't have to give the update twice.

I stood up and relinquished the chair to Renee. "Greg is finding Ina an attorney to help her with the police questioning," I explained to the moms. "He's also on his way here."

Renee put a hand over her heart. "Thank God." As soon as she said the words, she looked at me with apologetic eyes. "I'm sorry, Odelia. I know you're quite capable, but I always feel better when Greg or his father are around in times like these."

I caught my mother rolling her eyes and gave her my own brand of daughterly disapproval. The eye rolling froze.

I knew Renee Stevens had a core of steel. The woman had nearly single-handedly pulled Greg through the aftermath of his accident and the resulting paralysis. It was she who showed him his life wasn't over and that it could be full of love and success even if he was sitting in a wheelchair. And when Greg flirted with destructive drugs in his late teens, it had been Renee who'd reached into the depths of his black, hopeless depression and yanked him back into the light with tough love. Without Renee Stevens, Greg would not be the solid, positive, and accomplished man I love more than life itself. But Renee was of a generation of women that depended on their men for strength, even if they had more than enough on their own. My mother, on the other hand, had a history of hooking up with nice but weak men. She'd been an alcoholic, headstrong manipulator. She'd stopped drinking years ago, but I wasn't so sure her personality had mellowed with age.

"They're letting some people leave." My mother pointed in the direction of the gate closest to us.

Sure enough, the cop posted by the smaller gate was opening it to let a few of the auction-goers leave. The main gate — the one large enough to admit trucks — remained closed. Among those leaving were the two Latinos who had won the first locker. The one called Roberto was talking with Kim Pawlak, trying to find out when they could get back in to clean out the locker they'd won. I heard him arguing that they were not going to pay any rental fee on the locker because of the mess with Tom. Kim assured him they would let him know when the police cleared the area and that he'd be given ample time, free of charge, to clear out the items. Mollified, he and his nephew started to pass through the gate, but at the last minute a man in a suit called to the cop guarding the gate to stop them. Roberto froze, but his nephew dashed through the gate, only to be stopped on the other side by a cop with his gun drawn.

"Is that the killer?" asked my mother.

"I don't know, Mom."

While we watched, the man in the suit strolled over to Guillermo and said something to him we couldn't hear. Roberto stepped in to translate. After a short exchange, police cuffed Guillermo and stuffed him into the back of a police car while Roberto argued with the guy in the suit that he was making a big mistake.

I scooted back over to where Ina and Buck stood watching the drama. "Is he a suspect?"

Buck shook his head. "Nah, from what I overheard it sounds like Guillermo is an illegal. He almost made it past the cops with his phony ID."

I watched as the police car pulled away. Roberto Vasquez ran for his truck, a cell phone to his ear. "I saw them trying to leave earlier," I told Ina and Buck. "Guess that's why."

The man in the suit approached us with two uniforms in tow. "Mrs. Bruce, we need you to come down to the station for further questioning."

Ina said nothing. She stood rooted to the ground in defiance, as if expecting the order and challenging the man to carry it through. It was my guess the man was a detective, and I knew that Ina had a dislike of authority figures that permeated her very bones.

"Right this minute?" I asked, hoping to buy time until Greg got here.

"Yes," he answered, keeping his eyes on Ina. "And, Mrs. Bruce, I'll need to see your backpack."

"Why?" Ina asked him, pulling the backpack close.

"Is this legal?" I asked.

The man turned to me. He was average in height and slim, with dark eyes and short dark hair. He was young, maybe mid-thirties. "You're with Mrs. Bruce, correct? Family?"

I nodded, and he held out a card to me. "Detective Leon Whitman. Long Beach Homicide." I took the card. It confirmed the name he'd just given me.

"My husband is on his way here," I told the detective. "One of us would like to go with Ina."

Ignoring me, he nodded to one of the officers, who tried to steer Buck back to what remained of the crowd. Buck protested, saying he wanted to stay with Ina, but a look from Whitman caused the officer at Buck's side to insist on his departure. "We'll get to you soon enough, Mr. Goodwin," Whitman promised.

Once Buck was gone, Whitman slipped on latex gloves and held out a hand toward Ina. "Your backpack please, Mrs. Bruce."

Ina held on to it like a life preserver. Her chin was high, and now her eyes were bright with fear more than defiance.

"Mrs. Bruce, please." Whitman said the words like an invitation to a root canal.

With great reluctance, Ina handed the bag over to Detective Whitman, who promptly started pawing through it like he was looking for loose change. A few seconds later, he slowly withdrew his hand, bringing with it a handgun, holding it with one gloved finger through the trigger opening.

"You have a permit for this?" he asked Ina. She said nothing.

"Don't tell me," Whitman persisted, his voice heavy with sarcasm, "you've never seen this before in your life, and you have no idea how it got in your bag."

"It's . . . it's . . . ," Ina stammered. She cleared her throat and lifted her chin higher. "The gun is mine, and no, I don't have a permit for it." The words shot out of her mouth fast and challenging. "We'd had some trouble at the store recently, so I started carrying it."

"Trouble at the store, huh?" Whitman prodded with a straight, serious face. "And where did you get it?"

"We had it in the store. Tom got it. I don't know where."

The detective sniffed the gun. "Did you use it to kill your husband?"

"Of course not!" Ina insisted. "I've never fired that thing. Not ever!"

"But you admit you don't have a permit for it."

"Hold on," I interrupted. "I don't think Ina should be saying anything else until she has a lawyer present."

A small, tight-lipped smile, cynical and mean in nature, crossed Whitman's lips.

Without looking away from Ina, he called out, "Hey Fehring, look what I found."

FIVE

Fehring?

No.

It couldn't be.

I closed my eyes, then slowly opened one — my left. One eye could be mistaken, but not two. And I was praying for a mistake — a case of mistaken identity. According to my left eye, a trim woman dressed in a plain black pantsuit with a light blue blouse was coming our way. The eyelid dropped quickly, like blinds with a snapped cord. Slowly, I opened both eyes and worked my mouth into something resembling a smile of hesitant recognition.

"Detective Fehring," I said though semi-clamped lips. "How nice to see you again."

"Save it, Odelia," the lady detective said, recovering quickly from her own surprise. "You're not a good liar."

Detective Whitman's small eyes looked from me to Andrea Fehring with suspicion

— mostly of me. "You two know each other?" Next to me, Ina was also a study in curiosity. The cop on her other side was staying close, with one hand on Ina's arm, but his eyes and ears were drinking in the encounter.

"Yes," Fehring admitted. "This is Odelia Grey, a civilian with a nose for murder." Fehring turned to fully face me, hands on hips. "How do you do it, Odelia? Do you have some special olfactory gift like those pigs that smell out truffles?"

"It . . . it just happens," I stammered. "I thought you were working in Newport Beach." Last I'd seen Andrea Fehring, she had been a detective in Newport Beach, working with my good friend Dev Frye.

"That was temporary. I transferred to Long Beach a few months ago." She looked me up and down. She looked Ina up and down.

Fehring turned to Whitman. "What do we have here, Detective?"

Whitman held up the gun. "Concealed with no permit."

The news surprised the usually stony Fehring. "I thought you were smarter than that, Odelia."

"It's not her bag," Whitman corrected. "It belongs to this woman, Ina Bruce, wife of the deceased."

Fehring turned to the cop holding Ina. "Cuff her and take her in."

"But I didn't kill Tom!" Ina screamed as the cop read her her rights and cuffed her.

By now my mother and Renee were standing next to me, both in shock. "Leave Ina alone," Renee pleaded. "She didn't kill Tom. She wouldn't hurt anyone."

Fehring ignored Renee and stood in front of Ina. "You're under arrest for possession of an illegal firearm, Mrs. Bruce."

Just before being led away, Ina spit at Fehring's feet.

"Nice," Fehring commented to Whitman. "I can see questioning her is going to be a barrel of laughs."

Andrea Fehring turned to me. "So, Ms. Grey, what's your involvement in all this?"

"Ina is my husband's cousin." I pointed at Renee. "This is Renee Stevens, my mother-in-law, and next to her is Grace Littlejohn, my mother."

Fehring gave Renee a perfunctory nod, but her eyes lingered on my mother, who took it as a cue to speak up.

"We were here for the auction," Mom explained. "Ina let us tag along today. I really don't think she knew her husband was up for sale."

"Mom," I cautioned under my breath.

Fehring let a small smile crack her face. "I can see the apple didn't fall far from the tree."

By the time Greg arrived, I had gone through my questioning by the police and half of the crowd had been sent home. Ina was on her way to the police station.

"Ina's been arrested!" Renee said, rushing to Greg as soon as he was cleared through the gate. "Do something."

Greg put a comforting hand on Renee's arm. "Hold on, Mom. Let me get some facts first." He turned to me. "Ina was arrested for murder?"

"No," I told him, "on a gun charge. She had a gun in her backpack and no permit."

Greg's head dropped in disbelief. "Oh, Ina."

"Did you find her an attorney?" I asked.

"Yes." Greg pulled out his cell phone. "Steele's getting someone he knows." He placed a call. "Mike, it's Greg. My cousin was just arrested on a gun charge — concealing, I think — and has been taken to the station." He waited, listening. "Yeah, Long Beach. Have your guy meet me there. I'll be there as soon as I get Odelia and our moms squared away." He listened again.

"She's right here." He handed his phone to me, but I refused to take it. Greg shook it at me again. I shook my head at him and backed away. Greg put the phone back to his ear. "Sorry, Mike, she's busy. But I'll have her call as soon as she can. Thanks for your help." He paused, then said, "Okay, I'll tell her."

"Steele said you could take the rest of the week off if you need to, as long as you tell him where you put the Billings file."

I crossed my arms. "The Billings file is on his desk. I put it there last Monday, right before Mom and Clark showed up on our doorstep and I left for the holiday. This is just a ruse to get me to call him."

Greg stuck his phone into his shirt pocket. "You know he's not going to rest until he hears the whole story from you personally."

"Not my problem, especially right now." I turned to watch the police let a few more people go. One of them was Mazie Moore. As soon as possible, I wanted to know more about Mazie and Linda's relationship. When Detective Whitman had asked for Ina's bag, I'm betting he knew there was a gun in there. He seemed too sure and smug about it. Someone must have tipped him off. Maybe Mazie or Linda had set Ina up. Maybe one of them did the killing or knew about it and used Ina's gun possession as a distraction. Hard to tell.

"Sweetheart?"

"Huh?" I turned my attention to Greg to find both him and Renee watching me.

"I was talking to you, and you were definitely somewhere else."

Instead of answering, I returned my gaze to Mazie. I sucked my front teeth while watching her drive away in a white Toyota sedan.

"You know something," I heard Greg say. "Don't you?"

I turned to look at my incredibly patient husband. "I don't know squat except that the woman who just drove away might be teamed up with Tom's hoochie momma on something."

Greg looked around. "So where is this hoochie momma?"

"She took off before the police got here."

It was then I noticed Mom hadn't followed Renee over to where we greeted Greg, nor was she seated on a folding chair by the office. I scanned the small area where the remaining people were still being processed by the police and spotted her. She was cozying up to Buck Goodwin. It looked like they were having a friendly chat, which made me shiver with worry. Who knew what the old gal was saying to him, and I couldn't read lips. Maybe she was apologizing for smacking him with her handbag, but I doubted it.

"There you go again, Odelia," I heard Greg say. "Lost in space."

"I'm sorry, honey. I was just keeping an eye on my mother." I pointed over to where Mom stood with Buck. "That guy seems to be a friend of Ina's, but he and Mom had a small scuffle earlier."

"Grace knocked his phone out of his hand while he was taking pictures of poor Tom's body," Renee explained to Greg with disgust.

Greg laughed. "Sounds like something you would do, Odelia."

I cocked an eyebrow at my husband, warning him not to make any more comparisons. He read my silence with accuracy and only laughed more.

"By the way," he said, once he was over having a chuckle at my expense. "Was that Detective Fehring I saw when I arrived? You know, Dev's partner?"

"Yes, but she's not his partner any longer. She's with the Long Beach Police Department now." I knitted my brow. "Do you recall Dev saying anything about getting a new partner recently?"

"Not a word, but you know how Dev is. He doesn't like to talk shop when he's out socially, and he's had no reason to see us professionally — although who knows if that will change, considering this mess."

"This is out of his jurisdiction," I reminded my hubs.

Dev had had bypass surgery in March. After that, he had returned to work, but at a desk. He'd hated it, preferring homicide investigations to pushing paper. His doctor finally released him to return to his detective duties a few months ago.

"Fehring said she joined Long Beach a few months ago," I told Greg. "That would have been right after Dev returned to the field."

"Maybe she was sticking around to cover while they were short-handed?"

"You two know the detective?" Renee asked, her voice filled with cautious hope. "Maybe that will be good for Ina."

Greg turned his wheelchair to get a look at Fehring, who was talking to Kim Pawlak. "Hard to say, Mom. She and Odelia don't exactly exchange cookie recipes."

"Hey," I protested, "we managed to patch things up at the end."

"Was she involved with that little girl's case?"

"Yes, Renee," I answered. "She used to be the partner of our friend Dev Frye."

Renee took a deep breath. "That still might be a good thing." She hesitated. "Providing Ina's innocent."

"Mom." Greg swiveled around to face his mother. "Is there any reason why you might think Ina killed Tom? If so, we'd like to hear it, like right this minute."

Renee adjusted her shoulder bag and looked down at the ground, as if ashamed of her thoughts. "It's just that if those bruises on Ina's arms were made by Tom, maybe he was abusing her regularly." She took a deep breath and looked up at Greg. "You always hear stories about abused women snapping and killing their tormentors."

"Did you say any of this to the police?" asked Greg in a low voice.

Renee shook her head slowly. "They didn't ask specifically. They asked me if Ina and Tom were happy, and I told them about that Linda woman. That's all."

"Jealousy is a strong emotion," I said. "But abuse would really underscore a possible motive."

"Did I say something wrong?" Renee's worry skyrocketed to new heights.

"No, Mom, not at all." Greg took her

hands. "As soon as they release all of you, Odelia's going to take you back to our house. It's closer than yours."

Renee wasn't so sure. "But what about your father? I called him earlier and told him what's going on and that you were on your way here. I'm sure he's worried sick."

"Call Dad and ask him to come to our place to get you. I'm heading to the police station to meet Ina's attorney."

"All right," Renee agreed, then had a thought. "But what about Ina's car?"

"I'll talk to the police before I go." Greg turned to scan the parking lot, letting his eyes come to rest on Ina's Honda Element, which was parked next to my car. "I'm sure the police will search and impound it for now."

"You read my mind, Mr. Stevens." It was Fehring. She'd sneaked up on us like a panther wearing satin slippers. "Which vehicle is your cousin's? Or do we need to exercise the process of elimination and wait until all the other vehicles have left?" Her eyes scanned the parking lot, which was emptying as people were allowed to leave.

"It's the Honda," Greg admitted, pointing it out.

"We appreciate your cooperation." She called a uniformed officer over and gave instructions for the vehicle's processing.

Turning to me, Fehring said, "We have all of your statements and contact information, so if you and your family would like to go, you can. Just remain close in case we need to talk to you again."

I noticed Fehring catching sight of Mom talking to Buck Goodwin and saw her brows knit, though I wasn't sure if it was from the sun or curiosity.

"Is your mother the nosy sort, like yourself?" she asked, not taking her eyes off of Mom.

"I don't know what you mean, Detective Fehring."

Fehring gave me a long, slow look, conveying to me exactly what she meant.

"My mother will be going home soon," I assured her, "back to New Hampshire."

"In the meantime," the detective said, somewhat relieved, "why don't you keep both her and yourself occupied with sightseeing. Maybe she'd like to see Disneyland or Sea World before she goes home."

"I see you've become more subtle since leaving Newport Beach."

"Odelia," Greg said sharply under his breath. Next to him, Renee stood watching with worry.

"You want subtle," Fehring said, stepping

84

closer to me, "here's subtle: stay out of this investigation, Odelia Grey. I don't want to see you or hear about you anywhere near it. I don't want you poking around asking questions. Just answer the questions we ask you when we ask you." She stuck her right index finger out in my direction, nearly touching my face. "That's an order."

After Fehring left, Renee said, "Oh dear, that woman doesn't like you one bit, Odelia. For Ina's sake, I hope you listen to her."

"But Fehring said nothing about *me*." The words came from Greg. He was looking up at me with a determined and devilish eye.

Six

It was quiet around our kitchen table. It was midafternoon. Mom, Renee, and I were picking at chicken salad sandwiches my mother had whipped up. She'd made the chicken salad the night before with the grilled chicken left over from dinner. Mom put chopped celery and almonds in it, and sometimes golden raisins, never the brown ones.

"When Odelia was young," my mother said, trying to break the worry and tension that clouded the table like the odor of questionable food, "she loved my chicken salad. I made it for her quite often." She looked at me across the table. "Do you remember, Odelia?"

"I do, Mom. That's why I picked up a box of golden raisins yesterday at the grocery store, just so you'd make it." I tried a smile, but it was forced. All of us were thinking about Ina and what was going on at the police station. Chicken salad with raisins, no matter how good, wasn't bringing us any comfort.

"It is quite tasty, Grace," added Renee with little enthusiasm. "Ron would love this. Please give me the recipe before you go."

When the doorbell rang, the three of us jumped in our seats. Wainwright, our golden retriever, ran for the door, barking. From the tone of his bark, I knew it was someone familiar. Wainwright usually goes everywhere with Greg, but he'd been sent home with us while Greg went on to the police station.

I got up and answered, expecting to see my father-in-law. Instead, Mike Steele was on my doorstep. I groaned. "Don't you have any work to do?"

By my side, Wainwright was hopping with joy. He loved Steele, leaving it my job to growl through the screen door.

"Of course I do, and so do you. Since you won't return my calls, you gave me no choice but to track you down. Not to mention, I haven't met your mother yet and didn't want her to get away without the pleasure."

Steele gave me one of his signature shit-eating grins. He was dressed in his usual designer suit and tie, with the tie loosened a bit. With both hands he gripped a cardboard box without a lid. One glance told me it contained expandable files bulging with documents. I was tempted to slam the door and might have if I'd been alone. Instead, I caved and unlatched the screen door, holding it open for him to enter.

Once he got past me, Steele put the box down on the coffee table and went straight to my mother-in-law, holding out his right hand. "Renee, how nice to see you again. I think the last time was at Greg's fortieth birthday party."

In spite of her worry over Ina, Renee gave her hand to Steele with a warm smile. "Nice to see you again, Mike. Thank you for coming by to see how we're doing and for helping Ina."

He took her hand between both of his. "Happy to help. Odelia and Greg are like family to me, so that makes you family." Charm oozed out of Steele soft and slick, like a crayon left in the sun.

Wainwright was nudging Steele's leg with his nose. Usually when Steele visits, Wainwright is his first greeting. "Hang on, buddy," Steele said to the dog, "ladies first." I almost barfed.

From Renee, Steele made his way around the table to my mother. "Mrs. Littlejohn, I presume." He held out his hand to Mom. She took it. "I'm Mike Steele. I work with your daughter. I've been looking forward to meeting you."

"You're her boss, right?"

"Yes, though some would say it's really Odelia who's the boss." Steele turned to me and grinned.

"I can believe that." Mom gave Steele a warm welcome. "She can be a regular Miss Bossy Pants."

Steele let go of my mother's hand and squatted down to rub Wainwright's head and neck. The dog was in Nirvana. "Bossy Pants. I like that," he said to the dog. "Don't you, boy? We can add it to Corpse Magnet and Cheesehead Squirrel."

I was ready to hit Steele over the head with a fireplace poker, except we didn't have a fireplace.

I cleared my throat. "So what's with the box, Steele?"

He stood up. "Nothing much. Just a little work to keep you busy."

Steele had taken the position of managing partner of the Orange County office of Templin and Tobin over a year ago. I had joined him at T&T just after Labor Day of this year. With some negotiation, we had agreed that I only had to come into the office three

89

days a week. The rest of the time I would telecommute or, if we weren't busy, would have the other two days off. If we were busy, I worked a full work week but did much of the job from home. The T&T folks had set up my laptop so I could connect to the firm's main server. For the past two months that arrangement had worked quite well. I loved being able to work from home part of the time. Even though T&T was a much larger firm than my last one, the Orange County office was small. Steele had brought over a few familiar faces from Woobie, like his assistant Jill Bernelli and Jolene Mc-Hugh, a senior associate. We handled mostly business matters in the OC office. In addition to Steele and Jolene, there were two other attorneys. Jill was one of two assistants. I was the only paralegal. It was nice and cozy, and the mothership in LA pretty much left us alone.

"Greg said you told him I could have the rest of the week off if I told you where the Billings file was. I was going to text you about that in a little bit."

Steele held up an index finger. "No, what I said is that you did not need to come into the office the rest of this week. That doesn't mean this work doesn't need to be done. As for Billings, don't bother with the text —

the file is in the box. I need you to do a preliminary draft of a shareholder's agreement between Billings and his new partner, as well as the other necessary documents."

I glanced at the box again. "The Billings file is not that large. What else is in there?"

"Just the Wright Wood file and notes for the new corporation Ham Goldman wants to start. I think those should keep you busy until next week."

I grabbed Steele's sleeve and maneuvered him into the living room by the box, away from the two sets of mom ears, which I knew was useless because everyone knows mothers have hearing that can beat a dog's into the ground, even elderly mothers. Still, I made the effort.

"What's up, Steele?" I asked in a hushed but stern tone. "None of this work needs to be done this week. In fact, Jack Billings is out of the country through the end of the year, and Goldman specifically said he did not want to file the Articles of Incorporation for his new company until after the first of January."

"This is the day of technology, Grey," Steele pointed out, arching one brow, "or are you still in the dark ages? Out of the country or not, Jack can still review and sign documents. And it wouldn't hurt to have

91

Ham's documents ready ahead of time. And, if you haven't noticed, the end of the year is just a few weeks away. Not to mention, I'm going skiing over Christmas and want these matters taken care of before I leave."

"Aha, and there is the real motive." I paused, going through my recent memory. "Wait, you didn't have anything on your calendar about skiing. In fact, I remember you specifically telling Jill and me that you were sticking around over the holidays this year."

"Things change." He shot me another shit-eating grin.

I settled my hands on my hips in understanding. "So what's her name?"

"There is no *her,* Grey. If you must know, at the last minute some friends rented a chalet in Switzerland for Christmas and New Year's and asked if I wanted to join them."

Even though I was still sure a *her* was involved, I let the matter drop. "Okay, I'm sure I can draft up the documents you need this week."

"See, a win-win for everyone."

I squinted at Steele. "And how do you figure that? I see a win for you and one for the clients, but where's my win?"

"The work will help keep your mind off of the situation with Greg's cousin. And you never know what might happen in the meantime to get in the way of your work. It has happened before."

"You mean like a murder that might keep me from doing my job?" I aimed my best scowl at my boss. "Are you afraid I'll get bumped off and you'll have to do this stuff instead of me?"

"Actually, I was thinking that maybe this work would keep you occupied instead of fretting over this latest murder. Less fret — that's your win."

I leaned in close. "My mother's here. I think that will keep me occupied."

Steele put his head down closer to mine. "If she starts to drive you nuts, you can always use the work as an excuse for some alone time."

I had to admit, that was a fairly decent plan. "She's been here a week. Who's to say she's not already driving me crazy?"

Steele laughed, straightened, and headed back into the kitchen and the moms. "Sorry, ladies, just some confidential legal stuff."

"Would you like a chicken salad sandwich?" my mother offered. She was at the kitchen counter futzing with the debris of our lunch fixings. "I'd be happy to fix one for you."

"Grace's chicken salad is quite excellent, Mike," Renee added with a gracious smile. "You really should sit and have a bite."

Steele consulted his Rolex. "I'm meeting someone for tennis in just over an hour."

"On an empty stomach?" My mother appeared horrified with motherly concern.

If it weren't so rude and obnoxious, I would have grabbed my cell phone and recorded the exchange. Clark was never going to believe it when I told him about this.

Steele appeared to be considering something for a few seconds. "Is that chicken all white meat?"

"But of course," Mom answered. "Just the breast, grilled last night by Greg himself. And it's made with low-fat mayonnaise, not that you have to watch your physique." I swear, my mother almost giggled.

"Well, it's true, I didn't have lunch yet. I was too busy getting those files together for Grey."

That settled it. Fireplace or not, I was buying a poker to keep handy for Steele's next visit. I'm sure he'll give me reason to wield it at some point in the future.

Steele eyed my mother and twitched his mouth. "Would you consider it terribly rude if I said yes to the sandwich but asked for it to go?"

"This isn't Burger King, Steele," I said, snapping like a disturbed alligator.

"Odelia," Renee admonished, "don't be so rude to your guest."

"Yeah, Miss Bossy Pants," my mother chimed in. "Especially since he's your boss and all." She turned her attention to Steele. "But of course I can make the sandwich to go." She started pulling two slices of whole grain bread out of the package. "I'll have it ready in a jiff."

A few minutes later I was walking Steele to the door. In one hand he held a small paper bag containing the chicken salad sandwich, an apple, and a napkin. All that was missing was a juice box and a few cookies, and he'd be ready for school.

"Are you really going to eat that sandwich?" I asked him. "Or were you just wooing the moms?"

He winked. "I really do love a good chicken salad. Reminds me of my own mother. Is Grace's any good?"

"It's actually worthy of your elevated palate."

"Then I can't wait."

Steele started down the walk whistling a little tune. At the curb his Porsche, a new one, waited like a loyal steed. A large sedan drove up, parking directly behind Steele's car. It was Ron Stevens. Seeing him, Steele waited. When Ron got out of the car and approached the sidewalk, Steele greeted him with an outstretched hand and a smile.

From time to time, Greg tells me that I'm too hard on Steele, that he's really a great guy under all the fancy clothes, expensive trappings, and arrogance. And I know that. Really, I do. He's not only a brilliant attorney, but much of his character is built of higher quality materials than the suit on his back and the car he drives. He's annoying, it's true. He treats women in general as objects of amusement and turns a sarcastic nose up at the ordinary things the rest of us enjoy and love. But he's as loyal as the day is long to the people he cares about. If he weren't, I wouldn't have my job at T&T, nor would I have wanted to go there in the first place. If Clark is my big annoying brother, then Steele is my younger annoying brother, even if he isn't bonded by blood.

But I'm still buying that fireplace poker.

SEVEN

The day after the auction, I spent the morning taking care of some household chores. Although I work from home much of the time, we still maintained a housekeeper. Her name is Cruz, and she comes once a week on Wednesdays. Because she had a houseful of company for Thanksgiving, Cruz hadn't been to the house in two weeks and it showed. I try to keep it tidy, but Cruz works magic.

"Didn't you say your cleaning lady was coming this week?"

"Yes, tomorrow morning."

Mom was seated at the kitchen table, watching me sort through mail that had piled up on the counter in the past several days. I was discarding the trash and stacking the non-trash into specific piles.

"I don't understand why you're cleaning before she comes."

Mom had wanted to clean the guest

bathroom this morning, but I had stopped her, advising her of Cruz's pending visit. "I'm not cleaning, Mom, just tidying up. Cruz is paid to keep the house clean, not to pick up our clutter." I had already stripped our bed and the guest bed and had thrown the sheets into the wash — something I would normally leave for Cruz to do. Nervous energy was oozing out of me like an oil leak in an old jalopy, and in spite of what I was saying to Mom, I was tempted to grab a pail and start mopping just to burn it off. "As soon as I get this done, I'm going to dig into the work Steele brought by."

"Why do you call him Steele when everyone else calls him Mike?"

I stopped reading the junk mail in my hand. "I don't know, Mom. He calls me Grey and I call him Steele. It's always been that way between us. At work Steele calls everyone by their last name."

"But he calls Greg by his first name."

I sighed and set the mailer with grocery coupons to the side so I'd remember to stick it in my purse. "Greg doesn't work for him. He also calls Clark by his first name."

"Sounds very military to me. Like he's your commander and you're the troops."

"Uh-huh. It kind of is that way to Steele."

"Steele." Mom said his name carefully, as

98

if tasting hot soup. "Steele," she said again. "I think I'm going to call him that, too."

I kept my head down so Mom couldn't see me roll my eyes. "Knock yourself out."

She got up from the table. "I'm going outside to read, if you don't mind."

"Go ahead," I told her. "But wear a sweater. It might be warmer here than back home, but there's a chilly breeze coming in off the ocean."

Mom retrieved her sweater from the back of a chair and her Kindle from the kitchen counter and slipped outside. Greg and I had gotten the e-reader for her last Christmas when she complained it was getting more difficult for her to read as she got older. At first she'd balked about using it, but once Clark showed her how to change the fonts to larger sizes, she took to it in no time.

After I'd moved the sheets from the washer to the dryer, I grabbed my laptop and one of the folders from the box Steele had brought over and joined Mom on the patio. By her side in another chair was Seamus, our elderly feline. Muffin was off playing explorer among our shrubs. Wainwright was with Greg at work. Seamus is wary of strangers, usually spending most of his time on our bed or snoozing in front of a window, but in the past couple of days he and Mom had become close chums. Maybe Seamus sensed that, like him, Mom was in her golden years and just as cranky about it. Last night he even slept on Mom's bed. It had been the first time he hadn't slept with us since . . . well, forever. Mom was reading while her right hand gently stroked the cat, only moving it to change the page on her reader. I smiled to myself. Having Mom around longer wasn't proving to be the chore I'd thought it might be.

Mom looked up. "You doing some of that work Steele brought by?"

"I should be." As soon as I said the words, I wish I hadn't. I should have simply said yes. My fingers flew over the keyboard of my laptop as I fired up a search engine and plugged in some information. I hoped Mom wouldn't pry further, but today was not my lucky day.

"You're snooping around in Ina's mess, aren't you?"

"I'm *not* snooping, Mom. I'm simply checking out a few things, like the names and locations of the secondhand stores owned by some of the people Ina knows."

"That Detective Fehring told you to keep your nose out of it."

"She said no such thing."

"What I recall her saying as we left was

'under no circumstances are you to get involved in this, or I may have to shoot you.' In my book, that means keep your nose out of things."

Unfortunately, my mother's hearing and memory were not aging as fast as her eyesight.

"I saw you talking with Buck Goodwin yesterday. Did he happen to mention the name of his store?"

"So you're ignoring what the lady detective said?"

When I didn't answer, Mom pursed her lips and closed her eyes as she pondered the question and its possibilities. A good thirty seconds passed before she spoke again, making me wonder if she'd nodded off. "Goodwin's Good Stuff, I think," she finally said, keeping her eyes shut. "Or something like that."

I put in the name *Goodwin's Good Stuff* and up popped a couple of suggested links. One was to the store itself; other links were to review sites like About Town, which offered consumers the opportunity to review restaurants and other businesses they frequented, letting potential customers know if it was a good deal or should be avoided.

I opened the link to the website for Buck's store. Up popped a website that looked like it had been set up using an inexpensive service with preset templates. It was uncluttered and clean, giving basic details like location and hours. The store claimed to deal in used and vintage items, including furniture, appliances, and tools. The site also welcomed phone call inquiries about specialty items, proclaiming, "Looking for something special? We'll help you find it."

I scooted my chair over and turned my laptop so Mom could see the website while I hit the print button and sent the page to our wireless printer.

Next I checked out the About Town reviews for Goodwin's Good Stuff. There were just a handful, almost all very favorable, citing excellent customer service and help in locating specialty items. One man had been looking for a specific hood ornament for a vintage car, and Buck had located it for him. Other reviews commented on the nice selection of items in the store and the convenient parking. There was a photo of the storefront on the website. Like the website, it appeared basic and uncluttered. It was located in a strip mall in Torrance.

"Look at that." Mom was pointing to one of the reviews, the last one. Unlike the others, it had given Buck's store a bad review, saying the owner was surly and the store dirty and filled with broken junk. The review had been left by someone named Bob Y from Los Angeles. Unlike most of the reviewers on About Town, Bob Y did not use his photo but instead posted a cartoon of a goofy kid as his profile pic. I clicked the link to his profile and found it to be bare-bones. The profile did show, however, that he'd posted over twenty reviews and had given almost all of them one to three stars; only two had been given a four- or five-star rating. Based on the reviews posted on his profile, it looked like Bob Y frequented secondhand and consignment shops, along with Southern California–based food trucks. Food trucks had received the coveted four- and five-star ratings.

I scanned the list of reviews and saw that Bob Y had also reviewed Second to None, Tom and Ina's shop in Culver City. Like Buck's shop, Bob Y had found Second to None way under par, calling it a "rusty junk heap with rabid owners." Greg and I had visited Second to None once, and it was hardly a junk heap. I'd found a lovely side table that proudly sits in our living room and an antique dresser for the guest bedroom. Tom and Ina may have been "rabid" from time to time, but they'd kept the shop orderly and well stocked. It was a vocation they'd stumbled upon and discovered it suited them.

I clicked over to see other reviews of Second to None. There were some four-star reviews, but none with five stars. Several gave the store two and three stars, with most citing surly customer service for the lower ranking but liking the store in general. One went so far as to say, "Have the chick wait on you. She's the nice one." Only Bob Y had given Second to None the lowest ranking of one star.

"Does Ina's store have a website?" Mom asked. I was moving slower than normal through the information because she wanted to read it along with me.

"Yes, it does." I found the website. Unlike Buck's, the website for Second to None was custom. I knew that because Greg had designed it for them and had showed them how to maintain it. It was clean and uncluttered, containing photos of the shop inside and out, including all the pertinent information like address and hours. According to the website, Second to None boasted vintage furniture in addition to used household goods. I could vouch for that. Besides the two items I'd purchased, there had been a small but nice collection of gorgeous pieces in the store when we visited. Ina told me that most of their antiques came from estate sales in nearby Beverly Hills and Brentwood. She would have liked to expand that part of their store, but they could not afford to buy many pieces at a time. With their store very close to Sony Studios and not far from the Fox lot, they'd also built up a clientele that collected movie and TV memorabilia, which lately had become Tom's passion. Those items were usually smaller than furniture and were easier to store and sell.

"You done reading?" I asked Mom.

When she nodded, I went back to Bob Y's profile and checked out some of the other stores, hoping to find one connected to Mazie Moore. I remembered Buck saying she had several locations, but I had no idea what they might be called. I was hoping, like Buck, she used her own name in the store's name. A store among Bob Y's reviews caught my eye. It was called Otra Vez. Like Buck's and Ina's stores, it had received a bad review and even an ugly racist comment saying the proprietor could "make more money running drugs like the rest of his kind."

Following the links, I found the official

website for Otra Vez, which I knew meant "again" in Spanish. The website was very basic, like Buck's, but was in both English and Spanish. It was located in Lynwood right off the 105 Freeway. Besides the usual photo of the storefront, there was also a photo of a smiling family — a middle-aged mom and dad, a couple of younger adults, and two small children — all waving to the camera. The caption under the photo read in both languages: *The Vasquez family welcomes you.*

Vasquez. It sounded familiar. I searched my memory until a mental flash of a man being led away in handcuffs appeared, followed by another man yelling in Spanish into a phone. Vasquez. Roberto Vasquez. He'd been at the auction, and his nephew had been led away as an illegal. I looked again at the photo. The nephew was not in the picture.

Mom poked a finger at the family photo. "Wasn't that man at the auction? Was he the one the police took away?"

"Yes. That's Roberto Vasquez. But it was his nephew who was arrested for being undocumented."

My attention went back to the About Town reviews. The reviews had been done by a Bob Y — Bobby? Could it be Roberto

Vasquez was trashing his competition? He could have given his own business a bad review to put people off the scent, but it seemed counterproductive. I stored the possibility in the back of my mind for later consideration.

I continued going through the remaining secondhand store reviews by Bob Y, flipping back and forth between the reviews and searching for websites to the stores. In the few left, none appeared to be owned by Mazie Moore.

"Those shops have such cute names," Mom observed. "It used to be stores like that were just called Used Furniture or Thrift Store."

"Guess it's all about marketing these days and appearing to have better-quality merchandise."

A search of Mazie's name on Google did bring up several mentions of a store called Ladybug Vintage. A quick click and I was looking at a charming website for a store specializing in "gently used clothing, furniture, and gift items." A link at the top led me to Ladybug's locations. There were two: one in Pico Rivera and another in Inglewood, just as Buck had said. There was also an announcement of a third store coming soon to the Baldwin Hills district of Los

Angeles.

Somehow Bob Y had missed Ladybug Vintage, or maybe he just hadn't gotten there yet. I looked again at his review page.

"Why do you keep going back to that guy's nasty reviews?" Mom asked with keen interest.

"I want to see how long ago his reviews were posted."

"You mean it might be a clue?" She leaned closer.

I laughed silently at her enthusiasm. "Who knows, but I want to see if his attacks on these stores are recent or a phase he was going through."

Going down the list of reviews, both for the stores and the food trucks, it looked like Bob Y had only recently started reviewing. All were posted within the past four months. Not a single review of any kind was posted prior to that, not even for a food truck.

Mom noticed that, too. "Does that mean he's a fake?"

"Not necessarily. He could have just recently started posting reviews, but it does seem suspicious that he only posts reviews for secondhand stores and food trucks."

"We always called those 'roach coaches.' You saw them around factories and places like that where there was no place for employees to go for lunch. They weren't exactly known for food that was good, just quick and filling."

"They're big business now, Mom. And they serve up not only good food but great food."

Looking at the list of reviewed food trucks, I saw that Bob Y had left a couple for one food truck in particular, adding a running commentary to his initial review. It looked like he frequented this truck often. It was called Comfort Foodies. The menu on the website for Comfort Foodies showed a mixture of traditional comfort food with a trendy spin. The truck was operated by a family — a mother and her two sons — and served up fancy burgers and sandwiches along with new twists on comfort food, like fried mac and cheese, a meatloaf and mashed potato wrap, apple pie ice cream, and something called Not Your Mother's Chicken Soup.

I jabbed my finger at the computer screen. "I saw this truck featured on a local news show not too long ago. It's a very tragic story."

Mom looked at me with interest. "What happened?"

I combed my memory for the details. "The mom and dad were involved in a hit-

and-run accident several years ago. The father died, and the mother was badly injured and unable to work. Shortly after, the family was evicted from their home and scraped by with only part-time jobs held by the two boys, who were in their teens at the time. The eldest quit school to support his mother and younger brother."

Mom shook her head with sadness. "That is tragic, but it looks like they recovered."

"That's what the news story was about. Seems a local anonymous businessman heard about what had happened and came to their aid. He gave them a place to live and helped out so both boys could finish high school. The mother had always wanted to open a restaurant, so when she was well enough, he gave her the money to start one. She decided on the food truck business since that was starting to grow. Now Comfort Foodies pays it forward by going down to skid row in Los Angeles once a month and feeding the homeless lunch from their truck."

"What a lovely story."

"Yes," I agreed. "And from these reviews, it seems Bob Y loves Comfort Foodies and frequents it."

I toggled over to the Comfort Foodies website and checked to see their schedule.

Today they would be at two places. They were going to a food truck rally tonight at a Home Depot parking lot up near LAX, but from eleven to three they would be at a farmers' market in Manhattan Beach. I checked the time on my computer screen. It was almost twelve thirty and time for lunch. If traffic on the 405 Freeway cooperated, it would take about thirty to forty minutes to get there. Timing would be everything. If they were busy with a lunch crowd they may not have time to talk to anyone, but if I got there around one thirty or even a little after, there might be time to chat with someone from Comfort Foodies and see if they had any idea who Bob Y might be.

"Mom, I may have to go out for a bit." After sending more items to the printer, I closed my laptop and got up from the table. "You okay here by yourself? I think there's still some chicken salad for your lunch. Or you could heat up some soup."

"You don't fool me, missy."

That again. I sighed.

Mom shook an index finger at me. It was the second time in two days she'd said those words and made that gesture. If she did it again, I was going to bite her scrawny finger off at the first joint.

"You're going to find that truck, aren't you?" The finger stayed pointed, and I noticed it was shaking a tiny bit.

"I just need to run an errand." I did some quick calculations in my head. "I'll probably be gone two hours. Maybe only ninety minutes."

"You never were a good liar, Odelia. Must have gotten that from your father."

Fehring had also said I wasn't a good liar. I didn't know whether to be insulted or pat myself on the back.

"Dad was not a liar." I lightly stomped my right foot on the concrete of our patio to make my point. I felt like a kid defending my father to a bully on a playground.

"My point exactly. If you'd taken after me, you'd be good at it."

Speechless, I stood rooted to the ground, trying to sort out what Mom had just said. Was she condemning me because I was a bad liar, like I'd brought home a C instead of an A in duplicity on a report card? Or was she slyly acknowledging that she had not exactly been up front with the people in her life?

The real question was, when in the hell was Clark coming to get Mom and take her home?

The accusing finger was lowered, and my

mother got up from her chair. "If you leave this house, you're taking me with you," she insisted. Next to her, Seamus yawned and stretched, then settled back down to nap again. He wasn't asking to go anywhere.

"It will be boring, Mom. You'd enjoy yourself more if you stayed here and read or watched TV."

"I can do plenty of that when I get back to New Hampshire."

Traffic on the 405 moved along at a nice pace. We weren't able to go the posted speed limit but neither were we crawling, which was often the case during the week. Next to me, Mom looked out the window, taking in everything with eagle eyes as if she were on a life-or-death mission. No matter how much I'd tried to convince her, there was no way she was going to let me leave her behind.

Fine. Arguing with her was wasting valuable time.

"Just let me run to the ladies' room first," she'd said. She must have caught on that I was contemplating sneaking out and leaving her behind because as she started to go down the hall to the guest bath, she turned to me and said with a point of the annoying index finger, "And don't you even think

113

about running off without me. If you do, I'll simply call a cab and follow you."

"Mom, Manhattan Beach isn't around the corner. A cab would be exorbitant."

"You're forgetting, Odelia, I'm loaded, and although I'm not as spry as I used to be, I'm still quite capable of doing things on my own. I also have my iPad with me. I'm sure I'd be able to find all the information I need on it." With those words, my mother gave me a sharp nod to signal the end of the conversation. That settled, she shuffled down the hall.

Once Mom was out of earshot, I had a brief and quiet tantrum laced with swearing. I knew I was beat. Thanks to her first husband, who was also her third husband and Clark's father, Mom was very well off. But this was the first I'd heard about the iPad. She'd been here a week and I'd not once seen it. I was learning, albeit at a slow pace, that it was easy to underestimate my mother. Her corkscrew gray hair, sensible shoes, and shuffling frame belied a tough and conniving cookie, just like she'd been when she was younger. My mother wasn't a doddering old fool whom Boy Scouts needed to help across the street. She was the sort of geriatric who ended up in the news for beating an alleged assailant with her cane.

I glanced over at Mom, then put my eyes back on the road. "So when did you get the iPad? Did Clark buy it for you?" The question was a combination of small talk and curiosity.

"I bought it myself," she answered with an irritated sniff in the air. "When Lorraine, Clark's youngest, dropped by to visit this past summer, she had one with her. That old hand-me-down laptop I had from the house was about to die, so I asked Lorraine if she'd take me to the store so I could get one like hers." Mom turned to me. "We had a grand time, Lorraine and I. Before she left, she set it up and showed me how to use it."

"Don't they have computers at the retirement home for you to use?"

"Yes, a few, but there's always some old fart on them and our time is limited. This way I have my own."

"If I'd known you needed a new computer, we would have gotten you something like that instead of the Kindle."

"I like that Kindle just fine. It's smaller and easier to take with me when I just want to read."

This time I gave her a smile. "Between the iPad, Kindle, and that new phone Clark got you, you're one hi-tech granny."

Mom squeaked out a chuckle, something she didn't do very often. "That's almost word-for-word what Lorraine called me."

I checked the car's GPS to see how soon before we arrived at our destination.

"You're kind of hi-tech yourself," Mom noted, "with this fancy new car and all."

In March, my old car had been destroyed by an out-of-control van with a crazed driver behind the wheel. We'd replaced it with a new one — a hybrid — decked out with the latest in gizmos. The thing not only told me how to get someplace, but it synced with my phone and music and had a rear-view camera. It basically did everything but drive for me.

We rode along another mile in silence before Mom said, "Why are you so interested in this Bob Y? Shouldn't we be visiting those secondhand stores?"

We?

I swallowed a terse knee-jerk retort and replaced it with a nicer reply. "It's just a gut feeling. Bob Y might be a lead the police don't have. I'm sure they'll be all over the stores owned by the witnesses. Their first thought would be that a competitor might have killed Tom."

"I'd think Ina would be their first suspect."

"True — then they would be thinking about the competitors."

"What about the folks who owned that locker? Someone had to get Tom in there, and it didn't look like it had been broken into, did it?"

I tried not to show surprise at my mother's thinking. She was really looking at this from all angles with surprising clarity. Her body might be slowing down, but her mind was sharp as a tack.

"I overheard Kim Pawlak telling one of the officers that the storage unit had been rented to some people who'd left the area to find work. They ended up in North Carolina. They'd stopped paying for the locker and said they didn't care about the stuff in it." I put on my left turn signal and changed lanes. "I'm sure the police will give them a call."

"Whoever killed Tom had to know that locker was up for bidding."

"That's what I'm thinking too, Mom. But I don't think the lockers are known to anyone except for the storage company employees until the actual auction."

Mom and I glanced at each other at the same time.

"That Red guy and Kim," my mother noted.

"And others," I pointed out. "Elite Storage is a big place, and I'm sure they have many employees. I'm sure the police are going over all that with a fine-toothed comb."

"So you're hoping this reviewer guy will give you some information the police don't have?"

"You never know. If Tom was killed by a competitor and this Bob Y has been in all those stores, he might be able to supply us with some telltale gossip that could shed some light on who and why."

"Like who got along with who and who didn't play well with others?"

"Something like that." I saw our exit was coming up and slowly moved toward the right-hand lane to take the ramp. "And if it's a bust, at least we'll get a nice lunch out of it."

EIGHT

Our timing appeared to be perfect. By the time Mom and I reached the farmers' market in Manhattan Beach, it looked like the bulk of their business was winding down. We found parking with no problem.

For two to three blocks, booths lined the street like a makeshift shanty town of canvas and tables. Some were fancy, some basic, with most having overhead covering to guard against the sun. We made our way down the middle first, passing booths offering clothing and crafts. Next came a booth selling orchids and other live plants, and two offering up baked goods. Finally came the organic fruits and vegetables. The booths selling sandwiches and fresh cooked food were situated just past the produce booths. Glancing down the street, which had been closed off to traffic for the event, I saw two food trucks parked at the far end. One was Comfort Foodies; the other was a truck specializing in Asian food that I remembered from the reviews. A few plastic tables and chairs were set up in front of them for folks to sit and eat.

I backtracked a bit, stopping at a fruit stand to check out some pears. Grabbing a plastic bag, I dropped a few into it and handed them to the man behind the counter to weigh. I did the same with some oranges and squash.

"You're shopping?" Mom hissed. "Now?"

"It looks more natural than just barging up to the truck."

"I'll have to remember that."

I couldn't tell if the remark was serious or sarcastic.

Once the items were purchased, Mom and I slowly made our way to Comfort Foodies. The truck was large and shiny, painted in cheerful colors in a quilt motif. Facing us were two large rectangular windows through which food was ordered and picked up. There were two customers ahead of us, but by the way the nearby trash cans were overflowing, it looked like they had done a booming business earlier. The Asian truck's trash was equally filled.

The menu was written in colorful chalk on a blackboard. I looked it over. Mom stepped closer to the board and viewed it along with me. "See what you want, Mom?"

"I'd love some macaroni and cheese, but I don't eat fried foods." She pointed to an item — fried mac and cheese balls. The item below it had been erased, a sure sign of a sellout.

"We can serve the mac and cheese unfried if you like," said a voice behind us.

We both turned to see a young man of about twenty with an order pad in one hand and a pen in the other.

"Is it any good?" asked Mom.

"My mom's mac and cheese is the best," he said with confidence. "We sell out every time. Today we also had lobster mac and cheese, and it went like crazy."

"Paulie," called a woman's voice from the service window. "We have one more order of the lobster mac and cheese left if she wants it."

"Lobster macaroni and cheese," Mom repeated with near reverence. She stepped closer to the window. "Is it made with real lobster or that fake stuff?"

"Mom," I hissed. "Be nice."

Mom scowled in my direction. "I have a right to know if I'm going to eat it. So much of it isn't real now. Take crab, for instance. You can get real crab spelled with a C or fake crab spelled with a K."

A woman's head poked out from the window. Her hair was somewhere between silver and blond and pulled back tight from a wide face that resembled that of the young man waiting on us — minus the skimpy moustache. "She's right," the woman said. "A customer has the right to know." She gave Mom a broad smile, showing uneven teeth. "Nothing fake anywhere in this truck, except maybe my boobies." She gave us an exaggerated wink.

"Then I'll take it," said Mom with enthusiasm.

"Are you allowed to eat that?" I asked my mother. "Don't you have a cholesterol problem, like Clark?"

Mom turned on me and said loud enough for the woman and her son to hear, "You don't see me counting *your* calories, do you, Chubs?"

I swear, if there had been a bat close by, I would have been tempted to take a swing. I'm not sure at what, since I wouldn't want to rot in jail for matricide, but surely I could find something to hit that would only result in a vandalism charge.

I stepped up to the window. "Make hers a double, extra cheese and butter."

The woman shook her head and laughed. "Mothers. They always have a hold on us, don't they?"

"Tell me about it." It was the young man who spoke. Through the window, his mother shook her finger at him but was sending him a warm look of love while she did.

"And what would you like?" she asked me.

I looked back over at the chalkboard, then at my mother. "What's the most fattening thing you have?"

"That would probably be the fried mac and cheese," answered the woman, "although the lobster mac and cheese is no slouch in the calorie department. The meatloaf wrap will also put the pounds on."

"I'll take the meatloaf wrap," I told her.

"Mashed potatoes and gravy are also in the wrap."

"Even better."

I turned to Mom. "What would you like to drink, Mom?"

"Coffee, if they have it."

"We sure do," answered the boy. "All the other drinks are lined up in this other window."

I checked out the offerings. "Coffee for my mother and a lemonade for me."

"I thought you usually drank iced tea," Mom commented.

I took a deep breath. "I'm living on the edge today, Mom."

The boy gestured to one of the plastic tables. "Why don't you two ladies have a seat while Mom fixes your food." He scribbled our orders on his pad even though his mother had already taken them. "We'll call your name when it's ready."

"Put it under Odelia." I paid him and followed Mom to the closest table.

While we waited, I checked out the line at the other truck. A couple customers were lined up to order food.

"Who knows," said Mom, pointing at the customers. "That Bob Y might even be one of them. He could even be a she."

"True, you never know, but from the wording in his reviews, my gut tells me he's male, young, and more likely to hang out at the bigger food truck events like the ones held at night in trendier spots."

A few minutes later, the woman from the truck came over with three paper boats of food. She walked with a noticeable limp on her left side. Behind her came her son with our drinks. They placed everything on the table in front of us. It smelled heavenly, and the portions were far from skimpy.

Mom leaned over her food and took a deep whiff. "My, that certainly smells wonderful."

I pointed at the third boat. It contained a

single golden, crusty orb the size of a golf ball. "Is that the fried mac and cheese?"

"That's it, or at least a sample." The woman wiped her hands on her food-splattered apron. "I thought you might like to try it."

I nearly swooned. Macaroni and cheese is one of my favorite foods. I hadn't ordered it because my plan was to pinch a bite of Mom's. Meatloaf is one of my other favorite foods. So now I had both of my faves on one table. I was a happy girl, even if Mom did call me Chubs.

A shout came from the other food truck. They'd finished serving their last customers and were closing down their service windows. One of them was waving in our direction. "We'll see you tonight, Heide. Later, Paul."

The woman and her son waved back with promises to keep the deep fryers burning.

Heide turned to her son. "Guess we might as well wrap it up and get ready for tonight too."

"We'll take care of closing up, Mom. Why don't you sit down a bit?"

"Yes, please," I encouraged. "Grab a seat and join us."

Just then another young man hopped out from the truck. He was a bit older than Paul and had darker hair. "What's this 'we' business, little bro? I'm outta here."

"Eric," Heide said to him. "Can't you stick around long enough to help your brother?"

"I've been slaving over a hot grill, Mom. Let pretty boy get dirty for a change." He lit up a cigarette and blew out the smoke. "Besides, I've got people to see." As Eric walked away, he pulled the hood of his navy blue sweatshirt over his head.

Paul yelled at his brother's back, "Make sure you're back in time for tonight's gig — Mom can't cook all by herself."

Without turning around or changing his stride, Eric raised the hand not holding the cigarette and extended his middle finger high into the air.

"At least," his mother called after him, "use that finger to give us a call if you're going to be late."

Heide plopped herself down into one of the plastic chairs at our table. Her shoulders sagged with weariness. "I don't know what I'm going to do with him. Eric's really a nice kid and a whiz in the kitchen. I'm trying to get him to go to culinary school and become a first-class chef, but he won't listen. He cooked the food you're eating." Mixed with Heide's concern was pride.

Mom had a mouthful of lobster mac and cheese, so I made the introductions. "I'm Odelia Grey and this is my mother, Grace Littlejohn. She's visiting from the East Coast."

Mom swallowed her food. "New Hampshire, actually. I used to live in Massachusetts, but now I'm in an old folks' home in New Hampshire."

"I'm Heide van den Akker," she said. "That's my youngest son, Paul, cleaning up. The older boy is Eric."

I took a bite out of my meatloaf wrap and wanted to swoon with meat and gravy bliss. It smelled so good, I wanted to dab some behind my ears.

"You like it?" Heide asked.

"Mffhmmfgff," came out of my stuffed mouth along with a vigorous nod of my head.

"Mine's wonderful, too," added Mom.

"Glad you ladies are enjoying it." Heide beamed with pleasure at having her food appreciated.

"We don't have anything like this where I live," said Mom after wiping her mouth with a paper napkin that had been provided with the food. "I'm blogging about my trip to California and thought it would be fun to see one of these things. Catering trucks are a lot different now than in my day."

Blogging? I stopped chewing and stared at Mom through bulging eyes.

Heide leaned forward with interest. "You have a blog, Grace?"

"Yes, I do. It's called An Old Broad's Perspective."

Heide laughed. I nearly sprayed mashed potatoes across the table.

"It's nothing much," Mom continued. "Just the ramblings of an old woman with time on her hands. At first a lot of the old folks where I live were the only ones reading it. Now I have about fifty or so regular readers. Sometimes more than two hundred people view it in a month." Mom straightened in her chair with pride. "I thought it would be fun to blog about my trip. So far folks seem to be enjoying it. I've blogged about the flight, Thanksgiving Dinner, shopping — things like that. Even about Odelia here taking me and her mother-in-law to see *The Nutcracker* on Sunday afternoon."

I was waiting for Mom to add finding a dead body to her list of *What I Did On My Vacation,* but she seemed to be staying off that topic. Maybe she was right — maybe I did get my defective fibbing gene from my father, because she was lying like a champ.

"And you wanted to blog about a trip to a

128

food truck?" asked Heide.

"I'd seen trucks like yours on TV, so when Odelia asked me what I wanted to do today for lunch, I mentioned it." Mom looked to me to pick up the thread of deceit. I guess she wanted to get back to her food. And, of course, I'd just taken another big bite of mine.

After nearly swallowing my food whole, I said to Heide, "I went on About Town to look up reviews on local food trucks and remembered seeing a story on the news about your truck and how you got started."

"Odelia told me what happened to you and your husband," Mom chimed in. "I'm very sorry."

"Thank you." As she said the words, Heide's friendly face clouded. "But we're doing fine now, as you can see. Doctors told me I might never walk again, so I'll happily live with this gimpy leg." She slapped the thigh of her injured leg.

"Odelia's husband is in a wheelchair." The way Mom said it, I wasn't sure if she was bragging or looking for pity on my behalf.

Heide looked at me with similar confusion. "Really? A car accident?"

I shook my head. "It was an accident, though. A stupid stunt when he was a kid that almost turned deadly."

"But he's amazing," Mom added as if writing a review of Greg's skills for About Town. "Nothing stops him from doing what he wants."

"That's true," I agreed. "My husband is very athletic and competitive. He can do almost anything a man with working legs can do."

Heide gave me a lascivious wink. "Anything?"

"Anything," I assured her with the blush of a schoolgirl.

Mom pushed her paper boat away. She'd eaten most of it, which surprised me. She loved to eat, as I did, but didn't have a big appetite — unlike me. "Before we go, do you mind if I take a picture of you and the truck for my blog?"

"No, not at all, Grace," beamed Heide, regaining her prior cheerful composure. "And if you don't mind, could you e-mail me when it's posted? You'll find my e-mail on our website. But finish your food first. And don't forget the fried mac and cheese."

I cut the fried ball open with the side of my fork and popped half into my mouth, where it melted in cheesy goodness.

Mom looked at me with disgust. "Did you just moan?"

I nodded while the last bit dissolved in my

mouth. "It's fantastic," I gushed to Heide. "My husband would have an orgasm over these."

"Odelia!" snapped Mom.

"Don't worry, Grace." Heide laughed. "It's not the first time someone has said that."

I saw the perfect segue and grabbed it. "That reviewer on About Town was right about your food." I speared a bite from Mom's abandoned plate. The lobster mac and cheese was incredible, although I preferred the fried sample.

"Mom, you want a bite of my meatloaf?"

"Just a small one. I'm stuffed." Using her fork, she picked up a mouthful of meatloaf and mashed potatoes from the end of the wrap and guided it into her mouth.

"Which reviewer was that?" asked Heide. "I know there are a lot, but we've gotten to know some of them over time."

"His name was Bob Y." I turned to my mother, playing the game she started. "Isn't that right, Mom?"

Her mouth was full, so she simply nodded.

I turned back to Heide. Her face was cloudy again, but I couldn't tell if it was because she was thinking or because she didn't care for the person behind the review.

"He's written several great reviews for food trucks, but he absolutely raves about yours. It's like he's addicted to your food."

"And I can see why," Mom squeaked out after swallowing.

"Do you know him?" I prodded when Heide remained silent.

"Can't place him," she said, putting her game face back on.

"He only reviews two things," I continued. "Food trucks and secondhand stores." I took a drink of my lemonade. "Odd combination, isn't it? And as much as he loves food trucks, especially yours, he hates secondhand stores."

Heide held up her hand in surrender. "Kids. Go figure." She got up to go. "If you don't mind, let's take that photo now. I need to get back home and take a nap before tonight, and also get in some prep time in the kitchen. These nighttime events are usually jammed with customers."

"I think Heide knows who Bob Y is."

We were in the car, travelling on the 405 Freeway, heading back home.

"I think you're right, Mom. Her face totally changed as soon as I mentioned his name, and she called him a kid. Either she made an assumption or knows him, but it

132

still doesn't tell us who he is or if he'll be useful in helping us get the dirt on the stores."

Mom was looking at the photo on her phone. I had taken it of Mom with Heide and Paul in front of their truck. "It came out great."

"Do you really have a blog? Or were you making that up?"

"I do have a blog, just like I said."

"Why didn't you tell me?" My voice sounded peevish in spite of my attempt to appear cool and relaxed.

"I didn't think you'd be interested in the ramblings of an old woman."

"Did you post anything about the murder on it?"

"Sure did," she answered with enthusiasm. "Much more newsworthy than *The Nutcracker.*"

"But I thought you liked the ballet Sunday."

"I did, but let's face it, Odelia: no ballet can stand up to a murdered guy in a storage locker. And the blog has received more views than ever before. It might even go viral."

Did my aged mother just use the term *viral*?

NINE

Ina was still in jail, and it wasn't looking good. Greg returned from the police department exhausted and frustrated the night of the auction. He informed us that along with the gun, inside Ina's backpack the police had found a fake passport and a plane ticket for Paris. The plane ticket was dated for the day after the auction. When questioned by the police and her lawyer, Ina had clammed up.

"It's as if she's given up," Greg said after the arraignment two days later. We had all gone — Greg, Mom, Renee, Ron, and I; even Buck had shown up, but no one else I recognized from the auction. Ina entered a guilty plea to the gun charge. Since it was her first offense and Ina didn't have any other type of criminal record, we'd expected her to get released with just a stiff fine, which Greg was prepared to pay on her behalf. But the assistant district attorney effectively argued that since the gun was loaded when found and Ina was not the registered owner, that the charge should be elevated from a misdemeanor to a felony. He pushed for Ina to receive prison time.

The DA also stressed that Ina was a major suspect in a pending murder investigation, had been in possession of an illegal passport, and had proven to be a flight risk. Ina's lawyer pleaded vehemently against that course, underlining how Ina had not yet been charged with anything in connection with her husband's murder and likely had been fleeing the country to get away from her abusive spouse, not from a crime. Since her husband was now dead, there was no reason for her to flee the country. In the end, the judge took everything under advisement and set a sentencing date. He sent Ina back to jail without bail to wait until that time. When Ina was led away, she seemed reconciled to her fate; all her usual piss and vinegar drained from her like water from a bathtub.

"Do you think she's innocent of Tom's murder?" I asked.

Greg shrugged. We were alone in the house. After eating her lunch, Mom had taken Wainwright for a short walk. As with the cats, our dog had finally warmed up to her, especially now that he had another body willing to trot him up and down the sidewalks of Seal Beach, even if Mom did move at a much more leisurely pace than he preferred. As soon as they returned, Greg and Wainwright would head to Ocean Breeze Graphics for the rest of the day. Renee had been distraught after the hearing, and Ron had taken her straight home so she could rest.

"I don't know, sweetheart." Greg polished off the rest of his grilled cheese sandwich and reached for a pear from the fruit bowl in the center of the table. "Even though her gun wasn't used in Tom's death, there's some pretty compelling and damaging evidence that points to her having motive, not to mention her silence. Her lawyer told me she's shut down and is even refusing to talk or listen to him regarding the murder. She seems resigned to sit in jail for a year on the gun charge, but if she's charged and convicted of Tom's murder, that year could turn into life."

He took a bite of the fruit. As he chewed, he looked around. "Hey, wasn't Cruz supposed to come today?"

"She called and asked if she could come tomorrow instead. One of her grandchildren is home ill today, and she needs to take care of him for her daughter."

Our doorbell rang. When I answered it, I found Dev Frye standing on our stoop. "Dev, what a nice surprise!"

He grunted and entered when I opened the door. "Didn't Greg tell you he called me?"

Although caught off-guard, I tried my best to hide it while I escorted Dev to our kitchen table. "Would you like some coffee or some lunch? Or how about a soda?"

Dev had lost weight since his bypass surgery. He was still a very large man but had trimmed down around his middle. His once-blond hair was now completely gray.

"A cup of coffee would be great, Odelia." He took a seat at the table across from Greg.

"I called Dev when I found out Fehring was on the case," Greg explained as I went to the counter to fetch Dev's coffee. "I was hoping he could help us understand what was going on." He turned to Dev. "Did you find out anything?"

Dev jumped right into it. "It's not official, but it looks like Tom Bruce was killed by numerous blows to his skull with a long, thin, heavy object."

"You mean like a bat," Greg asked.

"More like a golf club or fireplace poker." Dev's answer took me back a bit. Seems

I'm not the only one thinking about pokers as weapons, although my thoughts are fantasies.

"From the blood spatter and wound," Dev continued, "forensics determined that he died in the chair in the storage locker where he was found."

I set the mug of coffee and a spoon in front of Dev and placed the milk within his reach. "But Ina's much smaller than Tom. Could she have the strength to kill him like that?"

Dev splashed milk into his coffee and grunted. "You'd be surprised how strong a woman can be when motivated by years of abuse. I've seen men my size killed by women under a hundred pounds. And it looks like he might have been unconscious when the assault occurred, possibly drugged, which might prove premeditation."

"So Tom was definitely abusing her?" I took a seat at the table between Dev and Greg.

Greg took my hand. "We suspected as much but didn't know for sure."

"Looks that way," answered Dev after taking a sip of coffee. "Although she's not talking about it. Andrea said there seems to be other bruises on Ina. And there have been past police reports filed by neighbors for domestic disturbances, but no arrests, and they couldn't find any incidents of emergency room visits."

I scrunched my brows in thought. "But if she killed him, why would she go to that auction knowing the body would be there?"

"It's not uncommon for killers to return to the scene." Dev took a long swig of coffee. "And it could have been used as a ruse to divert attention from her as a suspect. Even better that she had you ladies with her."

I didn't like the idea that Ina might have used my mother and her aunt as decoys. She didn't know Mom from Eve, but she seemed to have more respect for Renee than that.

I sniffed. "I'm surprised Detective Fehring is giving you so much information."

"I know you two didn't exactly see eye-to-eye last time, but Andrea's good people. I wish I could have hung on to her as a partner, but Long Beach offered her more opportunity for advancement. Besides," he said, chuckling softly before continuing, "she also thinks if she funnels you small details here and there through me, you'll keep your nose out of it. She'll tell us what she can, but there's a lot she can't." Dev looked directly at me. "I hope you understand that she still has a job to do."

Greg's hand let go of mine and combed through his thick hair — a habit when he was frustrated. "And her job is nailing my cousin's ass to the wall."

Dev put down his coffee mug with a soft thud. "Fehring's job is to find out who killed Tom Bruce. If your cousin killed him, then yes. If Ina didn't kill her husband, then she needs to cooperate and start talking so they can find out who did. I'll tell you this: having that plane ticket and fake passport did not help her case at all."

No, it didn't, but I wasn't about to let that seal Ina's fate so easily. "As her lawyer said in court, she was disappearing to get away from Tom. Or she could have been starting her life over after Tom left her for that McIntyre woman."

"The fake name would point to getting away from Tom," Greg agreed. "But if he'd already left her, would he still be a threat?"

"I've seen it before," Dev answered, "when the husband leaves but still controls his wife through fear. But what's really puzzling is now that Tom Bruce is dead, what does Ina have to fear? Andrea is pretty sure Ina knows something about her husband's murder but isn't talking, either out of fear or because she did it. I hate to say this, folks,

140

but it looks like she was planning a getaway, not just a new life. Seems she had also cleaned out their bank accounts, both personal and the store's, the morning of the auction."

Greg raked a hand through his hair again. "Did they find the money in her bag with the plane ticket?"

"No. Ina had a few thousand dollars in the bag, but not near as much as the withdrawal."

My nose twitched in thought. "I never figured Tom and Ina as having a bundle of cash. I mean, the store appeared to be doing okay, but it didn't seem like a gold mine." I turned to Greg. "Am I missing something here, honey?"

"I was just thinking the same thing." Another rake through his hair. If this kept up, I'd have a bald husband. "Dev, do you know how much the withdrawal was for?"

"Andrea said in the neighborhood of three hundred grand."

Greg gave off a low whistle. I stared at Dev as if he'd said he found Jimmy Hoffa.

"Are you sure Ina withdrew the money and not Tom?" asked Greg.

"The bank said it was her. One of the theories is that she used the money to pay someone to kill her husband."

Without another word, Greg and I looked at each other. I knew from the set of my husband's jaw that as soon as Dev was gone, we were going to talk about this some more. The missing money definitely added a new twist.

"What about security cameras?" Greg asked. "Don't all those storage places have them?"

"Yes, but nothing turned up. Not sure why. There was either a glitch in the system or the assailant knew how to bypass them. Either way, there's zip on the camera. Fehring and Whitman checked it out already."

Dev kicked back the rest of his coffee and got up to leave. "Gotta get back to work. I had an appointment nearby, so I thought I'd tell you in person what I'd learned." He glanced around the kitchen. "Is Mrs. Littlejohn here? I'd like to meet her."

"Mom's out with Wainwright," I said.

Dev laughed. "I thought I saw Wainwright prancing down the street when I drove up. At least I spotted a golden retriever walking with an older lady."

"That's them," I confirmed, "but they should be home soon."

"Another time, maybe. I really have to run. Is Clark still in town?"

"No," I told him. "He got called off to a job right after Thanksgiving, but he should be back in a day or so. He'll be accompanying Mom back to New Hampshire."

Dev and Clark got along famously, bonded by their years of police work. I didn't know if Dev knew Clark now worked for Willie. He did know Clark had retired from the job and was currently handling private security for a company, but I left it up to my brother to give Dev the details. Or not.

Greg rolled over to the detective and held out his hand. "Thanks, Dev. We really appreciate your help."

"I'll keep you posted as much as I can."

I stood up and gave Dev a hug. "When Clark returns, maybe you and Bev can come over for dinner and meet Mom before she goes." Bev was Dev's girlfriend, a schoolteacher he'd been seeing for some time.

Under my embrace I felt Dev stiffen. I let go of him and studied his face but saw nothing but his cop mask.

"Yeah, sure." His tone held the enthusiasm of being invited to a wake. "That would be great."

When Dev was gone, I turned to Greg. "What did you make of *that*?"

"Of what?"

"Dev's reluctance right now. He sure

didn't seem as friendly as usual."

"What do you expect, sweetheart?" Greg picked up his plate and glass from the table and wheeled them over to the sink. "He was here to tell us it looks like my cousin could be convicted as a killer."

I grabbed Dev's coffee mug and joined Greg in the kitchen. "I don't think it was just that." I put the mug into the dishwasher, along with Greg's plate and glass. "There's something he's not telling us." I paused, holding the dishwasher half open. "I could almost smell it." I shut the door as if punctuating my comment.

Greg laughed. "What you smelled is a cop being cagey about what he can and cannot tell us." He rolled back to the table. "Now let's discuss our plans before Grace gets back."

I rinsed my hands at the sink and wiped them on a kitchen towel. "Our plans?"

"We need to start checking out some stuff."

"What do you think I was doing yesterday?"

"Checking into that Bob Y character was a nice start, but I think we need to start digging deeper and faster."

"I was thinking of paying some of those secondhand stores a visit. I could do that today if I can shake Mom."

"I don't know, sweetheart, taking her along initially might be a good cover, as long as there's no danger. But as soon as things heat up, you'll need to get her out of the picture, not to mention yourself." Greg fiddled with the salt and pepper shakers on the table. "I'm sorry I can't join you today. I have a big customer order to take care of, and Chris is out." Chris Fowler was Greg's right-hand man at the shop. "But he should be back tomorrow, then you and I can hit the road together. In the meantime, call or text me with anything you find out, and I'll tackle any research I can from the office."

"Sounds good." I walked over to the table and stroked my husband's hair, using a lot softer strokes than he had earlier. I noticed a bit of gray starting to appear around his temples. It looked adorable — but then I'm biased. "But are you sure, honey, you don't want to wait and see what the authorities come up with or at least wait until Clark takes Mom home?"

He took my hand from his head and kissed it. "That would be the prudent thing to do, but I don't think I can sit around and wait knowing Ina may go down in flames. It would drive me crazy. It's bad enough she's in jail."

"What if she's guilty?"

"Then she's guilty. But until I know that for sure, I'm not going to stop looking into this mess." He kissed my hand again. "You with me?"

"Where else would I be?"

TEN

We weren't so lucky this time on the 405. It was bogged down, moving like a glacier as we headed north. Traffic was moving along nicely on the southbound side, but Torrance wasn't south of us. It was north — twenty miles north. As slow as traffic was moving, you'd think we were driving an ox cart across bumpy, unpaved terrain. My mission today was to hit at least two of the second-hand stores on my list. The first stop was Goodwin's Good Stuff in Torrance, but if traffic continued this bad, we'd be lucky to visit any stores beyond Buck's. Hell, we'd be lucky to get to Buck's at all.

Buckled into the passenger's seat next to me was Mom, buzzing with excitement like a Taser charged and itching to zap someone. I had tried my best to convince her to stay behind and rest, but no such luck.

"I'll rest when I'm dead," she'd shot back at me as she wandered down the hall. "Give me a minute to powder my nose and grab my pocketbook." I'd used that minute to squelch a moan of frustration.

I glanced over at her when traffic came to a halt for the umpteenth time. The weather had turned cloudy and damp. The weather-man had said to expect light drizzle off and on the rest of the week. She sat primly in the seat next to me bundled in slacks, sweater, and a light jacket. Her purse was on her lap. Her hands clutched the top of it as if she was worried someone might smash the passenger-side window and snatch it. Greg might be right. Mom could be good cover for my nosiness. An elderly woman standing next to a middle-aged woman might give off an air of innocence. It seemed to have worked with Heide at the food truck. Problem was, Mom was a loose can-non. You never knew what was going to come out of her mouth. Yesterday's blog bit had blown my socks off with surprise.

Last night I'd taken my laptop to bed and looked Mom's blog up while Greg read a book. The late news played on our TV. Reading and the news — it was our nightly ritual. I was still wondering if the blog had been a hoax to get Heide to talk, but it wasn't. As soon as I'd keyed *An Old Broad's Perspective* into the search engine, up popped the blog.

"Greg, did you know my mother had a blog?"

He looked at me over the top of his reading glasses. "A blog? Grace?"

"Yes. It's called An Old Broad's Perspective and covers all kinds of topics. She's even journaling about her visit here, including the murder at the storage locker."

"Is it any good?"

"Surprisingly good. There are a lot of grammatical errors and it's rather rustic and folksy in the wording, but it's very entertaining." I turned the laptop so he could see what I'd found. "And look," I pointed out. "She's already posted the photo of Heide van den Akker in front of the Comfort Foodies truck, along with an account of our day. At least she had the good sense to leave out the part about us nosing around."

Greg scanned the article, his lips pressed together to keep from laughing. "How'd she get the photo? Didn't you take it?"

"Mom insisted I take it with her phone."

"She's pretty IT savvy for an old broad. Maybe I could use her at the shop while she's here."

I looked Greg in the eye. "Did you know my mother had an iPad with her?"

"Yeah, I did. She asked about using our

149

WiFi while she was here. I set it up for her."

"And you didn't think of telling me that?"

He shrugged. "I thought you knew she had it."

"Not until today, when she threatened to do her own research if I didn't let her come along."

This time Greg laughed out loud, giving LOL a whole new emphasis.

"What's so funny?"

"Nothing." He straightened his glasses and went back to his book.

"Nothing, my fat behind. Tell me."

Greg put his book on the nightstand and set his reading glasses on top of it. After turning off his light, he turned to me. "No way am I telling you what's on my mind. I want to sleep in my own bed tonight."

My nose twitched. "Does it have anything to do with apples falling from trees?"

"Maybe." He tapped my laptop. "Now put that thing away so we can get some sleep."

While I shut down my laptop and turned off the light on my side of the bed, Greg turned off the TV. Quiet and in the dark, we cuddled. Greg kissed my ear, but I could feel a snicker vibrating behind his lips.

"I don't know how you people put up with this."

I turned to Mom. We were still inching ahead on the freeway. "You mean the traffic?"

"No, I mean the Rose Parade in January."

"No need for sarcasm, Mom."

She was right, though. I didn't know myself how we put up with the increasingly horrible Southern California traffic. It seemed to be getting worse daily.

"We just work around it best we can," I told her. "Although this is very unusual. There's probably an accident up ahead."

Mom leaned forward, peering out the front window with keen interest. "Or maybe another slow-speed cop chase like with O.J."

From the hope in her voice, I could tell she was already drafting her next blog entry.

"By the way, Mom — I read your blog last night and really enjoyed it."

She turned to me in surprise. "You did?"

"Yes. Greg and I both looked it over last night. You're doing a nice job with it. I can see why you have so many readers." I started to say something else but held my tongue.

"But?" Mom pursed her lips in my direction. She looked like a fish with lipstick. "*But,* what?"

"From the sound of it, you were about to tack on a bit of a scold."

"Not a scold at all. I'm just concerned

about you saying too much about the murder, or at least any information we might uncover in the next day or so."

"I do know how to keep my mouth shut about things that are important."

"I know you do." I started to point out she'd kept her mouth shut for more than thirty years but wisely decided I didn't need to open that can of worms again. I'd wanted Mom's visit to build a bond between us, not dredge up old pain we'd already discussed and beaten into the ground. She'd made it quite clear when I'd found her that she felt she had good reasons for leaving me all those years ago and had no regrets about her decision.

The car filled with silence as thick as the heavy dampness outside until Mom said, "Do you still see that woman?"

"What woman?"

"That woman your father married. The one with the stripper name — Koko, Bambam, Tata — something like that."

"You mean Gigi?"

Mom was staring straight ahead at the cars in front of us. As far as the eye could see, vehicles were lined up like lemmings waiting for a turn to jump off a cliff in mass suicide.

"I only saw her a few times after Dad died.

Gigi passed away a little over a year ago."

"Did you go to the funeral?" Mom stared at the bumper of the car in front of us as if it were an eye chart.

"Yes, I did. I heard her son, J.J., died shortly after from liver failure due to alcoholism."

My stepmother's funeral had been one of the few times Greg and I had disagreed vehemently. I didn't want to go, but he insisted we should, saying it would be closure for me and the right thing to do. I told him he was welcome to go without me. The day of the funeral, he put on a suit and started out the door, ready to do exactly that. In the end I caved and went with him. I had hated my stepmother and her two kids. They had been hateful to my father until the day he died. J.J. wasn't at the funeral because he was so ill. My stepsister, Dee Dee, a real harridan, was as imperious as ever, even in the face of her mother's death. She made some snarky remarks as Greg and I paid our respects, but much to my surprise I had no problem letting them slide. As usual, Greg had been right. Going to Gigi's funeral had been closure.

Closure. That word was invading my brain a lot lately. It felt like a schoolteacher nagging me to do a task over and over until I got it right — like having Mom visit when I really only half wanted her here. Greg and I had talked about it last night behind the closed doors of our bedroom.

"Would you come to my funeral?"

"What?" I'd been lost in thoughts of closure and wasn't sure I heard Mom.

"My funeral," she repeated. "Would you fly out for it?"

My first response was almost this: "Don't be silly, you're not dying." But in reality, Mom was in her eighties. She enjoyed relatively good health but was definitely slowing down.

"Yes, of course I would. Greg and I would both be there. Why would you think otherwise?"

She shrugged, not saying the words we were both thinking: that because she hadn't been there for me for decades, why should I pay good money on travel to see her put into the hard New England earth? If the car wasn't already at a near-dead stop, I would have pulled over for the discussion. Buck's store would have to wait. Instead, I turned to her, keeping half an eye on the car in front of me.

"Mom, if you ever need me to come back east to help you, just ask and I'll be there. You don't need to die to get me on a plane.

And you don't need to wait until Greg and I plan a trip."

She looked skeptical.

"No matter what," I underlined. "If you're sick and need me or just want to see me, call, and I'll find a way to get to you as fast as I can." I reached over and covered her hands with my right one. "Just because we're both pigheaded doesn't mean we have to wait until it's too late." When traffic moved forward a few inches, I put my hand back on the steering wheel.

"In fact, there's something I want to talk to you about." I did have something on my mind, something Greg and I had discussed last night, but I wasn't sure how to broach the subject with my often cantankerous mother.

Before I could say anything further, my phone rang. It was Clark. I answered it via my hands-free car console feature, something Greg insisted I get in the new car.

"Hi, Clark."

"Sounds like you're in the car," he said.

"Yes, and hardly budging. Mom's with me."

"Good," said Clark's disembodied voice. "It will save me a call. I have two issues to discuss."

"Issues?" Mom asked. Unsure of where

155

the sound was coming from, she leaned forward to speak into my dashboard. "You sound like you're addressing bad employees."

"Humph," said my brother. "If it were only that easy." A car to my left honked at the car in front of it.

"What was that?" Clark asked. "Someone honking at you?"

"We're on the freeway," I explained, "and there is a big traffic jam. And no, the honk was not at me." I glanced at the GPS. We still had five miles of this hell to go. "So what are your *issues*?"

"I'm basically calling to say I won't be back to pick up Mom this week. It looks like early next week is the soonest I can get to Cali. Is that okay, Odelia?"

"That's a stupid question," Mom responded on my behalf. "I'm right here in the car. Do you think Odelia can honestly say no?"

She had a point, though I was tempted to advise my big brother to tell Willie to function without him long enough for Mom to get home. In spite of the warm and fuzzy moment we'd just shared, I needed the freedom to dig into Ina's problem without a denture-wearing encumbrance.

"And," Mom continued before I could

answer. "What about me? What if *I* don't want to stay longer? Did you consider that, Clark?"

I jerked my head toward Mom. "Are you saying you don't?" Me not wanting Mom around was one thing, but I had never considered that she might be tired of us — of me. Then again, maybe she simply wanted to get back to her own routine in her own home.

Clark's sigh on the other end was not only audible, it was palpable, like his warm, wet breath was filling the closed space of my car, turning it into a steam room. "Mom, I can't break away from work right now. Do you mind staying longer with Greg and Odelia?"

"What are my options?" Mom asked.

Options? I was tempted to reach across Mom, open her side of the car, and tell her to get out and hitch a ride. There's an *option.*

"There are three options here, Mom." I turned my head forward and tried to pay attention to the traffic. "One, you can stay; two, I can take you home myself; three, you can fly home solo. Think about it; number three might be quite an adventure."

The issue with number three wasn't the flight east, which Mom was capable of handling, but what to do once she got there. Mom didn't live in a place easy to get to from the airport. She'd have to take a plane to Boston, then travel by bus or car to the small town in New Hampshire where her retirement home was located. We'd have to hire a car service for her, which would work providing they didn't dump her on the side of the road in frustration after ten minutes.

"Considering my second issue . . . um, concern," said Clark. "Maybe you should escort Mom home, Odelia, and as soon as possible."

"And why's that?" As I said the words, I noticed that up ahead the left lanes of the freeway were starting to merge into the right lanes. Whatever was causing the traffic jam must be up ahead on the left. I craned my neck and could see emergency vehicles with flashing lights in the distance.

"I read Mom's blog," Clark answered.

"You read my blog?" Mom asked with surprise.

"Odelia, couldn't you have put your murder business on hold until Mom went home?"

"It's not like I planned this," I snapped. "We went to the auction, and there was the body in the storage locker." From reading Mom's blog, I knew she hadn't given out any details, especially that the corpse was someone in our extended family. "Trust me, murder was not on our agenda for the day. Lunch, yes. Murder, no."

At this point I half expected Mom to jump in and provide the who and what, but she didn't. Instead, she answered, "I wouldn't mind staying here in California a bit longer. But I don't want to be a burden." She looked straight at me when she said the last bit.

"You're not a burden, Mom," I heard myself automatically respond. I turned and met her eyes so she'd know I meant my next words. "You're welcome to stay."

"Okay, then it's settled," Clark announced. "But Odelia, I don't want you getting mixed up in this murder thing, and I especially don't want you dragging Mom along for the ride."

"Clark," Mom admonished. "Stop worrying like an old biddy. We're on our way to go shopping. Odelia's only investigation involves getting a good deal and showing me more of Southern California. Didn't you read my piece about the food trucks?"

"Yeah, I did," Clark admitted. "Maybe having you there will keep Odelia occupied."

I slapped the steering wheel. "Stop talking as if I'm not here."

Mom gave me a raised brow. "You and Clark do it to me all the time."

I shot Mom a dirty look — one I hope conveyed that she was a heartbeat away from being shuttled back east on her own. But Mom wasn't interested in doing battle. Her face was relaxed, almost happy. It mellowed me considerably, at least for the moment.

"Don't worry, Clark," she said, changing her scowl to a half wink aimed in my direction. "I'll keep Odelia out of mischief. I'll stick to her like a second skin."

I turned my head to look out my side window. Next to me was a silver Mercedes. The driver was on his cell. I couldn't hear his words, but it looked like he was shouting. With his free hand, he was shaking a fist at the snarl of traffic in front of us.

Maybe *I* should use Mom's plane ticket. A quiet retirement home in New Hampshire was looking pretty great about now.

ELEVEN

"So what did you want to talk to me about?"

I stared at the bumper of the car in front of me. On it was plastered a bumper sticker touting the legalization of marijuana. In some ways Clark's call would help ease me into the topic on my mind, but inside I was chickening out. Then I remembered the look on Mom's face when she'd agreed to stay in California longer. I took a deep breath and jumped off the cliff.

"Are you happy where you live, Mom?"

"Why wouldn't I be? I picked the place."

Mom lived in a very nice place. It was one of those full-service retirement communities that offered independent living, assisted living, and nursing home services on one large property. It was located in a lovely part of New Hampshire surrounded by rolling hills and plenty of trees, not far from shopping and other services. It even had a van to shuttle residents to the mall and various appointments, and offered numerous activities geared for all levels of physical abilities. As residents became less able to care for themselves, they could change to a more full-service facility without actually moving off the property. Mom had a spacious one-bedroom apartment in the independent living section. She was on a plan where she could go to a common dining room for one hot meal a day, usually dinner. The rest of the time she fixed her own food. Every day someone looked in on her to make sure she was eating and active and taking her medications.

"Yes, you did, but that's not what I asked." I took another deep breath and asked the question again. "But are you happy there? If you're not, you can always move. We'll help you find another place."

"Like where?"

"How about here?" There it was, out of the bottle and unable to be taken back. "Greg and I have talked about it and wanted to offer it as an option for you."

"Greg may not mind my moving here, but I'm not sure you feel the same way."

We drove along, each encased in our own weighty thoughts on the subject.

"I guess your silence is my answer," Mom sniffed.

"Not so fast, Mom. I'm mulling it over. You want an honest answer, don't you?"

I glanced over at her. She was turned so all I saw was her profile. Her lips were tight, her chin uplifted in defiance. She looked ready to face a firing squad, and I held the rifle.

I cleared my throat. "Okay, here goes: the unvarnished truth."

Mom remained perfectly still, eyes ahead, chin still tight and lifted.

"Do I want you to come live with Greg and me? Absolutely not. I don't think any of us would be happy with that arrangement."

"I'm —," Mom began, but I cut her off.

"However." I paused for effect. "However, if you want to move to California and live *near* us, I'd be all in favor of that."

Mom's head snapped in my direction so fast I heard her old bones crackle and pop. "You would?"

"Yes. Greg and I discussed this before we invited you and Clark out for Thanksgiving, and we discussed it again last night. We worry about you. We know Clark travels a lot for his job, and you're up in New Hampshire pretty much on your own. Depending on how this visit went, we — I — was going to ask if you might consider moving out here. There are lots of very nice retirement communities in Southern California. There's even one right in Seal Beach."

She looked at me with suspicion. "Did you discuss this with Clark already? Is that why he's not coming to get me, so you'll have more time to convince me?"

"No, Mom, I haven't discussed it with Clark, and I don't think Greg has either. But I think if you left New England, he would relocate too."

Her jaw loosened and started moving in a circular fashion, like a cow chewing its cud on a sleepy summer afternoon.

After a few moments, she said, "He's always said he wants to live somewhere where it's warm."

"But don't do it for Clark, Mom. He'll be fine doing whatever. Do it only if you want to. I'll understand if you don't want to leave your friends behind or deal with all the congestion and people here. It's lovely where you live."

"It's boring is what it is." She nearly spat out the words. "It's nice and all and they treat me well, but some days I feel like I'm waiting at a bus stop for Death to come fetch me."

Mom turned to me. "Do you think I could see a few places while I'm here? You know, just to check them out and get an estimate of the cost."

"Of course. And we'll have more time to do it now that Clark has been delayed. We could even ask Ron and Renee about it. I'm sure they have lots of friends who live in such communities and who'd give referrals and recommendations."

"As long as it doesn't interfere with the investigation."

I sighed long and deep, the frustration starting in my feet and working its way up to be expelled from my mouth in a single gust. "Mom, there is no investigation. I'm just asking a few questions that might help Ina."

"Uh-huh." Mom turned back to stare out the window. "Remind me to call home in the morning and let them know I'm extending my stay. They get worried."

We crawled along the freeway a few more yards in silence.

"I think I could get used to this," Mom said, more to herself than to me.

TWELVE

Closed.

I looked at the sign on Goodwin's Good Stuff and wanted to bang my head against the glass door. All that time in traffic only to meet with a dead end. I probably should have called to make sure they were open, but we were well within the hours posted on the website.

Eventually we'd made it to Torrance. It had taken twice as long as usual. The cause of the traffic jam had been a very bad accident involving a couple of vehicles. It looked like a pickup truck had slammed into the middle divider and flipped. Two cars were near it, upright but smashed on their fronts and sides. One had spun around and was facing traffic in the far lane. A fire truck was standing by, along with two ambulances and several cop cars. Craning my neck like everyone else, I studied the carnage as we passed but couldn't tell the status of the drivers or any passengers. Once highway patrol waved us slowly past the accident, the road opened up and I hit the gas to our destination, but the damage had been done to our schedule.

"The little clocky thing on the sign says he'll be back a little after three," Mom pointed out.

She was right. The closed sign also displayed a small clock face. The little hand was on the three and the big hand was positioned somewhere between ten and fifteen minutes after the hour. I consulted my watch. It was almost three o'clock now.

"A lot of store owners don't bother with that, though," I said. "But since it's almost that time, it wouldn't hurt to wait and see if Buck returns."

I looked around the strip mall. It was good sized, with lots of the usual shops and services, including a liquor store, nail salon, and dry cleaners. There was also a sub shop, a donut shop, and a mailbox place. Next to the donut shop was a weight-loss clinic. Except for a major grocery store standing alone and taking up the bulk of the lot, Buck's store was the largest. It was located on the end of the line of stores, closest to the street. On the far end of the lineup of shops, closest to the grocery store, was the donut shop. Next to Buck's was the nail salon. Its door was open. I stepped inside, with Mom in tow. Like the shop I patronized, it was operated by Asians.

A petite young lady with jet-black long hair greeted me. "You want mani-pedi?" she asked in broken English.

I looked at her trendy American clothing and wondered if the accent was real or embellished for clients. It was a thought that often occurred to me at my own salon. I'd been going there for years, yet old hands and new employees alike, both young and old, spoke English like they'd just arrived in the country on a broken-down fishing boat.

"Thank you, but not today," I told her with a smile. "I'm looking for Buck Goodwin, the man who owns the secondhand store."

She tilted her head to one side like a puppy who didn't understand the command "sit."

"Buck Goodwin," Mom repeated. "Big guy who owns the store next to you." She pointed in the direction of Goodwin's Good Stuff, then pantomimed his size by holding her hands high and wide.

A slight middle-aged man stepped forward from the rear of the salon. He and the girl exchanged words in their language before he turned to me. "How help?" His English was better, but not by much.

I repeated my question. At Buck's name, I saw recognition flash in his eyes.

"Yes, know Buck."

"Have you seen him today?"

He thought about it a moment, then shrugged. "We busy. Not notice."

Realizing we weren't getting anywhere, I thanked him and the girl and left the shop.

On the other side of the salon was the liquor store. I headed in that direction.

"Are you going to hit every store in this mall?" Mom asked.

"If I have to. Buck's been here a long time. He must be friends with some of these people."

"When we get to the donut shop, I'd like a cup of coffee. It's getting a bit chilly."

I stopped just outside the liquor store. "You can go there now, Mom. You can get a coffee and wait for me if you're cold or tired." Mom putting her feet up with a cup of coffee would certainly speed up my questioning of the local merchants. Every time I asked a question, I'd be wondering if Mom was going to interrupt with her own inquiries.

"I didn't say I was tired," she clarified. "Just said I wanted a cup of coffee." She made no move to head for the donut shop. "But it can wait," she added. "We have work to do first."

We. I silently groaned and headed into the liquor store.

With its windows nearly blocked by ads, the store appeared small, dim, and crammed, like a tiny cave hidden in the side of a hill. Besides alcohol, it sold all kinds of beverages. It also displayed a lot of snack foods, tobacco products, and lottery tickets. My father always referred to these tiny liquor stores as package stores. With the convenience of buying booze at the grocery store or from one of those mega-beverage chains, I wondered how a place like this could stay afloat. Mom and I stood a moment on the threshold, waiting for our eyes to adjust to the dim light.

"Can I help you?" The question, uttered in a thick accent, came from a small brown woman stationed behind the counter. She appeared to be somewhere between Mom and me in age.

I approached the counter. "I'm looking for the man who owns the secondhand store. He's not there right now, and I was wondering if you saw him today?"

The woman looked at me with large, dark eyes but said nothing.

"Do you know Buck Goodwin, the owner of Goodwin's Good Stuff?" I pressed.

"We do not," came another accented voice.

I turned to see a male counterpart to the woman behind the counter. He was standing by the small vertical cooler that held soft drinks. In his hands was a small box. He approached, put the box on the counter, and nodded in our direction. "I am very sorry, but we do not get involved with our neighbors. We are too busy trying to run a business."

I looked from him to the woman, who was probably his wife, and saw that neither was going to say more. It was stamped on their faces along with very polite but closed smiles. I smiled at both in return and thanked them.

"Just a minute," said Mom as I was about to leave. "I want some of those lottery tickets."

I turned to her in surprise but said nothing as she surveyed the line of colorful scratch tickets behind the counter. "Give me five of the green ones and five of the red ones," she told the woman. "And five picks for SuperLotto."

"You're not playing Mega Millions?" I asked, stepping closer.

Mom looked over the advertisement for the lottery games, checking out the current jackpots. Obviously, she didn't catch the sarcasm in my voice or was choosing to ignore it. "Sure, why not?" She pulled a twenty-dollar bill from her purse and plopped it on the counter. "And give me five picks for that Mega game."

"I meant the question as a joke, Mom, not as encouragement."

"What's the harm? And who knows, I might win." She took the tickets from the woman and thanked her, giving both the store owners a rare smile.

Outside, I said to Mom, "I didn't know you played the lottery."

"I don't, but you can't go barging in questioning people without buying something; it's not polite. Not to mention you yourself said buying something during investigations looked more natural."

While I didn't like having my words thrown back in my face, Mom had a very good point. I'd bought many an item while trying to squeeze information out of people. I'd even submitted to a breast exam once. Mom's presence was definitely putting me off my game.

The next storefront was the dry cleaners. I was about to again suggest Mom go for coffee when she surprised me with the idea herself.

"If you don't mind," she began, "I think I will walk down to the donut shop for that cup of coffee." She pulled her jacket closer.

"Not at all, Mom." I tried not to show my enthusiasm at going solo. "I'll work my way down the line of stores and meet you there."

I got the same polite but stony response from the woman working the counter at the dry cleaners as I did from the liquor store. Next was the sub shop. Manning the counter were two teenage boys. One's nametag said his name was Luke and identified him as the manager. He couldn't have been more than nineteen — twenty, tops. There was only one customer, a man, who sat at one of the two tiny tables eating a sandwich while reading a newspaper.

"Do you know Buck Goodwin, the man who owns the secondhand store?" I aimed the question at the kid named Luke but hoped the other was listening too. Following Mom's example, I thought about buying something, but if I did that at every store in the mall, I'd be getting a manicure, eating sandwiches, and buying booze all the way down the line. And heaven only knows what I'd do when I reached the weight-loss clinic.

"The big guy?" he asked.

"Yes. Blond hair. Tattoos."

"Sure," Luke answered. "He comes in all the time for lunch." He turned to the other kid, who only nodded in response.

"Did he come in today? You see, his store is closed, and I'm wondering if he's coming back today or if it's closed for the day."

"No, he was in today," Luke answered. "I made his sub myself — turkey and ham with all the trimmings. I remember because usually he gets a meatball sub or a Philly steak sub."

"Did he say anything about closing early today?"

"Nope. Just grabbed a sub, some chips, and a drink, and left."

"Do you remember when?"

"Yeah, because that was odd, too. It was around eleven thirty. Usually he comes in around one."

Eleven thirty would have been shortly after returning from court — about the time Greg was home having his lunch.

As I made my way down the line of small stores and shops, I had no further luck. Even if people knew Buck, they knew nothing about his whereabouts. Skipping the weight-loss clinic, I doubled back to Goodwin's Good Stuff before entering the donut shop. I wanted to see if Buck had returned while I was checking with the neighboring merchants and before I reconnected with Mom. He hadn't returned, and it was now after three thirty.

I walked around to the back of Buck's store and found a wide service alley with access to the back of all the shops in the mall. This was where they took deliveries. Large commercial trash bins were lined up against the back walls. A quick glance told me none of them appeared full. While I was checking out the area, someone came out of the back door of one of the stores. It was the kid from the sub shop — not Luke but the other one. In his hand was a plastic bag full of trash. He heaved it into the trash bin behind the sandwich shop, where it landed with the hollow thunk of a near-empty container. The trash pick-up must have been yesterday or today. The alley was wider than I expected, and there was room for one or two parking spaces behind some of the businesses. These were probably for employees. Buck's shop was the only one with a garage-type door at the back.

Seeing nothing of importance, I returned to the front of the strip mall and called Greg. I reached his voice mail so simply left a short update about the bad accident on the 405, Buck's store being closed, and so far hitting a dead end. Finished with my message, I wandered down the sidewalk, past the shops I'd visited. It had grown cooler, and the promise of rain was in the air. A coffee or hot chocolate was sounding pretty good.

When I got to the donut shop, I saw that Mom was not alone. Sitting at a small, round table with her was an elderly man who instantly reminded me of a Hobbit, specifically Bilbo Baggins — the older one from *Lord of the Rings*. The image wasn't dispelled any when he politely got to his feet as I approached. He was short and portly, with thick, curly white hair and compelling blue eyes that twinkled from behind square-framed glasses. It took everything within me not to check for pointed ears and bare, hairy feet.

Mom introduced us. "This is my daughter, Odelia."

The pixie man held out his hand. "I'm Bill Baxter. Nice to meet you, Odelia."

Huh. Bill Baxter. Bilbo Baggins.

Bill indicated for me to join them.

"Let me get something first," I said, giving him a curious smile.

"No," Bill said, stopping me. "You sit down. I'll be happy to get you anything."

"That's not necessary," I protested.

"But I insist."

"Let the man be a gentleman, Odelia," my mother admonished. "It's so rare these days."

I hesitated, then said, "Okay, then. I'd like a hot chocolate. Very light on the whipped cream."

"Would you like something to eat?"

"No, thank you. Just the hot chocolate would be great."

With a nod and a wink, Bill left and went to the counter. It was then I noticed he used a cane and had a slight limp. I also noticed that for an old guy with a cane, he was pretty spry.

"Who is he, Mom?" I asked in a whisper as I hung my handbag on the back of my chair and slipped out of my windbreaker.

"He's a locksmith," Mom explained, her hands holding a paper coffee cup. "That's his shop in the parking lot."

I turned to look out the window of the donut shop and noticed for the first time a tiny shed almost on the edge of the mall parking lot. It was painted green, with white shutters. On top of it was a large sign that said "Keys — Locksmith." The diminutive house wasn't helping me rid my brain of the Hobbit reference. Next to the shed was parked a tan Honda Element. On its side was a smaller version of the same sign.

Before I could find out what Mom had told Bill, he was back with my drink and several napkins. I thanked him and wrapped my hands around the warm cup.

"I hope you don't mind my intruding on your time with Grace," Bill said to me. "But I saw this charming lady come into the shop all alone and couldn't help but introduce myself." He smiled across the table at Mom.

Charming? Mom?

I was about to remark that Bill didn't get out of his Hobbit hut very often but bit back the snide remark. After all, the man had bought me hot chocolate. Instead, I said, "I don't mind at all, as long as you're not a stalker or a serial killer."

Mom kicked me under the table just as I took my first sip. "Ow!" Bill looked at me funny. "Sorry," I explained. "The hot drink zapped one of my fillings."

"Maybe it's going bad, dear," Mom said, all sugar and spice. "At your age, teeth start to become troublesome."

At my age? Grrrrr. The fact that I was in my mid-fifties and had recently had not one but two root canals came to mind. Still, no one wants to be reminded of those things, especially not by one's eighty-plus-year-old

mother who wears dentures. It's like looking in a dental crystal ball and not liking
the reflection.

I was about to give Mom a little kick back
purely on principle when Bill chuckled. "At
my age I can hardly be either. You need
stealth for those endeavors. An old codger
hobbling along with a stick is pretty noticeable."

"Speaking of noticeable," interjected
Mom, "I was telling Bill about our trip up
to the secondhand store."

I was getting worried about where Mom
was going with this. How much had she told
this stranger?

Bill said, "Grace told me how you two got
caught in the backup from that nasty accident on the 405. I saw it on the news just
before I came to get my coffee. There was
at least one fatality."

"From the look of the pickup truck involved," I told him, "that doesn't surprise
me. It was totally smashed."

We had a few seconds of somber thought
for the dead before Mom added, "Bill here
said he saw Buck leave."

I perked up. "When did he leave? And do
you think he'll be back?" I toned down the
eagerness in my voice. "I mean, if he's

closed for the day, we might as well go home."

"I don't think he's gone for the day," Bill answered. "I could be wrong, but usually he pulls a security gate across the front before he leaves. A few years ago Buck had a short series of break-ins, so he had the gate installed. He's the only store with one and had to get permission from the mall owners to do it." He took a sip of his coffee. "I see pretty much everything that goes on around here from my little shop. The days are long unless I have customer calls to open their car doors or change their locks. And people tend to forget I'm there. You wouldn't believe some of the stuff I see." He shook his head. "Some of it is amusing. Others, downright shameful."

It was becoming clear to me that Bill Baxter could be useful. I glanced at Mom. She was watching me with a smug look, and I knew if I didn't tell her "good job" when we got back into the car, I would get an earful.

"How long have you been here?" I asked.

He closed his eyes as if counting on imaginary fingers. "About ten years or so. Right after my wife died, I bought the shop from a locksmith who moved out of state. I used to have a larger store, but as I got older it became more difficult to handle, and I didn't want to retire. My son thought this would be perfect for me, and it is, though some days it can be lonely. I have a TV and DVD player in there — in fact, all the comforts of home, just smaller. And I watch all the comings and goings."

"So you saw Buck Goodwin leave?" I asked, getting the conversation back on track.

Bill nodded. "Unusual day for him."

Luke at the sub shop had said something similar, that Buck's food order and lunchtime today were unusual. Seems Buck was breaking a lot of his patterns. Was it because of worry over Ina or some other reason?

"He opened late," Bill continued, "then went to the sandwich shop for his lunch, which he does almost every day. Shortly after, he got in his truck and left."

Mom asked the next question. "Is he the only one at his store? Doesn't make sense for him to close up every time he needs to make a delivery or go to one of them auctions."

"His daughter used to work at the store, but I haven't seen her for several weeks. She's a wild one. Boy, those two fought like cats and dogs. Not sure if he fired her or if she left on her own."

"Daughter? So Buck's married?" I raised an eyebrow in Mom's direction as I remembered how chummy Buck was with Ina at the auction.

"Not that I know of," Bill answered. "Though I have seen him with lady friends from time to time. He was seeing one particular lady for a while, but I haven't seen her lately. Tiffany — that's Buck's daughter — once told me her mother and Buck were high-school sweethearts. Her mother got pregnant just before he went into the service. They never married, but Buck has always supported and been close to Tiffany. She came to live with him after her mother died from a drug overdose. Tiffany was just a young teenager."

Reaching into my bag, I pulled out two photos of Ina: one taken at Thanksgiving just last week and another of her when she had long brown hair. I placed them on the table in front of Bill. "Ever see this girl?"

His eyes lit up with recognition. "Sure. That's Ina, a friend of theirs."

"Theirs?" Mom asked, looking for clarification.

"Yes. This girl hung around a lot with Tiffany. They're close in age. And I believe Ina and her husband are also in the resale business, like Buck. Ina drives a Honda like mine, just a different color. Hers also has a store logo on it."

So far Bill was spot-on with his observations. "So you saw her here with her husband?"

He shook his head. "No, I don't recall ever seeing him, just her. But Ina was here off and on. She and Buck seemed to get on fine."

Bill looked at the photos again, then up, giving me and Mom a closer look. "Ina's husband was found dead at a storage facility. I saw it on the news. Who are you ladies really?"

"We're Ina's family," Mom answered. "Odelia is married to her cousin. We were at that auction when Ina's husband was found dead."

So Mom hadn't told Bill everything over their intimate cup of coffee — until now.

Bill Baxter digested that bomb of information, taking a couple of small sips from his coffee. Mom started to say something, but a look from me stopped her. Normally a look from me would have enlisted a comment, but she seemed to sense we needed to give Bill a bit of space and not be too forthcoming with information.

"Do you think Buck Goodwin had something to do with that?" Bill finally asked.

"Buck was at the auction with us," I told him. "And we know he was friends with them, at least with Ina. We just wanted to ask him some questions — see if maybe there is anything he can tell us to help Ina. Right now she's their prime suspect."

"Yes, I heard she was arrested. Very sad."

"She wasn't arrested for Tom's murder," Mom clarified, "but they are trying to pin it on her."

Bill's interest sharpened. "The news just said she was arrested. I assumed it was for killing her husband."

I shook my head. "It was for carrying a concealed weapon and not having a permit for it." I leaned forward. "We believe Tom was abusing Ina, and she was scared. The problem is, she's not talking, so it's easy for everyone to assume she killed him."

Mom tapped a finger on the table in a staccato tune. "We should also talk to that Tiffany. She might know something if she was Ina's close friend."

I turned to Bill. "You said you haven't seen Tiffany around?"

"Not for several weeks." Bill rubbed his craggy chin in thought. "Now that I think about it, Buck used to have a young fellow who helped out in the store part-time. But I haven't seen him around for maybe, let's see . . ." He scratched his chin again, creating a raspy sound. "It's been maybe a month or two since I've seen him. He didn't work at the store long, just a couple of months. Started in the summer, as I recall."

"Do you remember his name?" I asked.

Bill screwed up his face as he tried to conjure up the name of the part-timer. When he relaxed his face, the news wasn't good. "Sorry, but I can't." He paused, then added, "But I would remember him if I saw him. He had dark blond hair worn short. Very tidy and clean-cut. He and Buck didn't seem to get along, which is probably why he didn't last long."

Mentally I was working hard, jotting down this information on my internal hard drive for later use. "Any idea why he and Buck had problems?"

"My guess, from what bits and pieces I heard, is Tiffany and the boy were becoming close, and Buck objected."

I played with my cup, turning it around and around. "Seems Buck has people problems. Does he have anger issues, too?"

Bill shook his head at my suggestion. "Buck's the kind of guy who either likes you or he doesn't. If he doesn't, he has no use for you. If he does like you, he'll give you the shirt off his back. I've seen him get angry at folks, but it's never for long and never to the point of violence. It's more like exasperation that turns into frustrated swearing."

"And how does he feel about you?" asked my mother, voicing my next question before I could get to it.

Bill smiled. "Buck and I have always gotten along very well. Right after I bought the little shop, my son and I went into Good Stuff to see if we could find a few things. Buck was very helpful. I keep an eye on his store as much as I can."

THIRTEEN

"Mom," I began once we were back in the car buckling up to leave, "did Bill come into the donut shop after you or was he there when you got there?"

"Why?" Mom was fiddling with her seat-belt strap and only paying half attention.

"It struck me that he might have seen us in front of Buck's store, then watched us go down the line of other stores. He did say he watched Buck's store for him."

Mom stopped playing with the seat belt and looked at me, her eyes owlish through her glasses as what I said sunk in. "Come to think of it, he did arrive shortly after I did. He struck up a conversation while I was at the counter deciding what to order. You know, decaf or regular? Donut or muffin? Takes me longer to sort these things out than it used to."

I smiled. "I see you went with the bran muffin."

"And the decaf. Bill and I shared the muffin." She turned to me. "So you think he approached me to find out what was going on?"

"Could be he was curious."

"You think that's why he wants to take me to Sunday dinner?"

"He asked you out?"

"Sure did."

She reached into her purse and extracted a business card and showed it to me. It was for Bill Baxter, Locksmith.

"Bill gave me this when you went into the ladies' room and asked if I was free on Sunday."

When Mom took her turn in the ladies' room after me, Bill had called Buck's store to see if he had returned. He hadn't. Bill never said a thing to me about seeing Mom on Sunday, not that he needed my permission. The idea of my octogenarian mother being asked out on a date threw me. On one hand, it was cute, and why not? On the other hand, did *Bilbo* Baxter have an ulterior motive?

"And what did you say?"

"I said I'd have to check and see if you and Greg had anything planned for me that day, and I'd let him know."

"If you want to go, don't wait on us." I

shot a questioning look in her direction. "Do you want to go?"

"Could be fun, and maybe I could pump him for information."

"You're on vacation, Mom. You're not here to pump anyone for information. Leave that to me."

"Are you saying I couldn't do it?"

Sigh. Conversations with my mother were like walking through a field of thick oatmeal laced with land mines camouflaged as raisins.

"I didn't say that. What I meant is, that's not your job. If you want to go out with Bill, just go out, have a nice meal, and enjoy yourself. My concern is he's going to be drilling you for information."

"If he does, I can hold my own."

"Of that I'm sure." I glanced at the clock on the dashboard. It was almost four thirty, and I had a decision to make.

My original plan was to go from Buck's to the Vasquez store in Lynwood if we had time. The stores weren't close to each other, but with good traffic on the connecting freeways it was doable, especially since Otra Vez was open until seven o'clock. But the earlier accident on the freeway had put us way behind time-wise, as well as the time spent with Bill, waiting for a no-show Buck

Goodwin. We were also at the beginning of rush hour; all the freeways would soon look like beach parking lots on a summer day, eating up more time. It would be bad enough heading straight home. If I didn't have Mom along, I might have given no thought to fighting my way through traffic to Lynwood, but she looked tired. And then there was dinner to consider.

Home it was.

I'd just started the engine when my cell phone rang. It was Greg.

"Where are you?" he asked as soon as I answered.

"At Buck's store. He never showed up. We're heading home now. I'm hoping the freeway isn't as slow as it was earlier today."

"Yeah," Greg said, his voice sounding tired. "About that accident earlier today — there was a fatality."

"We heard that," Mom added. "Bill told us."

"Who's Bill?" asked Greg.

"We'll tell you later at home," I said. "It's an interesting story. But first, what about the accident?"

"They identified the driver of the truck. It was the auctioneer, Redmond Stokes."

I was speechless, but Mom wasn't. She leaned closer to the dashboard. "You mean the big man who ran the auction?"

"Yes, Grace. That's him."

"That's awful. He seemed nice."

I know my husband, and from his tone and hesitation there was something he wasn't telling us. "And?" I asked. "I know you have more to say, Greg. I can hear it in the pauses."

"Ina's attorney called me. The police questioned Ina about Red's death today. A heads-up: they are probably going to question you two and my mother again just to see if there is anything else you can remember about the auction. They will probably question everyone again."

Mom looked at me with surprise. I looked back at her with similar wide eyes while I responded to Greg. "But it was a car accident."

"Yes and no," my hubs answered. "The police haven't made this public yet, but they have reason to believe Red was murdered. They think he was killed or died while driving, and that caused the accident. Fortunately, the other drivers involved are okay."

"That's really awful." I shook my head, shocked that someone I'd just seen was now dead. It never ceased to leave me a little traumatized.

"You coming straight home or heading

somewhere else?" Greg asked.

"Home," I answered. I looked over at Mom. She really did look exhausted. "We're both tired and hungry."

As if reading my mind, Greg asked, "How about I pick up some Chinese food on my way home? That way no one has to cook. You like Chinese, Grace?"

A wide smile crossed Grace's face. "Yes, quite a bit. Can we get some sweet and sour pork and egg rolls?"

I was going to comment about her choice again of fried food but stopped myself. Mom was old enough to police herself, and I certainly didn't want her calling me Chubs again. And I happen to love sweet and sour pork myself; egg rolls I can take or leave.

"Sure, and I know Odelia loves that, too. You like Mongolian beef?"

"Not sure I've ever had that," Mom answered.

I backed out of the parking spot in front of Buck's store and turned the car toward the exit.

"Honey," I said, "just get whatever you think goes best with the pork."

I turned right out of the parking lot and headed in the direction of the nearest freeway on-ramp.

"It might take us a bit to get home," I

continued saying to Greg, "so why don't you plan on ordering it about twenty or thirty minutes from now?"

"Sounds like a good plan," my hubby commented. "You girls get home safe and sound."

"Oh, and by the way, Clark called. He's been delayed, so Mom's staying a bit longer."

"Is that all right with you, Greg?" Mom's voice went from Chinese food glee to worried hesitation.

Without missing a beat, my darling husband answered, "Of course it's okay, Grace. You can stay as long as you need to." He laughed. "You can even move here if you like."

"Odelia's already asked me about that."

"And?"

Mom paused, but there was a small smile on her face. "It has possibilities."

Just as Greg's laugh came through the speaker, we heard a loud, head-exploding boom. Everything around us rocked and shook, including my car and eardrums. Around us, alarms on parked cars were set off, creating a symphony of honking horns. I fought to control the car as it vibrated and barely kept it from rear-ending the car in front of me that had stopped.

"What in the hell was that?" screamed Greg. "Odelia, are you okay?"

Mom clutched her purse to her chest, her eyeglasses crooked on her nose. "Was that one of them earthquakes?"

"Greg, we're fine," I yelled into the phone. I shook my head, hoping to clear the ringing. "I don't know what it was, but it was not an earthquake, Mom. It sounded like some sort of explosion. And it was nearby."

Around us, other cars had come to a stop. Drivers were looking out their windows, curious and worried about continuing. People came out of the buildings and businesses to look up and down the street. Seeing people yelling and pointing in the direction we'd just come from, I unbuckled and got out of my car, letting my eyes follow theirs.

My hand went automatically to my heart. Just a block and a half away, flames shot up from a building in the mall we'd just left. And it looked like it was coming from the end building, the one closest to the street. Goodwin's Good Stuff was going up in flames. Then came a second blast, smaller but still heart-stopping. I ducked out of instinct.

From inside the car I could hear Greg yelling at me, demanding to know what was going on. Not a peep was coming from Mom.

Mom!

My mother prefers using dainty handkerchiefs instead of disposable tissues, even though they require washing and ironing. She and Buck had that in common. When I ducked back into the car, she was partially slumped forward, holding one of the hankies to her face.

"Mom!"

"Odelia!" yelled Greg from the phone.

Around us, the noise of alarms and approaching sirens mixed with the honking horns of impatient drivers. They'd stopped long enough to see what was going on, and now they wanted to move along and get the hell out of Dodge. Spotting a parking space just a few feet ahead, I put the car in gear. As soon as the vehicles ahead of me started moving, I eased forward into the spot and turned off the engine. Mom was still bent forward, but I could hear small moans coming from her. I tried to check her out, but it was too cramped.

Hopping out of the car, I dashed to her side and yanked the door open. "Mom?" I scrunched down beside her and fought back the urge to scream hysterically. "Mom!"

"Grace!" yelled Greg.

Slowly Mom raised her right hand while continuing to hold the hankie to her face with her left. She held the upraised arm out to me, palm out in a halt motion. Around us, sirens screamed toward the burning secondhand shop, but all I cared about was my aged mother.

I reached in and placed fingers on her neck, hoping to find her pulse. She didn't stop me. I sighed in relief to feel her heart beating steady and strong.

Greg yelled, "Will someone answer me before I lose my mind?"

"Hang on, Greg, I'm checking Mom out right now."

Slowly I eased Mom back in her seat until her head was against the headrest. Then I reached in further and unbuckled her seat belt. She didn't protest. I recognized the handkerchief. It was brilliant white with one corner edged with thick lace. I'd found it in a Celtic linen shop, bought a couple, and had them embroidered with her initials for her last birthday. It was then I saw the blood on the delicate hankie.

I took hold of her left hand and eased it away from her pasty face. Seeing her color-less complexion, my breath caught in my throat and refused to leave my body until I forced it out. Carefully, I removed her glasses and put them on the dashboard. The blood was coming from her mouth.

"Mom, you okay?"

She gave me a slow, slight nod. "I bit my lip," she said with a slight lisp. She swallowed. "The last blast scared me so much I bit my tongue and lip. So stupid." She pressed the cloth back to her mouth.

"She seems fine, Greg," I called toward the phone. "Just startled."

"Thank God!" he said with loud relief.

I returned to the driver's side of the car and popped the trunk. I always keep several bottles of drinking water in the trunk and was thankful it was there now. I retrieved two bottles and went back to Mom. She reached for the bottle as soon as I unscrewed the cap, but I stopped her.

"Don't swallow it, Mom. Swish it around and spit it on the ground. You need to clean the wound first." She did as I directed. I steadied her as she leaned out the door to spit into the gutter. Around us the air was starting to fill with smoke. Even more people had filled the streets to watch the blaze, getting as close as the authorities would allow. Mom swished and spit a second time, oblivious to the chaos.

"Okay," I said to her in a calm voice, relieved to see color returning to her cheeks, "now take a drink and swallow if you want water."

After she took a drink, she opened her mouth so I could inspect the wound. It was getting dark so I snapped on the car's overhead light to its highest level. It didn't help much, but it was enough for me to see the bleeding was slowing down.

"I think it's going to be okay," I told her, "but I can't tell in this light if you need stitches or not."

She snapped her mouth shut like a mouse trap and shook her head back and forth. After a mixed sigh of relief and frustration, I took the hankie and soaked it with some of the water. After wringing it out, I handed it back to her. "Here, Mom, use this on the wound if you need it."

I reached past her to buckle her up again, but she stopped me. "I can do it," she mumbled.

"Okay," I said gently, giving her a re-assuring pat on the shoulder. I handed her back her glasses.

To the dashboard I said, "We're on our way home, Greg. I'll fill you in on what's happened then, but in the meantime check out the local news. There should be something there about the blast." He told us to be careful and ended the call.

After handing Mom the open water bottle, I pulled my head out of the car and returned to my side with the second bottle. I took the top off and took a long drink. I hadn't realized how thirsty I was until the water hit my mouth. I took another long pull from the bottle and watched the chaos. If Mom hadn't been with me, I would have locked the car and wormed my way closer to the strip mall on foot to see what was going on. I tipped my head back and took another drink.

Then it hit me.

Minutes before the blast, Mom and I were parked in front of the building now in flames. If the blast had occurred while we were there, who knows what would have happened? It could have been far worse than ringing ears and a bit lip. It could have been . . . I didn't want to think about that. I couldn't. And what about those other stores? Were the people in the nail salon okay? That store was next to Buck's. And what about the closed-mouth husband and wife in the liquor store? And what about Bill Baxter? I wanted to know. I needed to know. And Redmond Stokes — what about him? Were his death and this blast just a co-incidence — two people at the auction who happened to have horrible things happen to them on the same day?

Without warning, I seized my gut and bent over, releasing the contents of my stomach onto the pavement. People nearby glanced at me, then looked away. I vomited a second time just as a light rain started up. This time no one gawked. A sick woman was no competition for a roaring blaze.

"Odelia," Mom called with concern from the car, "are you all right?"

"Yeah, Mom, I'm okay. It's just my nerves."

After heaving a third time, I opened the back door of the car and pulled out a small roll of paper towels I kept stashed in a pocket behind one of the front seats. More emergency supplies. It wasn't a mono-grammed linen hankie, but it would do. I wet a length of towel and mopped up my face and hands, then took a mouthful of water and swished and spit, as I had directed Mom to do.

I could only imagine what my mother would write on her blog tonight and hoped my upchucking would not be a highlight.

FOURTEEN

Dinner was quiet — mortuary viewing-hours quiet. Greg had picked up the Chinese food, but the three of us were not very hungry. We picked in silence at sweet and sour pork, egg rolls, fried won tons stuffed with crab and cream cheese, Mongolian beef, shrimp with pea pods, sautéed eggplant, and both steamed and fried rice. I don't know who Greg thought he was feeding, but even without the trauma of the explosion we would hardly have made a dent in the feast.

I'd wanted to take Mom to the ER to have her mouth looked at, but she refused. When we got home she did let me check it out under the bright light of the guest bathroom. The injury looked swollen, and the bite appeared clean.

"You have any mouthwash?" she'd asked. "Some of that really strong stuff. I need to clean it."

I nodded and went to our bathroom to fetch it. While my mother took a mouthful, swished it slowly around, then held it in her damaged mouth for a few seconds, I winced with discomfort only imagining the pain as the alcohol in the mouthwash hit the injury. Her eyes became damp during the process. When she spit it out, the room filled with an antiseptic odor but there was no blood in the sink. Mom took several deep breaths. The old broad had moxie, that's for sure.

"You should do that again before bed," I told her. I got up to leave. "Maybe you'd prefer warm soup or maybe something smooth and cool for dinner."

She shook her head. "I had three kids. This is nothing."

"Nothing" still made her blow her nose and dab her eyes several times.

At dinner Mom had a few bites of the sweet and sour pork, but I noticed mostly she ate the rice and shrimp — the more bland of the dishes. She ate little and chewed with slow, careful deliberation. After pushing a piece of pork around her plate with her fork for a minute or two, she excused herself.

"If you kids don't mind," she said, getting up from the table with the same care used to chew her food, "I'm going to get ready for bed. It's not every day I nearly get blown to bits." She started to reach for her plate to clear it from the table, but Greg stopped her before I could.

"Don't bother, Grace," he told her in a comforting voice. "Odelia and I will get the dishes. You go relax."

Mom put the plate down and started to go. I got up and put an arm around her, giving her a quick hug. Mom wasn't a hugger, so I made it short. "I'm so sorry for today. I should never have taken you with me."

"Nonsense," she snapped, still lisping from her wound. "I'm the one who insisted on going." She started toward the hall that led to her room. Before she got out of sight, she turned back to us. She started to say something, then snapped her mouth shut and continued on. Seamus, who had been curled up next to Wainwright on his bed, got up and followed Mom to her room with his own slow, arthritic gait.

Once she was gone, Greg said, "Today might make her want to run back to New Hampshire and stay there for good."

"And something tells me Seamus will be petitioning to go with her."

I plopped back down into my chair. After pushing my plate away, I put my elbows on the table and covered my face with my hands. "I nearly got my mother killed today." I started sobbing, not gobs, but a slow, choked weep. "Surely there's special place in hell for people like me."

"Don't be silly, Odelia." Greg wheeled over to me and pulled one of my hands away. "No one is going to hell over anything. You heard Grace say she insisted on going, and you didn't cause that explosion."

I held up two fingers and sniffed. "Two explosions."

The early evening news had reported that a blast had occurred at Goodwin's Good Stuff, a resale shop in Torrance, around four thirty. Authorities didn't know yet what had caused the blast. It was suspected that the resulting fire had set off the smaller second explosion when it reached paint and refinishing materials. They also reported that it was believed the store was empty at the time. Neighboring businesses had suffered varying degrees of damage, with the nail salon getting the worst of it by nearly being destroyed by the blaze. Injuries suffered by the people in the salon ranged from numerous cuts and bruises caused by falls and flying objects and one broken arm. The liquor store also sustained serious damage when merchandise fell to the floor in heaps of broken glass. Fortunately, considering all the spilled alcohol, the blaze didn't reach that far. The owners of the liquor store were bruised and cut, the reporter had explained, but they had escaped any serious injuries. People in the other shops were badly shaken. One woman in the parking lot suffered a mild heart attack. Bill Baxter had been interviewed by the reporter. He seemed stunned but safe. He reported that some of his tools had fallen to the floor from the impact of the blasts, but his business had sustained no other damage.

I reached for a paper napkin and blew my runny nose with it. "I know, but still — that could have been Mom who had the heart attack. We could have still been parked in front of that store when it exploded." I started to cry again, then forced myself to hold it together. "And those poor people in the liquor store and nail place."

Greg rubbed my arm. It felt comforting. I could feel his love and concern seeping into my skin like warm, expensive lotion. It found its way to the center of my core.

"Do you think," I said to Greg, trying to reset my mind on the what and why and not what might have been, "Buck set that explosion himself? Or that someone did it to get him, same as Red?" I grabbed another napkin from the stack we kept on the kitchen table and mopped up my face. At this rate, I'd have no makeup left to wash off later.

"I'm not sure. You did say Buck showed up at the store, grabbed lunch, then left."

"That's what both the sub shop guy and Bill said."

"Maybe he did set it himself, though why anyone would want to destroy a business they worked hard to build is beyond me."

"For insurance money?" I suggested.

"Maybe, but say I decided to pull such a stunt with Ocean Breeze. Before the ashes would be cold, the fire department's arson investigators, the police, *and* the insurance company would be all over the remains like ants at a picnic and crawling up my ass with questions. In this day of advanced forensics, it's very difficult to do, otherwise you'd see more of it in this ailing economy. Not to mention it's a major crime, especially if people are injured."

I started pulling cartons of Chinese food toward me. While I gave Greg's words thought, I removed serving spoons from the cartons and closed them up. We'd have enough leftovers for several meals.

"Did Ina's attorney tell you anything more about Red Stokes?" I got up and started moving the food toward the refrigerator. Greg started to help, but I shook my head. "Let me, honey. I need to keep busy right now or I'll go insane."

Greg positioned his wheelchair so he could watch me move between the kitchen and the table. "Not really, just that they were questioning Ina about any reasons someone might have to want Stokes dead."

Also on the news tonight was the story of Red's death. They had reported that he was shot from a passing vehicle while driving on the freeway. Witnesses interviewed by the reporter said they saw a late-model car come up close behind Red's vehicle, then move alongside him. One witness who'd been driving one of the cars involved in the accident said he was driving behind Red's truck and saw a hand holding a gun poke out from the rear window of the car that pulled alongside Red and fire. He said he heard two shots just before Red's truck lost control and hit the divider. The news speculated that it might have been gang-related.

I stopped, a carton of food held in my hand, and turned to Greg. "Do you believe the accident was gang-related like the news said?"

Greg shrugged. "Hard to tell. From the little I saw of Red Stokes, he didn't seem the type to be involved with gangs, but you never know. Neither of us knew the guy, just what we saw the day of the auction. The attorney didn't know or tell me anything more than what we heard on the news, only that Ina still isn't talking."

I put the carton in my hand back on the table and sat down in my chair. "Honey, I want to talk to Kim Pawlak tomorrow. She was on my list already, but I'm moving her up."

"Wasn't she Red's assistant?"

"Yes. I don't know if she worked for Red in his auction business or for the storage company directly, but I'll find out. I want to see what she has to say."

"I'm sure the police have already questioned her about it."

"True, but I'll be asking about Tom's death, not Red's, and Kim might be emotionally vulnerable enough now to crack. I know that's mean, but we need to get to the bottom of this, and fast. Too much has happened in too short of a time." I pointed a finger at him. "And Ina needs to start talking before she's implicated in more than just Tom's death."

"I totally agree. I went to see her today after her attorney spoke to me, but she just stares off into space when anyone asks her anything. I think she's either involved or protecting someone. Maybe she's protecting Buck Goodwin."

"She might also be scared spitless."

A low, sad laugh escaped from Greg's lips. "I think that goes without saying. She was looking very pale and fragile when I saw her today. My mother is worried sick about her."

I got up and moved the final food carton into the fridge and started picking up the dirty plates. "I'd also like to locate and talk to Buck's daughter. Bill Baxter said she and Ina were tight."

"I'm going with you tomorrow, Odelia."

I stopped rinsing the plate in my hand and turned off the water. "What about the shop?"

"Chris is back in the saddle, and I've already told him I'd be taking tomorrow off, maybe longer, depending on how this goes. The shop will be fine. You're not going back out there alone."

From the set of Greg's jaw, I knew I'd never talk him out of it, nor did I want to. My husband made me feel safe and protected, and wheelchair or not, he could hold his own with almost anyone. I wiped my hands on a towel, went to him, and planted a big kiss on his lips. "What about my mother? She may want to come along."

Greg put an arm around me and hugged me close. "Even after today?"

"I'm learning my mother is made of steel. This might only scare her off temporarily."

Greg chuckled. "Then we better get out there and investigate while she's still frightened." He pulled back and looked at me. "You know, my mother needs something to keep her mind off of Ina. Didn't Grace say she wanted to look at some retirement places out here?"

"Yes, she did." I smiled, knowing where Greg was going with his thoughts.

"How about I call my parents and ask them to take Grace out for a look around tomorrow? I'm sure Dad would also like to keep my mother occupied with something other than this mess."

"Great idea, honey."

I rewarded him with another big kiss. He picked up his phone and called his parents while I went back to cleaning up.

"All set," Greg said with satisfaction. "Mom told me she'd call Grace around eight tomorrow morning to plan their day." He hesitated. "I didn't tell Mom about you and Grace being near the blast in Torrance, just that Grace wanted to check out a new place to live. Mom sounded pleased that your mother might relocate."

"I'm happy they're getting along. I wasn't so sure at first. As for today, I'm sure Mom will tell her tomorrow. No sense giving Renee something more to worry about tonight." I walked back to the table and voiced my next concern. "I wonder if Mom has blogged about the blast yet. If she does and Clark reads it, he'll have a meltdown."

Greg wheeled over to the counter where he'd dumped his laptop when he got home and pulled it from its bag. He brought it over to the table and fired it up. While he was doing that, our doorbell rang. Wainwright charged for it barking his happy bark, his nose and ears telling him it was someone friendly. I left Greg and answered the door, finding on our stoop a slightly damp Dev Frye.

"Hey, Dev," I greeted as I opened the door to let him in.

"Where were you today?" he asked without greeting me back.

"Um, out and about with my mother?"

"Is that a question or an answer, Odelia?"

I didn't care for Dev's tone one bit but kept my snarky self under control. "Mom and I were out all afternoon. I was showing her the sights."

"Torrance is a hot spot for tourists these days?"

"According to the news tonight," I shot back, "it's a big hot spot."

Greg wheeled in from the dining area. "What's this all about, Dev?"

Anxious to change subjects, I offered, "You look beat, Dev. We just finished dinner. Why don't you take off your jacket and let me heat up some Chinese food for you?"

"No, thanks, I grabbed something before coming over."

"Coffee, then?"

"This isn't a social visit, folks."

I headed for the kitchen. "Then let me get you some 'police business' coffee. Mom made a fresh pot right before dinner. It's decaf, though." To emphasis the invitation, Greg started rolling back to the kitchen table.

After a bit of hesitation, Dev blew out a deep breath of air in surrender and followed us. He shrugged off his jacket and draped it over the back of a kitchen chair before lowering himself into it. By the time I placed his coffee in front of him, Dev was giving Wainwright a hearty rubbing on his neck and head, and his frown had been replaced by a tired smile.

When we join forces, the Stevens family can be quite charming, but the dog is our secret weapon. A few minutes later, Muffin came out from under the buffet as backup and rubbed herself against Dev's pant leg. Seamus was still with Mom and was generally useless when it came to buttering up visitors.

"Excuse me a minute, Dev," Greg told him, going back to his laptop. He turned it away from the cop. "I have to check something for work real quick, then you'll have my full attention."

While Greg tapped along on his laptop, I settled at the table next to Dev. "Yes, Dev, Mom and I were in Torrance, and we were near the explosion. But you already knew that, didn't you?"

He took a sip of coffee, testing it for temperature, then followed up with a big, satisfying gulp. "According to Fehring, witnesses said a plump middle-aged woman and her elderly mother were asking questions about Goodwin right before the blast. One witness even provided your first names."

"That must have been Bill Baxter. Mom and I had coffee with him."

Greg closed his laptop. "Is Fehring involved because it was Buck Goodwin?"

"What do you think?" Dev took another sip of coffee. "In one day, two of the people at that auction have been involved in violence; one is dead. You do know about Redmond Stokes, don't you?"

Greg and I nodded in unison. "Mom and I were caught up in the traffic jam the accident caused," I told Dev. "The news mentioned something about it being gang-related."

Dev shrugged. "Easy to assume since most drive-bys are, but it's under investigation."

"So, Dev," Greg asked, "are you here on your own or at Fehring's request?"

Dev leaned back in his chair and studied the two of us. "You might say I'm the opening act." He played with his coffee mug, slowly turning it around in his hands. "There are people wondering if Odelia here had something to do with the blast."

"That's preposterous!" came an angry lisping voice from the living room.

We all turned to see my mother standing in the living room at the edge of the hallway. She was in a floor-length mauve satin robe, pulled tight and cinched at her waist. On her feet were matching slippers. She'd slipped in so softly none of us had heard her. She stepped closer and started shaking her right index finger at Dev.

"I don't know who you are," she said, the slight lisp in no way masking her outrage, "but to even suggest my daughter had anything to do with that mess in Torrance is despicable."

Dev got to his feet and extended his right hand with tired patience. "Is it safe to assume you're Mrs. Littlejohn, Odelia's mother?"

When Mom hesitated, I made the introduction. "Mom, this is our good friend, Detective Devon Frye. Dev, my mother, Grace Littlejohn."

Mom still looked like she wanted to bitch slap Dev instead of shake his hand. It didn't matter that he towered over her; like a missile waiting for liftoff, she stood ready to defend my honor — something that touched me in spite of the situation. Finally, she held out her hand.

"I've been wanting to meet you, Grace," Dev told her, taking her slender hand between both of his meaty paws. "I'm just sorry it's under these circumstances."

Mom withdrew her hand as if Dev had cooties. "Odelia did not set that blast. Any fool who's met her could tell you that." It was clear she wasn't giving Dev an inch.

"I know that, Grace. I'm just telling them what some people have suggested."

I stood up. It was clear by the stony look on Mom's face that she had no intention of heading back to her room. "Here, Mom, take my chair."

"Please," Dev encouraged her. "Join us. After all, you were there and at the auction, so you might as well hear this, too."

FIFTEEN

"Coffee, Mom?" I asked as she settled in a chair at the table.

She raised a hand to wave off my suggestion. "No, but I'd really like a cup of tea — some of that Sleepytime you have. Maybe it will settle my nerves."

"Coming right up." I filled the teakettle, set it over a flame on the stove, and got out two cups. Mom wasn't the only one with nerves that needed settling.

"That blast have you rattled, Grace?" Dev asked the question with sincerity, like he was speaking to his own mother instead of a witness. He was pulling out his tender side, which was considerable but seldom seem by suspects and witnesses.

Mom, however, was all jagged edges and sharp points. "Wouldn't it rattle you to be almost killed?"

"It would and it has," Dev answered honestly. "I've been in a few near-death scenarios in my career. I've even been shot."

I swiveled, a tea bag hanging from one of my hands like a Christmas ornament. "You have?"

Greg was just as surprised. "You never told us that!"

Dev shrugged. "It happened a long time ago, when I was in uniform for the LAPD."

Mom pushed her glasses farther up her nose. "I know who you are now. You've become friends with my son Clark when he visits here, haven't you?"

"That's me."

"It's hard on a mother when her son's a police officer. My son Grady died in the line of duty."

My half brother Grady hadn't exactly died in the line of duty, but he had been a police officer at the time he was killed. Clark had never made it clear to me exactly what he had told Mom about the whole thing, so I wasn't about to quibble. And if Dev knew the real story about Grady, he wasn't letting on either.

Dev reached over and patted my mother's hand. "I'm sorry for your loss. Truly, I am." This time Mom didn't withdraw her hand. "My late wife never liked being married to a cop. She liked it even less when our daughter became one."

Mom gave Dev a nod, letting him know she shared his wife's pain. "I was very happy when Clark retired and went into private security work. He travels a lot now, but at least he's safe and seems to make a lot more money."

At this point Dev looked away to his left. He appeared to be studying the wall next to the kitchen table, or maybe the edge of the picture on the wall caught his eye — hard to tell. Or maybe he was thinking about Clark and the job he had now.

Then again, maybe he was remembering what he'd stopped by to discuss.

Or maybe he was thinking about what to buy his grandchildren for Christmas. Dev had two now — a girl and a boy. But I knew that last option was a very long shot.

When he turned back to us, he was all business. "Like I said, some people have suggested that Odelia had something to do with the explosion at Goodwin's, but neither Detective Fehring or I buy that." Dev turned his steely gaze on me. "Unless you've started a sideline we don't know about."

I plopped the tea bag into a cup and held up my hands in surrender. "You've got me, Dev. When I don't work for Mike Steele, I make bombs in our garage."

"That's nothing to joke about, Odelia,"

Dev snapped. "People saw you snooping around Goodwin's right before the place went up like a rocket. Someone even claims to have seen you in the alley behind his store shortly before the blast."

"When was this?" Mom asked. "I don't recall that."

"Before I joined you at the donut shop."

I turned to Dev, ready to plead my innocence. "Yes, I was back there, Dev," I explained. "I was trying to see if Buck's truck was parked there instead of in front. But it wasn't 'shortly' before the explosion. It was at least thirty minutes, maybe even forty minutes before then. And if I had planted the bomb, would I have left my car parked directly in front of the store and gone for coffee?"

I noticed Greg paying sharp attention.

"Did you try to get inside?" Dev asked.

"No, I didn't. I did see one of the kids from the sandwich shop back there emptying trash. Bet he's the one who told you he saw me."

"I don't know where the information came from," Dev said, "just that someone saw you there and told the police. And be glad you weren't back there when the blast occurred. The bomb was planted in the office, in the back of the store. Anyone standing in that part of the alley would probably have been killed."

Silence fell over our little gabfest like a shroud soaked in motor oil. It was bad enough to think of Mom and me parked out front just minutes before the explosion, but the thought of me standing just feet away from the bomb turned my legs to jelly. I grabbed the edge of the kitchen counter to steady myself.

"Sweetheart, you okay?" Greg started for me, but I held up a hand.

"I'm fine, honey. Just rattled." I looked over at Mom. She was staring at me with wide, watery eyes, her face pastier than it had been in the car after the blast.

An awkward silence fell over the kitchen again, only to be shattered a moment later by the doorbell. We all jumped. Wainwright, who'd retired to his bed once he'd said hello to Dev, now shot like a rocket for the door. This time he was barking his stranger-danger bark. Muffin understood that tone and retreated under the buffet again.

"That's probably Detective Fehring," Dev said, getting up. "I'll get it."

At the door, Dev tried to muscle Wainwright aside, but the dog wasn't having any of it and continued pushing his strong body between Dev and the door. "Down, boy,"

Dev said to the animal, but with no luck. Dev wasn't his master or his mistress, and Wainwright was determined to guard the house against the intruders. It was his job, and he was good at it.

"Wainwright," Greg called sharply to the dog. "Here." He rolled his wheelchair from the kitchen area into the great room.

The animal looked to Greg, then to the door. He was still on alert, his bark reduced to a guttural growl of warning.

"Come here," Greg ordered again. This time the well-trained dog obeyed. He trotted over to Greg but kept glancing back at the door, ready to protect Dev should he need help.

Greg grabbed the dog's collar and pulled him close, patting him on the head to calm him down. "Don't worry, ol' boy, Dev's got this covered."

At the door was Detective Fehring and her partner, Detective Whitman. Dev let them in just as the teakettle started its high-pitched whistle. We all jumped again. Even Wainwright let out a few bottled-up barks.

While the battalion of detectives greeted Greg and made their way into my kitchen, I turned off the flame and poured hot water over the two waiting tea bags. Maybe no one would notice if I sloshed some Scotch into mine. With sadness, I abandoned the idea as coming too late.

After placing the two cups of tea on the table, one in front of Mom and the other in front of a chair by Greg's place, I pulled a plate of sliced lemon out of the fridge, removed the plastic wrap, and added that to the table. Both Mom and I preferred lemon in our tea, but I was really delaying the inevitable face-off with Detective Fehring. She'd already greeted Mom. Now everyone was waiting on me.

Maybe Wainwright needed a good, long walk.

"Odelia." Greg, seeing my hesitation, rolled up to me. "Come on, sweetheart. Let's get this over with."

He was right, of course. Even though I was guilty of nothing but nosiness, it always unnerved me when I was questioned by the police, like I was waiting for them to pin something on me — say, the Lindbergh kidnapping or global warming — and in my rattled state I'd confess to it all. I'd make an awful spy. At the first sign of trouble I'd take the cyanide, sure that if I didn't I'd surrender national security secrets within the first sixty seconds of questioning.

With my husband by my side, I plastered a smile on my face and went to the table to face the music. I really should have laced my tea with booze.

Detectives Fehring and Whitman were standing with Dev where the great room met the kitchen area. It was the border marking formal territory from cozy comfort. Friends gathered around our large kitchen table or the patio table in good weather. Company and insurance salesmen sat in the living room. Dev had a foot in each, waiting for either Greg or me to make the call on the current situation. Wainwright had been banished to his bed on the perimeter of the kitchen, but he watched the new people with canine caution. In the end, it was Mom who tossed the coin about their acceptability.

"Why don't you folks sit down?" Mom said. "I'll make a fresh pot of coffee." She started to get up from her chair. "And take off those coats, they're wet."

"Grace," said Greg, "I'll make the coffee. You enjoy your tea while it's hot. You, too, Odelia." My husband left my side and swiveled for the kitchen counter.

There were three chairs at the table already and an open space for Greg's wheelchair. Three other chairs were scattered around the wall waiting to be pressed into service. I grabbed one and Dev another. We placed them together at one end, near where Dev had been seated. Without thinking, we'd marked our territories — police on one end, civilians on the other — much as the living room and kitchen were divided as formal and casual.

"You want some pie?" asked my mother of our visitors. "We have pumpkin and apple." She turned to me. "Any of that pecan left?"

I shook my head. "That's all gone."

All of the detectives declined. A second later, Fehring said with a slight smile at Mom, "On second thought, Mrs. Littlejohn, I would like some pie with my coffee. Apple, please."

I started for the kitchen again, but Greg waved me back. "I got this, sweetheart." He glanced over at Andrea Fehring. "Would you like that warm with ice cream, Detective?"

"Just warmed up a bit would be great, Greg. Thank you."

In spite of the coffee klatch pleasantries, I took my place at the table as if facing a firing squad.

Dev began, "I just confirmed that Odelia was in the back of Goodwin's store."

Fehring looked at me with tired eyes. I noticed more gray strands in her dark hair than when I'd first met her months earlier. "And what did you do back there, Odelia?"

I shrugged. "Nothing. I was just checking to see if Buck's vehicle was back there, but it wasn't. I saw one of the sub shop kids come out and dump some trash, and then I left and went to meet Mom at the donut shop."

"And you never saw anyone in or around Goodwin's?"

"No one."

The bell on the microwave dinged. Greg brought Fehring her pie and a fork. Next to me, Mom carefully slurped her tea through her injured mouth and winced.

Fehring noticed. "Are you okay, Mrs. Littlejohn?"

Mom nodded. "The explosion frightened me so much I bit my lip and my tongue. Who knew dentures were that sharp?"

"You're lucky that's all that happened to you," Whitman said with a concern that was anything but sincere.

I really didn't like him. I wasn't crazy about Fehring either at the moment, but if Dev said she was good people, that was good enough for me. Maybe under different circumstances, we might actually like each other. Whitman I wasn't sure I'd ever like. He seemed too snaky, and I hate reptiles.

They make my skin crawl, both the animal and the human kind.

Mom matched his tone and answered, "So we heard. We also heard a woman in the parking lot had a heart attack. Is she going to be okay?"

"Yes," Fehring answered. "It was a mild one and she's in the hospital for observation, but she'll be fine."

Greg wheeled over with a tray across his lap. On it was the coffee pot, some mugs, cream and sugar, and a few spoons. He lifted the tray to the table. I poured the coffee and distributed it to Fehring and Whitman. Dev shoved his empty mug toward me for a refill.

During the coffee service, Fehring took several bites of pie. "Great pie, Odelia," she said, washing it down with hot black coffee. "My family never has pie for Thanksgiving. It's my father's birthday, so we always have cake and ice cream. Just doesn't seem right, does it?"

If she was trying to make me — all of us — more comfortable with her forced folksy charm, it wasn't working. "Sorry to disappoint you, Detective Fehring, but I didn't make the pie. My mother did."

In response, Fehring lifted her coffee mug in a salute to Mom.

227

"If you want her recipe," I barked, "I'm sure she'll share it with you after the interrogation."

"Odelia," Mom snapped. "These good folks just want some information. I doubt they'd be having pie and coffee if they were here to arrest us for something."

"Calm down, ladies," Greg intervened. "Just answer the questions you're asked."

Then my level-headed hubby looked at each of the detectives individually, one after the other. "In all the drama, we forgot one very important question. Should Odelia and Grace have an attorney present for these questions?" When no one answered immediately, he tacked on, "Or maybe we should just have coffee tonight and set a time for them to meet you at the police station after they've lawyered up."

"That won't be necessary, Greg," responded Dev. "No one here believes Odelia is a suspect; we just want to ask her questions to see if she can shed some light on the situation."

"You sure about that?" Greg prodded with growing agitation. "Seth Washington's out of town, but I'm sure I could get Mike Steele over here with a single call. Or maybe even Ina's attorney."

"While you're at it, Greg," Dev shot back,

"why not put in a call to Willie Proctor? Isn't he your caped crusader in times like this?"

Whoa! I've never seen Dev and Greg face off. I understood Greg's attitude. Like Wainwright at the front door, he was stepping forward to protect his loved ones. Dev was no stranger to sarcasm, but to throw out Willie's name like that was not like him, especially in front of other cops. He hardly ever shot off his mouth. He weighed his words; even his digs were carefully considered first. Something wasn't right with our friend.

Fehring was quick to catch the remark. "William Proctor, the embezzler? What does he have to do with this?"

Mom started to say something, but I reached under the table and put my hand on her knee as a signal to keep quiet. For a change, she followed my lead. We'd passed Willie off as Willie Carter, one of Greg's cousins, when they'd met a few years back. I don't know if Clark set her straight later, and I still didn't know if Mom knew yet that Willie employed Clark. But come to think of it, Mom didn't mention anything about Willie at Thanksgiving, so she'd either forgotten about Greg's other "cousin" or knew the truth, or at least part of it.

Clark and I really needed to sit down and share notes and formulate a common story. The family secrets were starting to need an Excel spreadsheet.

Dev remained silent a moment, then said, "Nothing. He has nothing to do with it. It was a private joke."

Both Whitman and Fehring turned their radar on Dev, trying to figure out what was true and what was BS, but it was clear Dev wasn't going to offer up any more information. They turned to Greg, but his face was also made of granite. I kept my hand on Mom's scrawny knee.

"What about Buck Goodwin?" I asked, hoping to get everyone's attention back on track. "Do you think *he* planted the blast? From information I got from Luke at the sub shop and Bill Baxter, it sounded like he diverted from his usual routine today."

Andrea Fehring pulled a notepad and pen from her shoulder bag and prepared to take notes. Dev did the same when questioning people. Whitman sat like a bump on a log, drinking his coffee and looking like he'd rather be having a proctology exam.

"And what about his daughter?" Mom piped up. "Bill said Buck and his daughter had a falling out."

"Buck Goodwin seems to be MIA," said

Whitman. "No one has seen him since he left his shop after lunch."

"We found his daughter," Fehring told us. "Or I should say she found us. She saw the store burning on the news and ran down there to make sure he was okay. She claims she hasn't spoken to Buck for several weeks, confirming they'd had a big fight. She quit his store and moved in with a friend. She's obviously still very concerned about her father but has no idea where he is."

I removed my hand from Mom's knee and took a sip of my tea, which was now only lukewarm. "It sounds like you already know everything we found out today and more, especially if you spoke to Bill Baxter."

The corner of Fehring's mouth twitched at the mention of Bill Baxter — not in a half smile, but with annoyance — reminding me of how my nose sometimes twitches when something bugs me. It made me wonder if she'd made the leap to Hobbitville as I had.

Fehring brought her lips to attention and said, "Did Mr. Baxter tell you why Buck and his daughter had a problem?"

"We heard the fight was about a boy who worked at the store."

Fehring dabbed at the pie crust crumbs on her plate before looking up at us. "Actually, it wasn't. It was about a girl. Tiffany's a lesbian who is newly out of the closet. Her father wasn't very happy about it, so she moved in with Kim Pawlak."

"Red Stokes's assistant?" I asked with surprise.

"The same."

"Are they lovers or just friends?"

"I'd say they're a couple. Kim came with Tiffany to Buck's store after the blast."

I looked to Greg and my mother. They seemed as surprised by the information as I was. I was betting even eagle-eyed Bill Baxter had botched this tidbit.

"What about Ina?" asked Greg. "Are she and Tiffany involved romantically?"

"Not according to Tiffany," answered Fehring. "She said Ina was like a big sister to her and encouraged her to come out. She didn't seem upset about Tom's death, even said he deserved what he got considering how he treated Ina. Tiffany is very concerned about Ina."

Greg swallowed hard, then asked, "Does she think Ina killed Tom?"

Fehring shook her head. "No, she doesn't, but she wasn't surprised that Ina was planning to take off. Tiffany said Ina had been talking about it ever since Tom took up with Linda McIntyre a few months back."

"Seems Bill got the boyfriend thing all wrong," Mom said, leaning forward. "But Bill also said until recently Buck had a girlfriend, but he didn't tell us her name or anything about her, just said she hadn't been around in a while. Did Tiffany mention that?"

"Not a word," Fehring said. "Neither did Bill Baxter."

Whitman added, "Considering the girlfriend is in the past, neither might have thought it important."

Fehring jotted the information into her little book with short, precise strokes of her pen, wasting no effort. The conviviality was over; the pie, forgotten. She looked up. "Anything else?"

I scrunched my eyes closed, wondering if I should say anything about Bobby Y. In light of Red's death and the destruction of Goodwin's shop, his reviews seemed trivial, but you never know.

"What is it, Odelia?" asked Dev. "I know that look. There's something you're not telling us."

"It's silly, really."

Whitman let out a long-suffering sigh and stood up. "I don't know about you two," he said to Fehring and Dev, "but I have real police work to do." He reached for his jacket. "I don't have time to coddle some busybody."

My eyes popped open. "Hey," I snapped. "You came here, remember? I didn't come to you. Maybe it's *my* time you're wasting."

Greg put a hand on my arm. "Settle down, sweetheart."

Detective Fehring stood up but didn't reach for her jacket. She took Whitman by the arm and led him away from the table. "Why don't you go home, Leon. It's been a long day. I can handle this from here."

Wainwright went on alert but stayed in his bed.

Whitman glanced back at me, then gave Fehring a short nod of agreement. "Okay. I'll see you tomorrow."

Fehring spoke low to Whitman as they strolled to our front door. Once he was gone, she returned to the table. "He's been under a lot of pressure lately," she said, "and it has been a long day." She looked around the table. "For all of us."

She took her seat and took a long drink of coffee before picking up her pen again. She latched her eyes onto mine. "If you have more to say, Odelia, spill it. Spill it all."

I told her about my research into second-hand stores and how that led to the online reviews and to Bob Y and his obvious bias

234

against such stores. While Fehring jotted in her notebook, I outlined our trip to the food trucks and our failure to date in finding out Bob Y's identity.

When I was done, Fehring asked, "So you think this guy might have a vendetta against resale shops?"

I shrugged. "I don't know. But he sure dislikes them and has taken potshots at several represented at the auction, including Tom and Ina's store and Buck's. He seemed particularly nasty in his review of Buck's store. My gut told me it might be something to look into."

Dev looked over at Fehring. "It might be a stone worth turning over," he told her, backing me up.

Fehring nodded while she wrote notes. "I'll contact the About Town office and see what info they can give us on this guy or are willing to give without us getting all legal on them."

Detective Fehring stopped writing and looked at me. "Anything else?"

I thought about the day we found Tom's body. "Yes, something I just remembered. It was something I overheard Ina say to him the day of the auction."

"To him?" Fehring asked. "To Tom Bruce?"

"Well, to his body," I clarified. "At the time it just seemed like something she might say in shock, but now I don't know."

"What was it?" Fehring was ready with her pen to take down the words like dictation.

"Right before the police arrived and pull us away from the crime scene, I overhead Ina say to Tom, 'You stupid, stupid bastard.' "

Fehring wrote down the words and studied them. "That's all she said? 'You stupid, stupid bastard'?"

I nodded. "Doesn't exactly sound like something a murderer would say to her victim, does it?"

"Hard to say, Odelia," Dev said. "You'd be surprised what people say after they've killed loved ones."

"But we'll definitely look into it." Fehring tapped her pen on the notepad. "And you just remembered this now?"

"Yes." What I didn't tell Fehring was that it popped out of my memory when I was mentally calling Whitman a bastard.

"Have you talked to Linda McIntyre yet?" I asked.

"No," Fehring admitted. "She's been rather elusive. No one claims to have seen her since the auction. We're wondering if she skipped town."

I forged ahead with an idea that had been fermenting in my brain since our talk with Bill. "I'm wondering if she was Buck's girlfriend before she started seeing Tom. You know, the girlfriend Bill mentioned who is no longer in the picture. We know Ina was close to Buck and Tiffany, but maybe she had feelings for Buck and didn't like him being with Linda. And then when Linda took up with Tom, it was too much."

"Are you giftwrapping a new motive for Ina and handing it to us?" asked Fehring without a hint of sarcasm. "Right on the heels of telling us something that might help her?"

"No, not at all," I quickly clarified. "I'm not saying Ina killed Tom over it. But maybe Buck did and used the blast in his store as a diversion."

Mom leaned forward and tapped an index finger on the table to make a point. "Or maybe Buck dumped Linda because of Ina, so Linda took up with Tom for revenge."

Fehring wrote it all down, then looked at us, waiting for more. Mom complied, working the angle on her mind. "Maybe things with Tom weren't working out, so Linda killed Tom, then went after Buck. She did flee the auction as soon as the body was discovered."

"And how do you figure Redmond Stokes fits in?" asked Fehring, who seemed mildly amused by Mom.

Mom zeroed her weathered face in on the lady detective like a heat-seeking missile. "How the hell do I know? That's your job, isn't it?"

SIXTEEN

Greg and I determined that our first stop Friday morning would be Elite Storage. We still didn't know if Kim Pawlak worked for them or directly for Red Stokes, so before going we called the Elite Storage office. A man answered and told us that Kim didn't work there; she worked for Acme Auctions. A quick Google search gave us the information we needed for location and ownership. Seems Acme Auctions was owned and operated by Redmond Stokes — or had been owned and operated by him. A calendar showed an auction scheduled for this morning at Elite Storage and another scheduled for later this afternoon in Downey. The man who answered the phone at Elite had said nothing about that. Maybe the auctions had been cancelled in light of Red's death. I placed a call to the number listed for Acme Auctions, half expecting to get a recording saying that due to the death of the owner, the business would be closed until further notice, or at least for a few days.

"Um, hi," I said to the woman who answered. "I read about Red's death and was wondering if the auctions scheduled for today were still going forward."

There was some hesitation, then the woman said in a low, sad voice, "Yes, both of them are still on the calendar. Seems making money trumps decency."

I thanked her and started to end the call when I tacked on as an afterthought, "Was Red the only owner of Acme? I mean, what will happen to the company now?"

"Guess it will go on as before. At least that's what Kim told us this morning."

"Kim Pawlak? Red's assistant?"

"She's also his partner. Red sold her half of the company recently."

"Oh, I didn't know that. Well, it's nice that the business will continue and your jobs are safe."

"We'll see about that," came the short, curt response that seemed anything but optimistic.

This was definitely getting more interesting. With Red out of the way, Kim probably had full ownership of the company, or at least full management. It would depend on what kind of business entity it was and what kind of an agreement they'd signed when Red sold Kim half the business. We did contracts like that all the time at the firm. Usually the agreement would provide the remaining partners with an option to buy the deceased partner's ownership from the heirs for a predetermined amount or calculation of value. If the remaining partners decided not to exercise the clause, then the heirs could sell it to someone else or keep it; Greg had made a similar agreement with Boomer when Boomer bought into Ocean Breeze Graphics. Or it could be that Kim got full ownership outright. Everything would hinge on the agreement made when she bought into the business. I shared this new information with Greg while he finished dressing.

"Acme Auctions." I rolled the words over my tongue. "Makes me think of anvils falling from the sky and a roadrunner squawking 'beep beep.' "

Greg chuckled in agreement. "Sure does." He pulled a Lakers sweatshirt over his tee shirt. "If Kim Pawlak directly benefits from Red being gone, it certainly opens up the possibility that she could have had something to do with his death."

"Well, it at least gives her a motive, but it doesn't tie her in with Tom's death."

Greg ran a hand through his hair, which was his equivalent of styling. "Two murders and a bombing all within days of each other and all having to do with people connected to the resale business. I'd say there's a connection." He turned to me and grinned. "As Dev would say, it's not a coinkydink."

"Speaking of Dev, I still think there's something wrong. He doesn't seem himself at all. I hope he's feeling okay."

We moved from the master suite into the kitchen and prepared to leave. "After last night, I think you might be right, sweetheart. Maybe I'll ask him out for a beer and see what gives."

"Good idea." I put on my earrings as I walked. "I hope some of the same people are at the auction today as last time, especially that Linda McIntyre."

After Dev and Fehring had left the night before, we gave Mom a heads-up that Renee would be calling. We didn't want her to feel blind-sided. She seemed very happy with Renee's offer to help and didn't say a peep about tagging along with us. Of course, we didn't tell Mom our plans either.

"Maybe I could get my hair done tomorrow," Mom had said. "Just in case my date with Bill is still on. Renee's hair looks so nice. Do you think she'd take me where she gets hers done?"

Greg had turned his head so Mom couldn't see his grin.

"Maybe," I'd said. "Or you can try to get an appointment at my salon. I'll leave the number on the counter for you." I hesitated, then moved forward with caution. "Do you think it's such a great idea to still have dinner with Bill Baxter?"

Mom had looked surprised by my question. "Why not? I doubt he planted the bomb. At least the police didn't say he was a suspect. And I might be able to pump him for more information, especially about that girlfriend of Buck's. The more I think about it, the more I think it might be that Linda tramp."

I threw up my hands, knowing I was talking to a wall.

About then, Seamus wandered out from the direction of Mom's bedroom. Slowly he made his way to his food bowl, scooped up a few pieces of kibble, and crunched away, ignoring us. Muffin went over to say hello, but the crabby old cat swatted her away and went back to eating.

"Did you know," Mom said, watching Seamus with affection, "that Seamus snores? He snores louder than either of my two husbands."

I laughed. "You ought to hear it when he and Greg get going in harmony."

"Me?" Greg pointed a finger at his own chest. "Don't believe her, Grace. It's more like Odelia and Seamus are in competition. I've seen Wainwright cover his head with his paws." I swatted at my husband, but he was just out of my immediate reach.

"You know, Mom, you don't have to let Seamus sleep with you. Just shove him out and close the door. He'll either bunk with us or on the sofa."

Mom shook her head. "It's okay. I rather like the company, snoring and all. I was never one for pets, but I'm thinking if I move out here I might get me a cat."

"You might not need to, Grace," said Greg. "The way Seamus has taken to you, he might adopt *you* full-time. As he's gotten older, he's become less patient with Muffin and Wainwright, and even with us."

I could tell by my mother's small smile, flashed just before she tottered down the hall, that it would be something she'd like. I'd miss Seamus if he moved in with Mom, but if it was something the two of them wanted, I would go along with it. He'd still be in the family.

■ ■ ■ ■

In the morning, just as we were getting ready to leave, Cruz showed up. I introduced her to Mom, who was waiting for Renee to come by and pick her up for their day of beauty and home hunting. We left Wainwright behind so we could move faster and not worry about his water and potty breaks. This was unusual and the dog let us know it, ladling on the guilt like mushroom gravy. As we went out the back, the dog pressed his nose against the glass sliding door and whimpered. By his side was Muffin, looking just as forlorn and abandoned. Seamus had given up saying goodbye to us years ago.

"Don't look back," Greg told me as he hustled me out to the garage. "If you do, we're toast."

Sometimes I wonder who really runs our household.

Long Beach is just north of Seal Beach, and Greg knew which streets to take to avoid the morning rush-hour snarl. We landed at Elite Storage just as the auction was beginning.

The crowd was larger than it had been on

the day Tom's body was found, making me wonder if some of the new people were lookey-loos who came to see where it all went down. I recognized some of the people present, but there was no sign of Buck Goodwin. No surprise there. Not only did he no longer have a viable store, if he did destroy it himself, he would be in hiding from the law. If he didn't do it, he might be in hiding from whoever did.

Right up front was Linda McIntyre, dressed again in jeans and a tank top. Over the shirt this time was a loose black jacket worn unzipped. In her ear was a cellphone earpiece. Even though she wore oversized sunglasses, I could see the events of the past few days had taken their toll. Her already hard face was gaunt and ashy, making me wonder what she was doing here. Ina had said Linda worked auctions on behalf of clients who could not attend them, so maybe she had to be here for work. If she was a contract worker, no work meant no pay, and she didn't look like she could afford to lose a day's pay.

I scanned the crowd but didn't see any sign of Mazie Moore and was curious about their alleged partnership. I was also still curious why Mazie's store had escaped the harsh critique of Bob Y. Did he not have time to visit her stores? Or was he only interested in certain shops and their owners? I spotted Robert Vasquez standing on the edge of the crowd. He appeared to be alone. I wondered what had happened to his nephew. Had he been deported already? With so many questions swirling around, I had to work hard to mentally sort them into priority piles.

I studied the faces of the people waiting for the auction to begin. A group of people mostly brought together by the common thread of wanting to purchase and sell used goods, yet each was an individual with their own peculiar history, dreams, and motives. It was true of any group of people of any size. Put four people together and you had four different dramas playing out, some quirky, some tragic, some fun and uplifting. The more people, the more story lines. In this group of thirty or so people standing together in the cool November morning, there could be an abuse victim, an alcoholic, a former priest, a millionaire, a wife-beater, even parents putting a kid through medical school. There might even be a murderer.

Kim Pawlak approached the crowd. She looked the same as the last time I saw her, only this time she was running the show. By her side, holding a clipboard, was a young,

247

slim woman with closely cropped blond hair, thick black eye makeup, and torn jeans. She couldn't have been more than twenty — twenty-two tops. My money was on her being Tiffany Goodwin.

Kim's eyes scanned the crowd. When she caught sight of me I saw no recognition reflected from behind her round framed glasses. I'd dressed very casual for the day in jeans and an old V-neck sweater over a turtleneck. My hair was pulled back into a clip, and one of Greg's baseball caps sat on top of my head.

"I'm Kim Pawlak, the auctioneer," she announced in a monotone. "As many of you know, Redmond Stokes died in a horrible accident on the 405 yesterday, but we at Acme Auctions thought the best way to honor him would be to continue with our scheduled auctions. For those of you who knew Red personally, you know he would have wanted that. Details of a memorial service for Red will be posted on our website shortly."

The announcement made me think of poor Tom. His body still had not been released by the police, and once it was, I didn't know who would claim it. Ina was in jail. Greg's dad had told us that while Tom's family had been called, they had made it clear they had no intention of taking possession of the body or of having or attending any funeral. He was dead to them in more ways than the obvious. They had also expressed the desire that Ina get "the chair." Although I never cared for Tom Bruce, it saddened me to see him tossed aside by his own people like garbage. Another individual with a tragic history. Knowing my in-laws as I do, they would see to it that Tom received a proper sendoff when the time came. It's who they are and why Greg is the wonderful person he is. Decency runs in that family like grouchiness runs in mine.

With the business of Red's death dispatched, Kim indicated the young woman. "This is Tiffany Goodwin, my assistant."

Bingo!

"When the auction is over, please pay her." Kim followed with a rundown of the rules, following a script similar to Red's.

I studied the young woman by Kim's side and wondered how long she'd been employed by Acme Auctions. Did she go there right after quitting her father's shop? Fehring never mentioned she also worked with Kim, just that the two women lived together. I pulled out my phone and texted Greg: *TIFFANY GOODWIN!* Even though he was standing next to me, I didn't want to whisper to him and alert anyone to my interest in Tiffany. He texted back: YEAH, CAUGHT THAT.

Kim announced that there were three storage units up for auction today. She also informed us that two of the units were originally up for auction on Monday but had to be postponed due to unforeseen circumstances. Talk about an understatement. She made it sound like they'd been postponed due to missing paperwork.

"Is another body up for auction today?" A tall, skinny guy in flannel yelled out from the back. Everyone tittered nervously. "If so, that's the one for me." More laughter.

When an Elite Storage worker cut the lock and raised the door, I held my breath, just in case. I expelled it when I saw the unit was corpse-free and packed with miscellaneous goods. There weren't a lot of items, and they appeared to have been thrown in helter-skelter. Many were automotive. There were rims and tools. To the left was a heap of greasy rags. Some beat-up boxes lined the back wall. The stuff looked abandoned and without much value.

"Not a very good locker," I whispered to Greg.

"I don't know, sweetheart. Those tools could fetch a nice price. Good tools are very expensive, and so are those rims if they're in good condition. It all depends on what type of items you're looking for."

While the serious auction-goers stepped forward with their flashlights to examine what they could of the unit, Greg and I eased back into the crowd.

With a sigh, I texted Greg again: *BLND BLK JKT LINDA*.

He texted back: *GOT HER.*

YOU? HER. I'LL TAKE KIM/TIF.

Linda struck me as the kind of woman who might respond better to questions from a handsome man, although if she decided to make a break for it, Greg would not be able to pursue her. Then again, neither could I, considering my size and age matched against hers. We also needed to divide in order to conquer. When the auction at Elite was over, the non-winners would probably clear out quickly, either on to the next auction location or back to their businesses.

Greg texted back: *OK.* Then followed up with: *TELL DEV RE LINDA?*

Not exactly sure what he meant in his last text, I glanced over, trying to read his face. Then it dawned on me. The police were trying to locate Linda. If they had already, no harm done except we would tip our hand that we were pursuing information on our own. But if the police hadn't located her, we needed to give them a heads-up. It might help Ina.

I quickly texted back: *I'LL TELL FEHRING.* Yeah, I'd tell her . . . once we got what we came for.

Since getting a smartphone, I'd become quite adept at typing with one index finger. Some people were great with their thumbs. I tried that for a bit, but my messages were so loaded with errors, no one could read them.

While the auction was in progress, I located Fehring's number on my cell phone directory. It was the number she'd given me several months earlier, and I hoped it was still good even though she'd changed police departments. I plugged in the message: *AT ELITE. LINDA MAC HERE. ALSO TIFFANY.* The message drafted, I did not send it.

The auction got underway, and the bidding was lively. Linda McIntyre was the only woman in the thick of it. Kim kept the bids moving at a good speed but not with Red's fast-talking frenzy. As bidders fell off, the speed slowed until there were only two bidders — Linda and the man from Otra Vez. The bids continued climbing in steady, reasonable increments until Linda bumped the price with a very large bid. The next bid was to Roberto Vasquez. He hesitated, looking between Linda and the items in the locker, weighing whether it was worth another raise in price. In the end, he waved a hand at her in disgust, letting Kim know Linda could have it.

As soon as the auction was over, Linda closed the door and slapped her own padlock on it. As the crowd moved toward the next locker, she turned away and started speaking in a low tone into her earpiece. I pretended to drop something and edged closer. Before she noticed me and moved farther away, I caught her saying, "Got it."

"What's that all about?" asked Greg when I returned to his side.

"Ina said Linda comes to these things to bid for other people. Could be it's a client on the phone. Whoever it was, she was telling them she'd won the locker."

I studied the closed unit door. "Honey, didn't that seem like a very high bid, even for those tools?"

He shrugged. "It did to me, and by making that last huge jump, Linda showed everyone she was determined to get it, no matter the cost. Maybe her client had given her an order to buy lockers with tools and car stuff."

We hung back, concerned that Linda might decide not to participate in the next auction or that her client, thinking the last purchase broke the budget, decided one locker was enough for today.

"What do you think?" asked Greg. He kept an eye on the crowd as it moved away and glanced back at Linda, still hanging behind. "Should I stay with Linda while you go to the next auction?"

"Something is telling me we should both stick with Linda. Kim and Tiffany aren't going anywhere until the auction is done, and then they'll have to come back this way. We can cut them from the crowd then."

"Did you contact Detective Fehring?" he asked.

"Not yet. If I do, she and the cops might be here in a flash, giving us no time to talk to Linda or Tiffany. But it's ready to send."

"Good thinking."

Following my lead, Greg rolled alongside me as we approached Linda McIntyre. With each step I braced myself, ready for the barrage of rudeness sure to come.

"You speak to her first," I told my husband. "Butter her up."

If Wainwright was our family's star charmer, Greg was his understudy. Seamus and I battled for last place.

SEVENTEEN

"Hi," Greg began, getting close to Linda as soon as she ended her call. I hung back a couple of steps. "You Linda McIntyre?"

"Who wants to know?"

"I'd like to speak to you a moment if I could."

Linda McIntyre turned to look Greg full in the face. As she took in his rugged good looks and his wheelchair, her face softened from stone to newly poured concrete.

"What do you want?" Her voice was scratchy, like a zipper, and not as steady as it had been during bidding. She turned and studied me from behind her sunglasses before taking them off for a better look. Her face turned to granite again.

Greg moved closer. "I'm Greg Stevens. This is my wife, Odelia. My cousin is Ina Bruce."

Linda's lip curled into a sneer. "I've got

nothing to say to you." She started to turn away.

Undaunted by Linda's rebuff, Greg pushed on. "Please. We're not interested in getting you involved. We just want to help Ina. You may not like her, but I think you know her well enough to realize she'd never kill Tom, even though they were having problems."

"Jealous women do a lot of things you'd never expect them to do."

I moved up next to Greg. "Are you speaking about yourself?"

"Are you saying *I* killed Tom?" Linda squared her shoulders. It made her sizeable boobs and buffed arms stand at attention and ready for defense. "Tom and I were together. Ina was old news. Tom was even going to buy out her half of their business so we could run it together."

Now there was some new information to consider. It made me wonder if the money Ina had taken from the bank was the buy-out money, but I doubted it. If Tom had bought her out, Ina would not have had a reason to go to that auction. Then again, why go to the auction at all if she was going to leave town? None of that made sense.

"But," I said, moving as close to mad dog Linda as I dared, "I thought you were going into business with Mazie Moore."

"More old news," Linda said. "Mazie and I decided to go our separate ways."

"Before or after Tom Bruce was found dead?" asked Greg.

Without answering, Linda elbowed roughly past me. "I'm outta here."

"Don't you have to pay for the locker you won?" I pointed over to the locker Linda had just padlocked.

She stopped short and looked back at the rows of storage lockers. We couldn't see the auction going on, but we could hear the lively bidding. After that, they would move on to the third and final locker. Linda swiveled her head to look up the row of units in the other direction, which led back to the front gate. It was clear she wanted to bolt rather than speak with us, but she'd bid a lot of money for that locker. I didn't know the exact rules of storage auctioneering, but I doubted you could walk away without making the cash payment immediately. And if you did disappear, were you still on the hook for the money or did you get penalized? And if Linda had purchased that unit for her clients, they might be pretty upset if she did walk away.

"They're in the middle of an auction," I told her, "and there's another after that. You have a little time to talk to us before Tiffany's available to take your cash."

"I don't have to say nothing to you."

"What about Buck Goodwin?" I pushed. "We heard you two were an item before you took up with Tom Bruce." It was a bluff. We had no concrete evidence she had ever been Buck's girlfriend. It was simply a possibility.

Linda threw back her head and laughed. "Me and old man Buck? That's a laugh. Buck may look like a badass, but he prefers women his age or older. Less drama, he claims."

"Then maybe Buck killed Tom to protect Ina. We also heard she was close to Tiffany and like a daughter to him."

Linda pointed an index finger in my direction. She was in bad need of a manicure. "Now that's a good possibility. Buck was very protective of Ina, and he and Tom had gotten into it good a few times about how he treated her. Why don't you go bother him and leave me alone."

"We'd love to talk to Buck Goodwin," Greg responded, "but he's disappeared. You heard what happened to his store in Torrance, didn't you?"

Linda hesitated. I couldn't tell if she was using the time to consider the question or to fabricate a story. "Of course I did." She snapped the words like a crocodile snagging dinner. "Saw it on the news. The ass probably did it to his own store to cover his tracks on Tom's murder."

Greg tried another question. "What about Red Stokes? Do you have any theories on that murder?"

Again, hesitation. When she finally did speak, her words were noticeably softer. "Red was a nice man. His death was something that didn't need to happen."

After mentioning Red, Linda became noticeably edgier. For some reason his death had hit a nerve that mentioning Buck had not. I pushed her on it. "Why do you think it happened?"

Linda seemed lost in her thoughts, forgetting we were there. Off in the distance, the bidding noise had stopped. The group must be moving on to the final locker up for grabs. I decided to nudge her. In my hand my cell phone itched, just waiting for me to hit the send button and notify Fehring.

"The news said Red was killed in a gang shooting. Why would a gang target Red? Was he involved in dirty dealings?"

When Linda looked up at the sky, lost in her thoughts, I looked down at Greg. He was watching the cell in my hand. He looked up at me and gave an almost nonexistent nod, suggesting it was time to get the cops involved, but I wasn't so sure. I wanted to see if we could squeeze something more out of her first.

When Linda's thoughts returned to the here and now, she resumed her nasty stance. "How the hell do I know what Red was involved in?" This time her tough words were coated with a false, shaky bravado that I didn't believe for a minute. Dollars to donuts, Linda knew something about Red's murder, and maybe a connection to Tom's. I hit the send button on my phone and prayed Fehring saw the text ASAP.

Mustering my own swagger, I faced Linda. Problem was, hers was real; mine was only trotted out from time to time, like fragile holiday decorations. If she called me on it, I'd crumble like spun sugar. "There's something stinky about this whole mess. I think you know more than you're letting on — a whole lot more."

Next to me, Greg placed a firm hand on my arm in warning. Tough or not, Linda was a woman. Greg could clean most men's clocks in a tussle, and although he'd come to my assistance if needed, I knew he would be hesitant to mix it up with a female opponent.

"You have no clue, lady." Linda spat the

words at me like expelling tobacco juice. She seemed unperturbed by Greg's presence. Maybe she sensed he'd have a moral dilemma with her gender or maybe she thought he wouldn't be capable. She stepped forward and lowered her head, going almost nose to nose with me.

"Ah, but I do have a clue." Determined to pick at her until she bled answers, I didn't back down, even though my legs were starting to feel like jelly. "Lots of clues that I'm going to piece together." I shook a finger in her face. "And something tells me, Linda, that I'm going to find you smack in the middle of this mess, leaving poor Ina to hang for something you did or something you know about. And, trust me, Greg and I will never allow that."

"You're nuts." Linda sneered, showing off dull teeth. "Probably going through that menopause shit. I hear it turns people crazy." She took a step back. "Go home and knit something before something bad happens to you."

Determined to keep her unbalanced, I pushed again. "You know what happened to Red. I can see it in your eyes — they're full of fear. Maybe you're worried the same thing will happen to you. Who knows, maybe today, maybe tomorrow, someone will drive up next to you on the freeway and open fire. No place to go. Nowhere to hide. Just you, a moving vehicle, and a bullet with your name on it. Red didn't stand a chance. And you won't either."

She measured me with her eyes, weighing what I'd said, probably wondering if I was bluffing, perhaps worried I had information to back my bluster. She was definitely dirty and involved in some way; I'd bet my next mac and cheese on it. She glanced down at Greg, then back to me. For a moment, I thought she might forget about her unit and make a run for it. I hoped not. I really wanted to hand her over to Fehring and Whitman for questioning. Under their pressure she might spill information that could lead to Ina's innocence.

The fist came at me like a wrecking ball. I lay on the rough pavement, stunned. A few seconds that felt like minutes morphing into hours passed, and then the pain hit me. My nose gushed blood. It felt like it had been used as a chew toy by a pit bull. I never saw the punch. I never even felt it until I shook off the initial stupor. I clutched my bleeding nose with one hand and sat up. My ears rang like church bells.

I tried to yell to Greg to stop her, but all that came out was a gurgled cry of pain.

But I need not have worried. Greg was on the job. He had grabbed Linda by her arms and was trying to pin them behind her back. She thrashed around, kicking back with her legs, connecting with the wheelchair that Greg used as a block, but it was no use. Even with her buffed biceps, Greg was much stronger than Linda.

As Linda struggled with Greg, the back of her jacket came up, exposing a gun tucked into the small of her back.

"She has a gun," I yelled, but I wasn't sure the words came out clear enough to be understood. I was relieved when Greg spied the weapon and tightened his grip on her arms.

"Hey, what's going on?" someone yelled.

I turned to see someone running toward us. It was a man wearing an Elite Storage shirt, and he was yelling something into his phone. I braced myself against the pain in my face and slowly got to my feet, hoping he'd see we were the attackees, not the attackers.

About the time he reached us, Fehring and Whitman came around the corner from the front of the complex. When she saw the struggle, Fehring broke into a run.

EIGHTEEN

My nose did not appear to be broken, but the paramedics told me I should get it x-rayed just in case. They stopped the bleeding and offered to take me to the nearest emergency room, but I turned the offer down. "My husband will take me if I think I should go."

I always keep ibuprofen in my bag and now pressed it into service. I swallowed two, washing them down with bottled water offered by the paramedic. I swallowed two more two minutes later. Something told me this was going to hurt even more in a few hours. The paramedic told me I might even get a black eye. Great.

Once again we were giving the auction-goers a memorable day, but at least a dead body wasn't involved. While the paramedics took care of me, Fehring was questioning Greg. I didn't like not being part of that little party, but I had no choice.

Whitman was with Linda, who was now in handcuffs and more subdued. Fehring had ordered Greg to let her go, but he refused until someone removed Linda's gun. As soon as Fehring saw the weapon, she took it into custody. Like Ina, Linda wasn't licensed to carry a concealed weapon. She was calmer now but still agitated. Uniformed cops had been called. I looked over just as Whitman handed her off to a patrolman. As she was being led to a squad car for a trip to the station, her eyes caught mine and she grinned. It took me aback. Was she smirking because she'd hit me or because she wasn't worried about being arrested? She certainly didn't seem concerned about a police record. Then again, she probably already had one, so what's a little thing like a weapons charge?

Released by the paramedics, I made my way to Fehring and Greg. While the cops dispersed the crowd, Detective Whitman approached Tiffany Goodwin and Kim Pawlak.

When I reached Greg's side, Fehring said to me, "I see you still have a knack with people."

"Yeah," I answered, carefully touching my nose. "It's a gift."

"Cut the smartass remarks. You're lucky."

265

She looked from me to Greg. "Both of you are lucky that McIntyre didn't pull the gun and start shooting. People like her don't carry guns as fashion accessories."

"People like her," I parroted. "So she's a criminal?"

"Nothing major on record, but she's a very tough cookie. No telling who her friends are."

"Someone like her has friends?" In spite of just having the snot smacked out of me, I couldn't help myself or my mouth.

"The way I see it," Greg said to Fehring before she could scold me, "there are only two reasons to carry a gun — offense or defense. I have no doubt the gun Ina had in her backpack was for defense, but why would Linda McIntyre be carrying one? I'm guessing for the same reason or else she would have pulled it on us."

"Which means she's afraid of something," I added, quickly seeing where my hubs was going with this. "She didn't have a gun the last time she was here. The way she was dressed, there was no place to hide it."

Fehring gave us a look that said loud and clear we weren't telling her anything she hadn't already thought of on her own. "Listen," Fehring began, "I really appreciate you letting me know Linda McIntyre was here. We weren't very far away at the time. But you two are too smart for your own good. Hopefully this altercation will put the fear of God in you, since I can't seem to. I have no doubt Linda is afraid of something. I wouldn't be surprised if a few others here today have weapons of some sort on them."

Greg and I looked at each other, both knowing what Fehring said about the others was probably true.

Whitman came up to us. "Any news on Buck yet?" I asked him.

He ignored me and spoke to Fehring as if she was the one who had asked the question. "Tiffany still claims he hasn't contacted her. Says she's worried sick."

"Do you believe her?" asked Fehring.

Whitman ran a hand over his chin. "Yeah, I do. Seems he's gone to ground."

When a wave of pain passed, I said, "Linda thinks he set the blast at his store to cover the fact he killed Tom Bruce."

Fehring nodded. "It's a definite possibility."

She closed her little notebook and stashed it in a pocket of her trousers. As usual, she was dressed very masculine. Not for the first time, I wondered what Andrea Fehring would look like in a dress and heels. She was fairly attractive in a no-frills way, and I had to admit she was growing on me.

"By the way," Fehring said, "where's Mrs. Littlejohn today?"

"She and my mother are getting their hair done," Greg answered.

"Good," Fehring said with a hint of a smile. "Just where she belongs. Last thing I need is another nosy Nellie." She turned to me. "You should have gone with them."

I placed a hand gently on the side of my face and winced. "No argument there."

The auction crowd had dispersed quickly after the third and final auction of the day. Some stood around hoping to see more girl-on-girl Fight Club, but when Linda was hauled away in the patrol car, they also left.

Kim Pawlak approached us with Tiffany in tow. Up close, Tiffany looked more worried and exhausted than she had before. "What am I supposed to do with that storage unit?" Kim asked the police. "Linda McIntyre hasn't paid for it yet."

"Give her a few days," Whitman said. "Unless we find something more serious than a concealment charge, she'll probably be released in record time."

"That's not how this works," insisted Kim. "It's a cash business. You bid. You pay. Elite needs that locker. Acme needs their money."

"A couple of days," pressed Whitman. "It won't kill you or this dump to give her that. Just charge McIntyre rent on the unit until she clears it out."

Seeing Kim wasn't sold on the idea, Fehring added, "My partner is right. You can always put it back up for auction, but won't that take several days to set up again anyway?"

Her eyes rolled behind her glasses as Kim weighed her options. "Yeah, you're right. Linda has always been a good customer. I'll talk to Elite about extending the time on the unit for her, but I'm sure they're going to charge her for the extra time."

She turned to Tiffany. "I'll be right back. Why don't you stay here in case the other bidders have questions." Leaving Tiffany behind, Kim took off at a trot for the front of the complex.

Whitman zeroed in on Tiffany. "Anything you want to add or remember before we go?"

The young woman shook her head, her eyes down, giving the appearance of being meek and mild.

"You have my card," Whitman added. "Give me a call if you do remember something or if your father contacts you."

In response, Tiffany held up a white business card pinched between two fingers like something sticky and stinky.

Whitman and Fehring started to leave, but not without a parting gift from Fehring in my direction. "Go home, Odelia. Put your feet up. Put some ice on that face. We've got this from here." The detective took a few steps, then turned again. "Or should I stay to make sure you leave?"

"We're going, we're going," I confirmed. To emphasize my point, I wobbled a little when I took a step. "Trust me, all I want to do is go home and take a long, hot bath."

With an assured nod, Fehring left.

"You okay, sweetheart?" Greg asked, putting a strong hand on my elbow.

"Dandy," I replied. I turned my attention to Tiffany Goodwin, who was watching the detectives leave with a relief similar to my own, although I doubted it was for the same reason. I wanted to talk to her without them around. Tiffany probably just wanted them gone, which was confirmed when she crumpled Whitman's business card and threw it to the ground in disgust.

"Hi," I said, approaching her. She gave me a steely look of wariness and studied the blood stains that had dribbled down my boobs. "We're related to your friend Ina Bruce," I told her. "My husband here is her cousin."

When Tiffany's eyes moved to Greg, her defensive demeanor changed and her shoulders relaxed. "You're Greg?"

He wheeled closer. "That I am. And this is my wife, Odelia. We're trying to help Ina and would like to talk to you."

"Ina's told me a lot about you." She took a solid stance and hugged the clipboard to her chest like armor. "Like I told the police, I don't believe Ina killed Tom. It's not who she is, even if he did smack her around."

"We don't believe she did it either," Greg assured her. "Did you know she was leaving town right after that auction?"

Tiffany pursed her lips and stuck a hand in the pocket of her jeans. "Yeah, I knew. She told me the only way she'd ever be rid of Tom for good would be to disappear."

"But Tom was with Linda McIntyre," I pointed out.

"That wouldn't have lasted. Tom and Ina have broken up before, but he always came back to Ina and she always took him back. This time she was going to put some serious distance between them so he couldn't find her. She didn't tell me where because she didn't want Tom to try and squeeze it out of me."

"It was Paris," I told her. "She had a plane

271

ticket for Paris and a fake passport."

A sad smile crossed Tiffany's lips. "She always said she wanted to see Paris."

"Linda just told us Tom was going to buy Ina out of their business," Greg said.

Tiffany scoffed. "With what? Tom was always broke. If not for Ina, he'd have spent every dime they made from the store."

"My cousin must have been a good little saver then," commented Greg, "because the day she was supposed to fly to Paris, she withdrew three hundred grand from their bank accounts."

Tiffany's mouth almost hit the pavement. "Wow! I didn't realize their store was doing that well."

"Can a secondhand store generate that kind of money?" asked Greg. "Seems unlikely to me."

"Yeah, they can," Tiffany answered, "depending on the type of merchandise and the turnaround time. The less time merchandise is in the shop, the sooner you can restock and make more money. Some of these guys have a good eye and stumble onto very valuable stuff from time to time. I've been around these resale shops most of my life. My dad has one." She looked down at the ground. "Or did have."

"Is that how you hooked up with this

job?" I asked.

She nodded without looking up. "I used to come to the auctions once in a while with my father." She glanced up at us. "That's how I met Kim. Since I already knew the business, when she became an owner of Acme, she asked if I wanted to work for them."

"Did you also work with Red Stokes?"

"Sometimes. And sometimes Kim still acted as his assistant."

Before we could say anything more, Tiffany started to edge away toward the bowels of the storage complex. "Look," she said, "I have a job to do here. I want to help Ina, but all I know is that she was leaving right after the auction."

"But," I persisted, "why would she bother coming here at all if she was leaving?"

Tiffany stopped walking. "She came for a couple of reasons. She wanted to say goodbye to Tom and to tell him it was over for good, and she wanted to say goodbye to my dad. She was like a second daughter to him. The night before the auction, she dropped by my place and said there were things she wanted to tell Dad, but she couldn't reach him."

"Do you know what those things were?"

"I think it was about me. About him being more understanding and not pushing me away."

"About you being gay?" I ventured.

She was surprised by my question, but only for a second. "Yeah. He didn't take it well. He was really pissed off when I moved in with Kim."

She started walking away, and we followed. We could walk and talk with the best of them.

Greg pulled alongside her and kept pace with her strides. "Tiffany, do you have any idea where your father is?"

She'd stopped short in front of the locker where Tom's body had been found just days before in a lounge chair. It was difficult to miss the unit since yellow police tape was still stretched across the front like tape at a finish line — Tom's finish line.

From the look on Tiffany's face, Greg's question had hit a nerve. "As I told that slimy cop, I don't."

"You mean Detective Whitman?" I asked. I wasn't a big fan of his either and was pleased to see someone else had my good taste.

"Yeah," Tiffany spat. "He couldn't keep his hands off of me while he talked." She shivered. "Kept calling me 'sweetie' and rubbing my arm. He said he could help my dad if I'd cooperate. I got the feeling he didn't mean cooperate with the cops either."

"Are you sure?" Greg asked.

"He even put his private cell number on the back of his card." She shivered again. "Pissed at me or not, my dad would have knocked his block off if he'd been here. For all his faults, my father has a soft spot for women, especially women being mistreated or in bad situations."

"He likes to save women?" I asked, interested. "Like be their knight in shining armor?"

"Yeah, kind of, but not like make them dependent on him — nothing like that. Dad likes to empower women, help them stand on their own two feet. I think it's something he does because he was raised by a single mom. That, and he always felt it was his fault my mother never kicked her drug habit."

I thought of the big bruiser of a guy in the muscle shirt standing next to my mother and taking her crap without so much as a blink of an eye. He certainly didn't look the part of a sensitive feminist-supporting guy, but, as most of us discover in life, looks were often deceiving.

"You sound sad but very proud," I told her.

"I am proud of him, but it also surprised me how angry he got when I came out and moved in with Kim. He always told me I could do anything I want as long as it made me happy. Guess that didn't include sexual orientation."

I shook my head at the mix-up caused by Bill. Guess he wasn't as observant as he thought. "Bill Baxter told us that you and Buck had a falling out about a young man who worked at the store."

"About Paul?" Tiffany seemed very surprised. "Please — even if I was straight, he wouldn't be my type. He's one of those creepy goody two-shoes types, always kissing ass and sneaking around. Dad only gave him a job as a favor to his mother, and even Dad thought he was weird. Paul hated the resale business and sucked at it."

"So his mother was a friend of Buck's?" Greg asked.

"Dad helped her out several years back when she lost her husband. Last year she and Dad started dating." Tiffany looked thoughtful. "I think Paul was one of the reasons they broke up. Too bad, too, because I really liked Heide."

Paul. Heide. Was Buck Goodwin the Good Samaritan who came to Heide van den Akker's rescue after the accident that took her husband's life? My brain itched with possibilities.

"Maybe Heide had other children who objected to the relationship?" I was thinking of the surly Eric. He seemed more likely to cause a problem than the polite Paul.

"She has another son named Eric. He wasn't around much but seemed cool the few times I met him."

I was on a roll and didn't want it to stop. "Does Heide have a third son, one named Bob or Robert maybe?"

Tiffany shook her head. "No, just the two, but I think her late husband's name was Bobby. Why?"

"No reason," I lied. "I thought maybe it was a Heide I met once. She also has a son named Paul and is a widow. Did you tell the police about Heide?"

"No," Tiffany said with defiant tilt of her chin. "They asked if Dad was seeing anyone, and I told them no. It's the truth. They broke up a while back, and I couldn't see dragging Heide into this mess if it wasn't necessary."

Greg gave me a look that said he could tell I smelled a lead, even through an almost broken nose. He turned back to Tiffany. "We know you have to get back to work, but I want to ask you one more question.

Do you think your father caused the blast that burned down his store?"

"Absolutely not!" Tiffany fixed Greg with a tough look. "As I told the cops, my father loved that store. He built it from scratch and made a very good and respectable living from it. He'd sooner cut off his arm than destroy it. And he certainly wouldn't do anything to hurt those other people at the mall or their businesses."

Greg gave her a reassuring smile. "That's good enough for me."

From down the lane, Roberto Vasquez waved to Tiffany. "I gotta go," she told us. "Mr. Vasquez bought the last unit at auction today, and I still need to collect his money so he can start cleaning it out."

After saying goodbye to Tiffany, I stood in front of the locker with the police tape and studied it, wishing it would talk to me. Give me a clue. Tell me what it saw that night like some oracle made of steel and concrete. "This is where Tom was murdered," I told Greg. "I wonder what will happen to all the stuff in there?"

"If they still auction it off, I'm betting someone will buy it just for the ghoul factor."

I turned to my husband and touched his hair, glad he was mine and fairly normal and with me for this journey. "I like it when we question people together. Makes me feel all Nick and Nora, but without the drinking."

Greg laughed and took my hand, kissing it before releasing it. "Where to next? Comfort Foodies?"

"You read my mind. If Heide van den Akker is not the woman Buck was dating, I'm a twenty-year-old pole dancer. I'm also betting on one of her sons being Bob Y."

"My money's on Paul," said Greg. "He probably thought those reviews did his mother a service and harmed Buck at the same time."

"Hard to say. Eric is the one with the bad attitude, but Tiffany seems to think Paul is the one with problems."

As we moved back toward the front of Elite Storage, I pulled out my smartphone and started the search engine. By going to the Comfort Foodies website, I should be able to find out where the truck would be parked today.

I was looking down at my phone when my eye caught something on the ground. It was Leon Whitman's crumpled business card. I stooped to pick it up. Sure enough, on the backside he'd written a phone number. Then I noticed something else. I stuck

Whitman's card into my pocket and squatted down again. We were in front of the unit
purchased by Linda McIntyre. When Tiffany
tossed the business card, it had landed
directly in front of the left bottom corner of
the door. On the corner, just above the
pavement, a black X had been crudely
marked on the metal door.

I stood up and looked at the doors of the
units to the right and left. Neither had an
X.

"What are you doing, sweetheart?"

"Checking something out." I checked a
few more. Still no X. I waved to Greg. "I
want to go back to the other unit — the one
with the police tape."

Together, we traveled down the short
road, turned left, and found the unit with
the tape. I checked the lower left corner of
the roll-up door: a black X.

"What do you think those mean, Greg?"

"Could be Elite marks the doors of the
units up for auction."

"Come on," I said to him. "Let's find the
other units in today's auction."

We followed the short road in the direction where Tiffany had disappeared to help
Roberto Vasquez. They weren't far. Tiffany
was in front of the unit, speaking with Vasquez.

"If Linda doesn't claim that unit, I'll take it," Vasquez was saying to her. "And for my last bid amount."

"I'll make a note of that, Mr. Vasquez, but under the circumstances, I believe Elite is going to give her a day or so to take care of it. If she doesn't, I'm sure both Elite and Acme will come up with a fair plan to dispose of the unit."

I was impressed. Tiffany looked like a tough young chick, but once in working mode she was very professional and knew how to handle customers. It was probably something she had learned at her father's store. Vasquez wasn't happy with the delay but seemed satisfied by her response.

We were in front of the unit he'd purchased. It was jam-packed with household goods that looked to be in very good condition — a much nicer unit than the one he'd lost to Linda McIntyre. Unfortunately, the door was up and I couldn't check for the mark.

Tiffany turned to us when Vasquez received a call and walked a few steps away. "Odelia. Greg. Did you guys forget something?"

"We were wondering, Tiffany," said Greg, "how Elite notes which units are up for auction?"

"Each unit is numbered. The auctioneer gets a listing of the units up for auction." To show us what she meant, she turned her clipboard toward us. On it was a simple list of numbers and columns next to each number. "This list tells us which units are up for auction. Once the unit is bought, we add the name of the buyer and what the winning bid is."

"So," Greg said, "they don't physically mark the units in any way so you don't miss them?"

"Nope. Everything is done by the unit number."

Vasquez returned and said to Tiffany, "My truck is delayed, so I'm going to grab something to eat while I wait. We all through here?"

"Yes," she responded. "Thank you for your business."

Vasquez pulled a padlock out of his pocket. He lowered the door to the unit he'd bought and slapped the lock on it. The lock closed with a sound metallic click. With a nod to us, he left in the direction of the parking lot.

"We should be going too, Tiffany," Greg told her. "Thanks for all your help."

"Anything, if it will help Ina." She hesitated, then asked, "Can she have visitors?

I'd like to see her and give her my support."

"She'd like that, I'm sure," Greg said, "but don't be surprised if she refuses to see you or doesn't respond when you visit. She's not saying much to anyone."

When we were back in Greg's van, he asked, "Did you see a mark on that unit Vasquez bought?"

"Nothing. But I do recall at the last auction, Linda told Ina not to bother bidding on the last unit they bid on, the one Tom was found in, because it was going to be hers."

"Could be just smack talk."

"Maybe — or maybe the marks are a signal to Linda to buy the ones marked."

"But didn't you say she bid on the others last time?"

"Yes, but her bidding wasn't as lively or determined as today. Last time, Ina said Linda was bidding just to drive up the cost to those who really wanted it, especially her. And she did stop bidding as soon as Ina stopped and let someone else scoop up the unit. Today she was taking no prisoners to get that locker."

I thought about the last auction and ran a replay of it against the information I now had. "In fact, Ina wasn't bidding very hot and heavy last time either."

"Could be," Greg said, "Ina was just going through the motions so no one would be suspicious about her leaving. Kind of like why she might have gone to the auction at all. She was giving the appearance of business as usual."

He looked at me with concern. "You okay, sweetheart?"

I touched my nose with a cautious fingertip. It still hurt like hell. "The drugs haven't kicked in yet, but I'll be fine."

Greg put the van into gear. "So, where to, boss?"

With this new possibility, I'd forgotten about the search to see where Comfort Foodies was dishing up food. I pulled my smartphone out of my purse and started running the search. "Let's see where Comfort Foodies is right now."

I was checking out the truck's web page when my phone rang. The display said it was Cruz calling. When I answered, Cruz was in hysterics. I got a cold rush of worry that something had happened to Mom.

It took almost thirty seconds before I could calm Cruz down enough for her to speak clearly. When she was done, I turned to Greg. "Head home," I ordered. "And step on it."

NINETEEN

I sat on our sofa and stared at the wall. Muffin hopped up next to me and nudged my hand for attention, but I couldn't lift it to pet her. I felt dead, emotionally paralyzed. Greg wheeled over to the sofa and gently pushed Muffin out of the way before lifting himself from his chair and transferring his body to the sofa so he could sit next to me. Without a word, he bundled me into his arms. I wrapped an arm around him and laid my head on his sturdy chest. I could hear his heartbeat, steady and strong. I took comfort in the sound.

And then I cried.

I sobbed without consolation, soaking the front of Greg's sweatshirt. Cruz quietly brought me a cup of tea and set it on the table next to the sofa. I didn't need to look at her to know she was crying too. I could hear it — a soft, wet sniffle. She'd been the first to cry, even before it was over. She disappeared into the bathroom and returned with a box of tissues. Plucking a couple out, she tried to hand them to me, but I wouldn't let go of Greg long enough to grab them. He took the tissue and thanked her for me.

"Is there anything more I can do for you?" Cruz asked in her comforting voice with the soft accent.

"No, thank you, Cruz," Greg quietly told her. "Why don't you go home. It's been a hard day for you too."

On the way out, she laid a work-worn hand on my head and patted it softly and with affection. "I am so sorry. Please call if you need anything."

The good news was the call from Cruz hadn't been about Mom. The bad news was there had been an illness.

The trip from Long Beach to Seal Beach had been short but seemed to take forever. Before the van came to a complete stop in our driveway, I was hopping out and running for the gate to the patio and through to the back door. Cruz met me, tears running down her face. Wainwright was agitated. Muffin peeked out from under the buffet. I'd told Greg to wait in the van and keep the motor running.

I returned to the van with a large bundle wrapped in a blanket. Tucked inside was

Seamus. He was breathing, but barely. On our way home from Long Beach, I'd told Greg what Cruz had said: that Seamus was ill and not responding to anything. Greg had called our vet while I was in the house.

According to the vet, Seamus, our old codger of a cat, had had a stroke — a bad one. There was nothing that could be done, and putting him down was one of the most difficult decisions I've ever had to make. During his last few minutes on earth, the animal, unable to move, had stared at me with big, frightened eyes, not understanding what was happening to him. But there was also trust in those eyes. Trust that I would do the right thing. Trust that I would ease his suffering. Trust that I loved him enough to let him go.

I spent several of those minutes stroking his champagne fur, still soft and fluffy, and cooing to him. When he stuck out his little pink tongue and licked my hand, I almost lost my mind to overwhelming grief. Our paths had first crossed years ago on St. Patrick's Day, when some kids had tied him up and colored his fur green with food coloring. I had come to his rescue, and after that he never left my side, adopting me and winning me over. In a final gesture, I thanked the cat for his years of faithful company and love and kissed the top of his furry head, then I nodded to the vet to proceed. Greg and I were with Seamus until the very end.

I don't know how long our little family sat locked in a dark, heavy sorrow. Greg and I stayed huddled together on the sofa. Muffin was on Greg's lap. Wainwright was curled up on the floor in front of us. Even the animals seemed to sense what had happened. They were feeling the loss too. We didn't move from our respective spots until Mom and Renee walked through the door, chattering and giggling like a couple of schoolgirls. Only Wainwright stirred to welcome them.

When Mom saw us, she said, "What's the matter? You two look like someone died."

"Is it Ina?" a worried Renee asked.

"Sit down, ladies," Greg said, not moving from my side. Both turned pale at the tone in his voice but sat as directed. "Seamus had a stroke today." Greg tightened his grip on me. "We had to put him to sleep."

"Oh, no!" Renee's hand went to her mouth.

Mom sat rigid, gripping the handles of her purse with white knuckles. She said nothing, but after a few moments she slowly got to her feet and shuffled down the hall to her room.

"I'll make sure she's all right," said Renee, standing. "She was chattering about that cat a good part of the day. This is going to hit her hard."

"No, Mom," Greg told her. "I think it's best to let Grace be for now."

"Yes, Renee," I said, finally finding my voice. "Mom likes to be left alone at times like these. I'll check on her in a little bit."

"Do you two need anything?"

"No, Mom," answered Greg, "but thanks."

"Then I'll go, but call if you do need something." She got to her feet, then hesitated, the mother in her not wanting to leave until she'd made everything bad go away or at the very least slayed a few dragons on behalf of her offspring and his family. It didn't matter that we were middle-aged. She was a mother-warrior. "Are you sure I can't make you something to eat?" she offered as a last attempt to be helpful.

"We're good, Mom," Greg answered for the both of us. "We'll call you later."

Renee approached the couch, leaned forward, and stroked Greg's face before kissing his forehead. He kissed her cheek in return. She turned her attention to me and did the same, her hand lingering against my face, still warm from crying. "Oh, Odelia," she said in a trembling voice, "I know you must be absolutely heartbroken." Before leaving, Renee stroked Muffin's head and patted the faithful Wainwright.

Dinner that night was quiet and early since we'd skipped lunch. While Greg puttered in the kitchen, heating up the Chinese food from the night before, I went to check on Mom. She wasn't in bed, as I had expected, but was sitting in the upholstered chair we kept next to the window. Beside the chair a soft reading lamp glowed, but Mom wasn't reading. She was just sitting there, staring at the wall, her glasses folded in her lap.

"You okay, Mom?"

"I should have been here."

"What do you mean?"

"I should have been here. Seamus would be alive if I'd been here."

I moved into the room and sat on the edge of the bed closest to her. "That's not true, Mom, so don't blame yourself. The stroke hit Seamus hard and fast. None of us could have done anything. Even the vet said that."

"Where's the cat now?"

"Still at the pet hospital. At our request, they are cremating the body. We'll pick up the ashes next week. Greg and I thought we might scatter them under the bougainvillea in the back. That was one of his favorite hiding spots."

Mom continued staring at the wall. "I should have been here all along."

"You couldn't have done anything," I repeated. "And Seamus wasn't alone when the stroke happened. Cruz was here, and she couldn't do anything to stop it. Greg and I were with him until the very end. He died knowing he was loved."

"No," Mom said, without looking at me. "I should have been here, with you, all those years. I shouldn't have left you when I got pregnant with Grady. But I was a coward."

Whoa. Where was this coming from?

I reached over and placed a hand on her knee. "You're here now, and I'm very glad you are. So is Greg."

"I want to die like the cat, knowing I was loved."

"You are loved, Mom. Clark and I love you very much. So do Greg and his parents. Clark's children love you. Didn't Lorraine visit you and help set up your iPad?"

If she heard me, she gave no indication. My grief over the loss of Seamus was battling with worry about my mother. Was she selfishly making the death of my beloved pet about her, or was there something else going on with her?

"Mom, are you okay? Are you ill and not telling us?"

She closed her eyes. She was so still, for a second I thought she'd nodded off or possibly died in the chair right in front of me. I'm not much on praying, but I sent up a quick petition to whoever or whatever might be in charge that Mom was just taking a snooze.

A few seconds later she said, without opening her eyes, "I *am* sick, Odelia. I'm absolutely heartsick."

"Do you mean you have heart trouble?"

She shook her head. "No, I mean I'm heartsick with regret."

I patted her knee. "I know you and Seamus bonded during your visit. Losing him will be difficult for all of us, even the other animals, but, trust me, you couldn't have stopped it from happening."

Her hand covered mine, but her eyes remained closed. "I'm not talking about the damn cat now, Odelia. Please try to keep up."

Annoyed, I started to pull my hand away, but Mom's closed over it like a claw in one of those stuffed-animal vending machines. She opened her eyes and looked directly at me. Her eyes were wet, and without her glasses they looked small and weak. "I'm

292

talking about you. Do you remember what I said to you when you found me in Massachusetts?"

I eased my hand away. This time she let me. "Yes, I do." I sat up straight and squared my shoulders. "You said you had no regrets about leaving me behind when I was sixteen, and you had no intention of apologizing for your actions."

"I lied, Odelia. I have regrets — mountains of them. I had them when I left, when you found me, and all the years in between and after. I have them right now, this very second."

I was speechless. Did Seamus's death unlock my mother's cold, selfish heart?

"I'd been wanting to visit," she continued, "to clear the air. I came here to apologize to you but couldn't find the words until now. You didn't deserve to be abandoned like an old, worn shoe. You were my daughter, and I tossed you aside. I failed you. And in spite of everything, you turned out so lovely and wonderful." She plucked a hankie from a pocket and held it to her eyes as she softly cried. "You've opened your heart and your home to me, and I don't deserve it."

I sat on the edge of the bed in stunned silence. These were the words I'd been hungering to hear since I was sixteen years old. There were times I was sure if I ever came face to face with my mother, I'd beat the apology out of her. Then, when I did finally find her, all I could do was tell her how I felt. I'd beaten her with my words, and she'd taken the pounding and thrown insults back at me.

I heard a light jingle and recognized the sound as Wainwright's collar tags. Turning, I saw Greg in the doorway of the guest bedroom, Wainwright at his side. I don't know how long he'd been there, but from the look on his face and the tears in his eyes, it had been long enough. He blew me a soft kiss and rolled away, taking the dog with him, leaving me alone again with Mom.

Getting off the bed, I knelt in front of my mother and put both of my hands on her knees. "Thank you, Mom. I accept your apology."

She raised her head. Cupping my chin in one of her hands, she stared into my face a long time, memorizing every line and large pore, perhaps searching for the teenage girl she'd left behind. We stayed that way until my knees ached and I had to get up. I took my place on the bed again.

"What happened to your face, Odelia?"

"I bumped into Linda McIntyre's fist." I didn't say more, and she didn't ask. We fell back into a soft silence.

"Your hair looks wonderful, Mom." And it did. The old permed ends had been clipped into a short, feathery silver bob. The new hairdo highlighted her bone structure and took several years off her lined face. Her lipstick looked new, too.

"Thank you, Odelia. We did have fun today." She dabbed at her face with the handkerchief. "Can I still come live here in California? If you don't want me, I'll understand."

"Do you want to live here?"

She blew her nose and nodded. "Very much."

"Then consider it done." I smiled at her. "Did you girls look at retirement communities today?"

"We saw two in the morning, then went to lunch — my treat. After lunch we went to the hair salon." Mom bent close as if telling a secret. I expected her to say something about the salon, but instead she dropped a bomb. "By the way, I think we found that Buck person."

TWENTY

Mom wasn't happy about being left behind, but she was so tired, emotionally and physically, from the day before that she didn't put up much of a fight when I suggested she stick around the house and relax.

Over leftover Chinese food the night before, we had compared our findings for the day. It wasn't with much enthusiasm, but it helped to keep our minds off of Seamus and our terrible loss. Mom had tracked down Comfort Foodies, and she and Renee had gone there for lunch. When I asked Mom why she didn't call me on my cell phone when she located Buck Goodwin, she said she had. I checked my phone and, sure enough, there was a message. It had been left during the rush to get Seamus to the animal hospital.

"I thought I saw Buck working inside the truck," she told us while spearing a shrimp, "but I wasn't sure."

"Were Paul and Eric there, too?"

"Heide's sons? I didn't see them. I just saw Heide and someone I thought was Buck. I was worried he'd recognize me if I got too close, so I sent Renee up to the window to order for us. They had crab cakes today, and they were excellent." Mom went to her room and returned with her cell phone. "Renee took these photos from the side while they were helping customers. It was very busy and I don't think anyone saw her, but she only got a couple."

"My mother is now taking surveillance photos?" Greg's tone sounded like a cocktail of annoyance with a garnish of amusement.

"Just a few," Mom assured him. "And it is for Ina." Mom leaned toward me. "Renee is a good sport, but I don't think she has real talent for this like you and me."

"Now there's a blessing." Greg stuffed some sweet and sour pork into his mouth.

I took Mom's phone and looked at the photos. They weren't very clear, but the man helping a customer at the window in one did look kind of like Buck Goodwin. The next photo was a bit clearer. The man handing a drink through the window to a woman did look a lot like Buck.

"Pairing this with the info we got from Tiffany," I said, still studying the photos, "it's likely this is Buck."

"Makes sense," added Greg. "He helped her out when she needed it, and she's returning the favor."

"Honey," I said to Greg as a thought crossed my mind. "If Paul is Bob Y, as we think, do you think he might have planted the bomb in Buck's store?"

Greg shrugged. "Seems kind of sophisticated for a kid who doesn't like his mother's friends, but you never know." He took the phone and checked out the photos. "That adds another suspect to the blast. It could be whoever killed Tom and Red or it could be the kid. But I doubt Paul van den Akker killed Tom and Red. What would be his motive?"

I swallowed the rice in my mouth. "I can't think of a single one. Maybe we're looking at two unrelated things here. Buck could have been spooked by Tom's death and think maybe the blast was done by the same people."

"I think," said Mom, tapping a finger on the table to make her point, "that some people know exactly who killed Tom and Red and aren't talking. Maybe because they're afraid. And I'll bet Ina knows, too."

"Could be," I said, putting down my fork, "that Ina is worried someone else will die if

298

she talks. She might not have been leaving town to get away from Tom, but maybe away from whatever and whomever Tom might have been involved with. That could be why she called him a stupid bastard."

"You may be right, sweetheart. Didn't Ina say at Thanksgiving that she and Tom were fighting about the business?"

"She sure did," I confirmed. "And if she wasn't leaving to avoid Tom, then it makes sense for her to go to the auction to say goodbye. I don't think it's normal for abused wives to say goodbye to their abusers when they hit the road."

I pushed my plate away, too busy thinking to eat, which is very abnormal for me. I closed my eyes and ran the possibilities like flashcards on the inside of my eyelids. It wasn't working, so I got up and retrieved a legal notepad from our home office. Back at the table, I started jotting down information and people's names, and tried to link them.

"Okay," I began, "say Tom is involved with something bad or illegal, and Ina doesn't like it. That could have caused the fight they had before Thanksgiving."

"And it's so bad she's frightened enough to take off," added Mom. She tapped the legal pad. "Write that down."

With a small huff, I noted that beside Ina's name.

"And the money," added Mom. "What if that three hundred thousand came from something illegal, and Ina was taking off with it?"

"But," I pointed out, "the cops said she didn't have the money on her, just that she withdrew it. And there's no record of where it went. The cops are thinking maybe she used it to pay someone to kill Tom. But if that's the case, why would she have been so distraught over his death? I don't think she was acting that day." I looked up from the pad to Greg and Mom. "What other reasons could there be?"

Greg stopped eating. "Payoff, maybe?"

I tapped my pen on the notepad directly under Ina's name. "Tom's in trouble. Ina pulls ill-gotten cash from their bank account and hands it over to the bad guys. They kill Tom anyway. Maybe as a warning?"

Mom nodded. "That's how it would be in a TV movie or on one of those crime dramas. You can never trust bad guys to do what they promise."

"And what about Red?" Greg asked. "Do you think he knew what Tom was involved with? Maybe that's why he was killed."

"If he did," I noted, "then it's connected

to the auction or resale business, which makes me wonder if Kim knows anything. We haven't been able to talk to her yet."

"If Kim knows, maybe Tiffany knows," Greg suggested.

"I don't know, honey. She seemed worried about her father, but I didn't get the vibe she was hiding anything."

"Neither did I, but she could be a good liar."

Mom punched the table with her finger again. "I'll bet that tramp Linda knows." Mom couldn't seem to say Linda's name without tacking on the word *tramp,* like it had become part of her name or a royal title — Tramp Linda McIntyre.

"I think you're right about that, Mom." I thought about the marked storage lockers. "Linda was going to go into business with Tom, leaving Ina out of it. Maybe that's why her and Mazie's plan didn't work out, because she decided to throw her lot in with Tom instead. If Linda only bought specific lockers for her unknown clients, I'm betting something valuable was inside those lockers."

"Something her clients wanted more than used furniture," Greg said, finishing my thought.

"Exactly."

"Drugs?" Mom suggested.

"Very likely," said Greg. "Or something else valuable, small, and easy to hide."

"But what about the other stuff?" Mom asked. "Do you think they wanted that too?"

It was a good question. I thought about it as I pushed rice around my plate, arranging the grains into little neat piles. "Maybe that's why Linda needed someone like Mazie or Tom. She doesn't have a store herself, so if her clients didn't want the goods inside the lockers, she'd have to find a way to dispose of them."

Greg ran a hand through his hair. "Those storage places all have security cameras and gates, so whoever marked those units had to be someone who could get inside and who knew the limitations of the cameras."

"True," I confirmed. "Dev did say whoever killed Tom managed to avoid the security cameras, but he didn't say if they were disarmed or just avoided."

I went to the counter and picked up my cell phone and started punching numbers.

"Who are you calling, sweetheart?"

"Detective Fehring. The police need to know about this theory. If Linda McIntyre is still in custody, they need to pin her down on it now. If she's released on bail, she might disappear."

Detective Fehring was all ears, hearing out our idea about the tagged storage units. She did say two marked units with only one bought by Linda didn't exactly prove anything, but it was more than they currently had to go on and said she'd check it out.

"And stay away from Elite Storage," she ordered before she hung up. "If I see you or Greg anywhere near that place, I'll arrest you for obstructing justice. You got that?"

"Loud and clear," I told her. When the call was done, I filled Mom and Greg in on what Fehring had said.

Mom got up from the table and started a kettle on the stove for her tea. "You didn't tell her about Buck. Was that an oversight or intentional?"

"I don't know what you're talking about, Mom." I started clearing the table.

"Like I said, Odelia, you're a very bad liar."

TWENTY-ONE

Greg and I had two items on our agenda for the day: we wanted to talk to Kim Pawlak and we wanted to find Buck Goodwin. Before we left the house, I called Acme Auctions and asked if Kim was in. The same woman I spoke to the day before informed me she wasn't, that she was "out in the field," which I assumed meant she was at a storage facility handling auctions. When I asked for a schedule of auctions being held today, I was told to check their website. So much for customer service.

"You know, honey," I said to Greg while I called up the Acme website on the laptop, "Linda's clients may not know Linda is in police custody. I wonder if she was scheduled to go to an auction today on their behalf?"

"Could be, but how would we know which ones? There are probably several places holding auctions in the area today."

"True, but since Red Stokes was murdered, I'm thinking Linda might have favored the ones conducted by Acme Auctions. Red could have been involved in the scam or found out about it. Either way, he became a liability."

"Good thinking."

As I maneuvered around the web, Greg reached out and placed a hand on my left arm. "Sweetheart, are you sure you're okay? We don't have to do this today."

In the middle of the night I'd woken up and began crying over Seamus. Greg wrapped his arms around me and held me tight until I fell asleep again. Feeding Wainwright and Muffin this morning had been tough. There were three bowls lined up against the kitchen wall, but only two needed kibble. Without a word, Greg picked up Seamus's bowl and took it to the sink. The other animals ate their breakfast but not with the same gusto as usual. We would all need time to heal.

"I need to keep busy, Greg. This will help."

He gave me a nod of understanding. "Just say the word, though, and we'll go home."

I gave him a smile of thanks and went back to checking out Kim's schedule for the day.

According to the Acme Auctions website,

305

there were two auctions today. The first was at a storage complex called Busy Boxes in Bellflower in about two hours. The second was at two o'clock in Santa Ana.

I placed another call to Fehring and gave her an update on my theory since she was checking out the marked units.

"It would be interesting to know," I told her, "if any of the units up for sale today have an *X* on the door."

Fehring had agreed. "We'll check it out. We're also going to talk to some of the other larger facilities and see if Linda was a regular buyer." Before hanging up, Fehring added, "And thanks, Odelia. Knowing you, I'm sure you wanted to snoop around yourself on these. I appreciate you handing it off to me."

A wave of guilt washed over me. I'd only given Fehring the information on the Santa Ana facility, not on the auction in Bellflower. She was right: I did want to check some of this out on my own. I was willing to share 50-50 but not 100 percent. When I ended the call, I turned to find Greg watching me, arms folded across his chest.

"I'm guessing that we're going to the auction in Bellflower?"

"Do you think I should call her back and 'fess up?"

He gave it some thought, then grabbed his jacket. "Nah, but if we're going to Bell-flower, let's go soon just in case traffic's bad. And if we get there early, we might be able to talk to Kim Pawlak without any interruption."

Before leaving, I checked on Mom. She'd just had her shower and was sitting in the chair by the window, wrapped in her robe. On her lap was her iPad.

"We're leaving now, Mom." I walked over to her. "Are you updating your blog?"

"Yes. I hope you don't mind, but I thought I'd write a piece about Seamus."

"That would be lovely." I sat on the edge of the bed. "I noticed you haven't said anything more about the murder in the blog. You didn't even mention the blast."

"And I won't," she said with clipped finality. "At least not until this nonsense is over."

"That's probably for the best. You never know who might stumble across it. Might be one of the bad guys, and we have enough problems right now."

"Humph. I'm not worried about them. It's your brother I'm trying to keep in the dark. If he ever found out how close we came to being blown up, he'd have a conniption."

I couldn't argue with that. The way Willie

kept tabs on Greg and me, Clark might already know. "He'll find out sometime."

"When it's over, we can tell him."

"We're leaving Wainwright home again today. If you feel like it later, I know he'd love a walk to the beach."

Mom looked up from her iPad and smiled. "I think I'd like that too. Too bad Muffin can't come along. I'd hate to leave her with no one home, just in case something happens."

"Don't worry about Muffin, Mom, she's young and healthy. Seamus was old, and he was starting to have health problems."

"True, but Wainwright's hardly a pup. If something happens to that dog, it will kill Greg."

I thought back to when Wainwright had been shot. It had been touch and go at first, and Greg had been incredibly calm and steady about the whole thing — at least on the outside. Inside he'd been a pile of weepy, worried jelly that only I witnessed.

"We almost lost Wainwright a few years back," I told her. "It was very hard on Greg — on both of us. But when that time comes for real, we'll manage to get through it, as we will with Seamus. They will always be in our hearts."

I stood and started to leave, then went

back to Mom and planted a kiss on her forehead. "I love you, Mom. If you need anything, don't hesitate for a minute to call my cell or Greg's. Okay?"

"Don't worry, I will."

The drive to Bellflower was uneventful, and we arrived early. Busy Boxes was set up a lot like Elite but on a smaller scale. There was also very little parking in the tiny lot in front of the main security gate. Two cars were already there. Other than that, it looked deserted. According to the posted hours, the office wouldn't open until 9 AM, although the facility was available to unit renters 24/7. It was twenty minutes to nine and a bit chilly out. A small storm was supposed to move in by late afternoon or early evening.

"Honey," I said as we passed the place, "that was it."

"Yeah, I saw it, but I was thinking since we're so early, let's grab a cup of coffee while we wait. I saw a Starbucks a block or so back."

"Sounds good to me."

Greg drove to the first side street and pulled over to let a few other cars pass. Once the road was clear, he made a U-turn at the small intersection and headed back to the coffee shop.

Armed with two fresh lattes, we returned to Busy Boxes, where Greg parked curbside just a car length away from the driveway into the facility.

"There's a handicapped spot in the lot," I pointed out.

"Yeah, but it looks kind of cramped. I'd rather park here."

We were enjoying a quiet moment when a man came into view from a side street and started walking toward us. He was slim, of average height, and wearing jeans and a navy blue hoodie. The hood was pulled low over his forehead; his hands were burrowed into the pockets of the sweatshirt. He turned and I saw just enough of his face to tell he was fair-skinned.

"Greg, look at that guy. I think that's Eric van den Akker."

"Who?"

"Heide van den Akker's eldest son. She's the owner of the Comfort Foodies truck. And he's acting kind of funny." Instinctively, I scooted down in my seat when Eric turned to check out the street one last time before approaching Busy Boxes' front gate.

Following my lead, Greg ducked. "I thought I saw him slipping on gloves," Greg whispered, his head close to mine. "Why would he need gloves?"

"I saw that too." I raised my head to look over the dashboard.

"Careful, sweetheart," Greg cautioned.

When he reached the individual entrance gate next to the large vehicle gate, he punched numbers into the security pad and entered.

"He had the entrance code," I told Greg. "Maybe he has a unit. Could be he and his mother store extra equipment here."

"So why would he wear that hood? It's not raining yet. He's hiding his identity."

I knew Greg was right. I knew it the minute Eric slipped on those gloves.

As soon as Eric entered the facility and disappeared, I opened the van door.

"Where do you think you're going?" Greg asked, slapping a strong hand on my arm like a vice.

"I have to see what he's up to."

"It's too dangerous."

"I'll be careful. I can pretend I'm going to one of the lockers. He's only seen me once in his life and then barely. He won't recognize me."

"No, Odelia. The gloves. The hood. Stokes was killed by gang members. This van den Akker kid might be part of that gang. It's too much of a risk."

"But Greg, it might help Ina."

"And how are you going to get into the facility? You don't have a security code. And don't even think about trying to haul your ass over that fence. Even if you could do it, that office is about to open and you'll be caught. There are two cars in the lot now. That means people are around, and I'll bet some of those are employees."

As usual, my hubs was right. I shut the van door, careful not to slam it in frustration. "So what do you suggest?"

In response, he pulled out his phone. "We'll wait until he comes out and take more photos. Set your phone for video. I'll take stills."

"You're absolutely right," I agreed. "We should have more information before we react." I plucked my coffee from the cup holder and took a long drink. I wasn't very good at waiting games. Greg watched me, ready to grab me if I tried to leave the van. He also knew patience wasn't my strong suit even though, ironically, it was my middle name.

We didn't have to wait long before Eric returned to the front gate. I nudged Greg. We both slunk down in our seats just enough so we could still spy over the dash and got our phones ready to record his departure. As soon as he slipped out of the gate, Eric stuck something into his pocket and removed his gloves. Without removing his hood, he quickly retraced his steps down the street and turned onto the small side street.

"Did you get it?" Greg asked.

I replayed the video. "It's choppy, but it clearly shows him leaving the place, though it doesn't have a view of his face. How about you?"

"My photos of him are clear but also no shot of his face. If we need to prove something, maybe we can do it by his clothing."

"Eric was wearing a navy blue hoodie just like that the day I saw him at the food truck."

"It's a common sweatshirt, but you never know. It might be enough to at least cause the police to question him."

I turned to Greg, needing to sort out the confusion. "Okay, Heide is or was dating Buck. Her youngest son, Paul, worked a short time for Buck and they didn't get along. Now her oldest son shows up slinking around at an auction facility before it opens."

"Maybe he's the one marking the units," Greg suggested.

I looked to Greg for more of an explanation.

"We are already thinking," he continued, "that maybe something small and valuable like drugs is hidden in the marked units. Maybe Linda's clients are really one client: a gang. One side brings in the product and hides it in units about to be put up for auction. They mark the units. Linda comes in and buys them. Her people remove the goods, hand over the drugs to her client, and no one thinks twice. Maybe this kid is marking the units. He certainly didn't appear to have anything to put inside one, nor did he have anything in his hand when he left, unless it was small enough to slip into a pocket."

I mulled it over. It was a plausible theory. "It would mean an inside person is involved, like a facility employee." I looked at Greg, not wanting to state the obvious. "Or an auctioneer."

He nodded. "Could be either Kim or Tiffany, or both, are involved. Tiffany has had contact with Heide's sons."

I thought more about what Tiffany had said to us. "Didn't Tiffany say she liked Eric but that his brother was a goody two-shoes who was always sneaking around? Maybe Paul found out what was going on."

"Could also be that Buck knows what's going on or is involved himself."

My head was starting to hurt from taking in all the information. I held it between my hands to let everything settle, careful not to touch my bruises from the day before. I'd been lucky and had avoided a black eye. "Could be any or all of them are involved. Pick a suspect — any suspect." I took a deep breath and raised my head. "Tom gets involved with Linda, who works for the gang. Something goes sour and Tom is killed, maybe as a warning or maybe he's done something to cross them. Ina's spooked enough before then to flee, but she comes to the auction to have final words with Buck and Tom? That's the part that doesn't make sense."

"Unless she was warning them or at least one of them. And it was Tiffany who said Ina came here to say something to them. What if Tiffany's lying about that?"

"This has more layers than an onion." I threw up my hands in frustration. "Could be they are *all* involved: one big unhappy criminal inbred family. The only thing we know for sure is that Tom and Red are dead, and Ina was going to leave the country."

"You know, sweetheart," Greg said, looking straight at me. "If Ina wasn't involved, I'd drop this right here and now. I'm tempted to do it anyway."

"And leave Ina to rot in jail?" I was surprised.

"I don't want to do that," he admitted, "but if she's involved in something this sinister, then she needs to face the consequences or start talking." Greg kicked back the rest of his coffee with one gulp.

I waited a few heartbeats, then said, "So what do you want to do now?"

"We're already here. How about we go to the auction and check those units for *X*'s like we planned. And we still haven't spoken to Kim directly. I'd like to hear what she says." He looked at me. "Maybe you can distract Tiffany long enough for me to get some one-on-one with Kim."

"Okay," I agreed.

We waited in the van just a few more minutes before we noticed someone coming out of the office and heading for the rows of storage units. I checked the clock on the dash. It was nine o'clock on the dot. After another ten minutes, I opened the van door.

"Where do you think you're going?" asked Greg, his hand on my arm again.

"To the office. I need to pee. It's a long time until the auction starts."

He looked at me with suspicion but said nothing. He knew I had a bladder the size of a child's play teacup.

"Don't you trust me?" I asked with a downturned mouth.

"With my life," my husband answered. "But when it comes to snooping, absolutely not."

"So what if I pick up a little information while I'm there? They probably won't tell me anything anyway."

"Uh-huh." He let go of my arm. "Go ahead." He started opening his door.

"Where are you going?" I asked.

"Maybe I need to take a whiz too."

"Tell you what," I said, ready to offer up a compromise. "If we both go in there, we might miss Kim and Tiffany's arrival, and it would be easier to talk to them before they get down to auction business. How about I go first and you wait for them? Then I'll come out and wait while you go in."

He considered the proposal. "That sounds fair. Just don't take forever."

I looked around. "There's a nice clump of bushes just behind the van. It looks wheel-chair accessible."

Before Greg could hit me with a snappy comeback, I was out of the van and heading for Busy Boxes' office with a lot more on my mind than peeing.

The office was small and sparse, with a clean counter painted robin's-egg blue with a pale gray countertop. Behind the counter was a middle-aged African American woman with an elaborate braided hairdo. She was wearing a light blue knit shirt with the Busy Boxes name over her heart.

"Hi," I said, entering and shutting the door. I spotted the sign for the restroom off to the left of the counter and pointed at it. "My husband and I arrived early for the auction today, and my coffee is going right through me. Mind if I use your restroom?"

Her lips, slick with the color of a ripe plum, parted to give me a toothy, white smile. "You go right ahead, hon. It's through that doorway to the left. It's unisex, so make sure you lock the door or you might get unwanted company."

I did my business but dawdled when I left the bathroom, wondering how to make my next move. The woman working the counter was still alone. With the auction starting soon, I knew I didn't have much time before people started arriving, including Kim and Tiffany. I wanted to know if Eric van den Akker had a storage unit at Busy Boxes, or even if his mother had one. It still didn't explain the gloves and hoodie, although a lot of young people wore hoodies, but if the van den Akkers had a unit, it would give Eric a reason to be here.

Sidling up to the counter, I noticed a list of storage unit sizes and prices posted in large letters on the wall behind it. "My husband and I are considering getting a unit here," I told the woman with the braids. "Do you have a price list I can take with me?"

She gave me her 1,000-watt smile again and held out a sheet of blue paper with the same information on it as was on the wall. I took it and scanned the sheet. Below the price list was a list of rules and information about the rental.

"A friend of ours rents a unit here and highly recommended your facility," I told her, hoping her lips could be loosened with casual chitchat. "It's also close to our home."

"That's so nice. A lot of our customers have been with us a long time. What's your friend's name?"

"Um, van den Akker. Heide van den Akker."

The woman appeared puzzled. "I don't recall that name at all, and I've been here a long time, nearly ten years."

I put on my puzzled mask. "I'm sure she said Busy Boxes. Maybe it was one of your other facilities?"

She shook her head. "Nope, we don't have

but just this one. Busy Boxes is family owned, not one of those big chains, and that name is fairly unusual. I'm sure I'd remember it. I handle the billing, so I know all our customers' names, even the ones I never see." She thought a minute. "Maybe she rents at U-Box-It. They're located in El Segundo and are much larger."

"Maybe," I said, faking a puzzled look.

"But I still hope you'll consider our facility." Another big smile. This woman was good at her job.

"We'll certainly consider it," I lied to the nice woman. I started to leave, then paused for effect before laying my next question on her. "Do you happen to know which units are up for auction today and their sizes? My husband is only looking for big units today. If they're only small ones, he'll want to leave and try to catch another auction."

Still hoping to land a new customer, the woman punched a few keys on her computer. Soon the printer behind her whirred to life and spit out a sheet of paper. "Here you go," she said, handing it to me. "This is what we'll give to the auctioneer today. Looks like it's going to be two of our mid-size units, but they're still pretty good size."

I took the sheet. It was in the same format as the listing Tiffany had shown me the day before except with different unit numbers and size notations. I gave the woman a wiggly finger wave as I left. "Thanks a lot. You've been quite helpful."

Heading out the front door, I saw an SUV pulling up in front of the gate. The driver lowered his window and punched in a code on the security box. The large gate opened. With nonchalance that could win me an Oscar, I strolled through the gate after the vehicle. I didn't look back, not even when I heard Greg call my name.

From the numbers on the list in my hands, it looked like the two lockers up for auction today were located fairly close to each other. Following the numbers posted on the units, I kept walking, getting closer to the first one. When I got to a T in the road, I turned right and easily found the unit. It was just past the intersection and well out of view of the front gate. I studied the bottom left-hand side of the door of the first unit and saw no marking. I looked over the door in general and still saw nothing. Moving over to the next unit, which was only a few doors down, I scrutinized it. No X. But there was a spot in the lower left-hand corner that looked badly scuffed, like someone had kicked the door or run into it with something sharp.

The storage units at Busy Boxes were the same color as its office décor. The walls were a pale gray stone and the doors painted blue. I bent down to examine the lower corner of the second unit up for auction in less than thirty minutes. If it had the mark, it would be exactly where the scuff spot was now. I felt the scuff with a fingertip. It was rough and flaky, and the paint was coming off. The area was also not dented. This was no abrasion left by a careless bump or an angry kick. The paint appeared to have been scraped off, and the attack on the door looked fresh. It also looked about the same size as the marks left on the doors at Elite. Eric could have been removing the X from this door, not putting one there. Maybe it had been scraped off to alert someone of something — a warning, perhaps, to not buy the unit. Last I knew, Linda McIntyre was still in jail. If she wasn't available to purchase the unit, did her clients have someone else to stand in for them? Or did they know Linda was out of the picture and had sent Eric in to remove the mark?

Possibilities were coming at me like tennis balls shot from a runaway ball machine, and I didn't have a racket to defend myself. Matching up ideas with the players was getting difficult without my trusty legal pad.

Taking a photo of the mark was out of the question since I'd left my purse and phone in the van.

I heard voices coming from the front. Most likely the noise was coming from people gathering for the auction. I wanted to get back to Greg and tell him what I'd discovered, but I didn't want to just pop out from among the units. It would be difficult to explain to Kim and Tiffany what I'd been doing, and if they were involved, it would only tip them off that we might be onto something.

Remembering there had been a map of the facility on the back of the price sheet the woman in the office had given me, I turned it over and studied it. Like Elite, Busy Boxes was a warren of small roads winding in and around the storage units, just smaller. I prayed not all the roads eventually turned into dead ends, forcing me to head back the way I'd come and right into the crowd. I was in luck. From the map, it looked like if I backtracked a few steps to the primary road but kept going instead of turning toward the gate, I would eventually be able to circle around the property back to the front gate from a different direction, arriving at the gate after the auction crowd was at the first unit and out of sight.

I took a few cautious steps down the road to the intersection and glanced around the corner. A lot of voices, joking and chatting, filled my ears, but they were still in front of the gate, not inside. I dashed across the intersection to the other side of the road and started following the map to circle behind everyone, and just in time. I had barely made my first left down a small side drive when I heard the crowd making their way to the first unit. From the sound of it, they were just on the other side of the bank of units I was passing. We were parallel, just moving in different directions.

My calculations were correct. By the time I made it to the front gate, the crowd was gone, leaving me to make my escape. Waiting for me by the van was Greg, and he didn't look too pleased.

TWENTY-TWO

"I'm never letting you out of my sight again," Greg said, his arms crossed in front of him.

"Sure you will," I shot back. "Especially when you hear what I found."

"Glad you were productive, because I got nothin'. Kim and Tiffany wouldn't even talk to me."

"They wouldn't say a thing?"

"Well, not exactly nothing. Kim did tell me she's said everything she's going to say to the police and no one else. And while she's very sorry about Red and Tom and what's happening to Ina, she doesn't give a damn what happens to Buck Goodwin after the way he treated Tiffany." Greg aimed his key fob at the van and unlocked the door for me. "Tiffany stood next to her, looking sad and compliant."

As I climbed into the van, Greg made his way to his side. "Aren't you going to use the restroom?" I asked when he opened his door.

"I used the bush." He shot me a boyish grin. "You were right, it was up to ADA regulations."

While Greg tucked his wheelchair behind his seat, I grabbed my cell phone and called Andrea Fehring. I got her voice mail.

"Call me," I said into the phone. "I think . . . no, I *know* we've stumbled onto something important." Just to be safe, I also left her a text message: WE MAY HAVE PROOF ERIC VAN DEN AKKER MIGHT BE INVOLVED. CALL ME.

"Where to now?" asked Greg after I told him of my findings at the unit.

"I don't know. There are so many moving parts to this thing, I'm not sure where to start. Did you recognize anyone among the bidders today?"

Greg nodded. "That Vasquez guy was here, and an Asian couple I remember being questioned the day Tom was found."

"Did you see Mazie Moore? She's a very short, very stocky black woman."

"No one like that. There were a few African Americans in the crowd, including one couple. Someone called the guy Ted."

I thought back through my mental list of the people at the initial auction. "That might be the Hudsingers. I think his name was Ted. He took off as soon as the police were called. Someone said — I think it was Buck — that Ted Hudsinger had had scrapes with the police in the past."

"Think he might be a good candidate to be mixed up in this?"

"Who knows who's involved, but I'm sure if he has a record, he was at the top of the police questioning list." I dropped my head in weariness. "The way this is going, for all I know, my mother could be the mastermind behind it." I looked up. "I'd love to know why Mazie Moore changed her plans to go into business with Linda, but she has a couple of stores, so if she's not here, it's difficult to say where she'll be."

"We could call her stores and ask if she's in," Greg suggested.

"True, but if she's involved, a call could spook her into running for cover. I'd also like to talk to Buck Goodwin before he goes underground again. I wonder if he'll be with Comfort Foodies again today?"

I got out my cell phone and looked up the food truck's schedule. "Looks like they will be at Cal State Fullerton from eleven to two today."

"Good. I'm dying to give them a try. At least I hope we can eat and talk at the same time." Greg started up the van. "If we hustle and traffic isn't bad, we might get there just before they open and the kids start to swarm."

It wasn't difficult to find Comfort Foodies once we got to the campus and parked. There were several food trucks lined up in one of the school's main plazas. Greg had made it to the school in record time, and we arrived at the stroke of eleven. Some students were milling around, waiting for the trucks to open for business, and when the trucks lifted their service windows, the hungry kids surged forward. It was still early and the lunch trade probably wouldn't hit its stride for another forty to forty-five minutes.

We approached Comfort Foodies from the side with the idea of seeing them before they saw us. Since Heide had never met Greg and Buck had, Greg took the side closest to the service window where Heide was clearly visible, taking orders and money. I took the side closest to the back door at the end of the truck. It was open slightly and I tried my best to peek inside. From what I could tell, there were three people inside the truck — two men and a woman. The two men were working in the back, probably cooking and preparing the food, while Heide worked the front. I looked again and identified both Eric and Buck slinging hash. Good. They were both on my chat list for the day.

I caught Greg's eye and nodded to let him know that Buck was present, then circled back around the truck and motioned for him to join me under a nearby tree, out of sight of Comfort Foodies.

"They're not going anywhere with the crowd building," I said to Greg. "It will be easier to talk to them when they close down at two."

"I agree, but what if they suddenly close up and make a run for it?"

"We'll just have to stop them somehow. Eric doesn't know we saw him today, and Buck is obviously helping but staying out of sight. Unless Tiffany or someone mentioned Heide as Buck's former girlfriend, who would think to look for him here?"

"You going to tell Fehring he's here?"

I shrugged. "I should. As soon as I tell her about Eric at Busy Boxes today, I'm pretty sure she'll hunt this truck down and locate Buck on her own. I'd like to talk to Buck and Eric before then."

Greg started rolling toward the truck. "In the meantime, I'll order us something to eat. Why don't you grab us a table?"

I looked around and spotted one close to

where I'd been standing on the other side of the truck. It would give us a view of both the service window and the back door without being too close or obvious.

"I'll be over there," I said to Greg as he wheeled away. He noted the table I pointed out and nodded.

Two guys were already seated at one end of the table, wolfing down burgers from one of the other trucks. I sat at the opposite end and waited. I hadn't been seated long when Detective Fehring called.

"What's up?" she asked.

I put the phone to my ear and turned away from the two college kids. "Just some interesting stuff. Did you have a chance to look into the marks on the storage units in Santa Ana this morning?"

"Yes, and you were right. They had four units going up for auction today, and one was marked with an *X* just as you described. We searched it with dogs and found drugs stashed in one of the storage boxes. From the condition of the other stuff in the unit, it looks like the box with the drugs was a recent deposit. Acme handled another auction elsewhere this morning. Units are on their way there now to stop any winning bidders from cleaning out the units until we search them."

"Well, that's what I called to tell you." I put my hand over the phone in case the two kids stopped eating long enough to eavesdrop. "You mean Busy Boxes in Bellflower, right?"

There was a long pause on the other end, followed by, "So did you have amnesia about Bellflower when we talked this morning or did you decide you were making it too easy on us?"

I didn't answer her question. Instead, I said, "Listen, there were two units being auctioned off this morning in Bellflower. One was marked, but it looks like the mark was scraped off by someone . . . um . . . recently, before the auction."

"I told you to stay away from those places," Fehring snapped, totally missing what I was telling her.

"As I recall, you thanked me for giving you a heads-up about Santa Ana."

Another long pause. I'm glad we were on the phone, because I was pretty sure Andrea Fehring wanted to shoot me at this point.

"I think," I continued, "that whoever is handling the drugs, receiving or placing them, might have had other workers like Linda and knows she's in jail. Scraping off the mark might have been a warning to their other buyers to stay away."

"Good theory, Odelia, but you need to leave this to us. Drug runners are dangerous people. I won't tell you again: stand down!"

Stand down? Now she was getting all official on me. Good thing I watch a lot of TV or I might not have known what she meant.

"But don't you want to know who I think scraped the mark off?"

"You saw them do it?" Her voice went up an octave.

"Not exactly, but we did see someone suspicious. Greg and I got photos on our phones."

"Text them to me," she demanded, "and get out of there now."

"We're not at Busy Boxes. We left there almost an hour ago." I looked up and noticed Greg making his way back to me, a cardboard box of food resting on his lap. "And we'll send you the photos. Mine is actually a video."

"Did you recognize the person you think removed the marks?"

"I think so, but I'm not 100 percent."

"Then be a good girl and text me the name, too." Sarcasm dripped from her voice like her chassis had sprung a gooey oil leak.

"I'm sure we'll be able to locate him . . . or her."

"I'm looking at him right now."

"Was it Buck Goodwin?"

"No, but you're warm."

"Dammit, Odelia, quit playing games before I lock you up for obstruction of justice."

I heard the rustling of paper and turned to see the two boys wadding up their lunch trash and leaving.

"Who's on the phone?" Greg asked as he placed our food on the table. Also nestled in his lap were two bottles of Snapple tea. He twisted the cap off of one and put it in front of me.

I put a hand over the phone. "Fehring. She just threatened to arrest me for obstruction of justice."

"Just you?" He sounded hurt.

"She likes you more than she does me, kind of like my mother does."

Greg laughed and stuck something in his mouth that looked like a sweet potato fry on steroids. "What is that?" I asked, still ignoring Fehring, who was on a rant.

"It's called a sweet potato pie fry. Tastes just like the sweet potato pie Zee makes. You have to try one."

He held one out to me. I took a bite. It

was amazing.

"Yes," I said into the phone with my mouth still full. "I'm still here."

"So who's in the photos?" Fehring asked.

"I think it's Eric van den Akker," I told her without fanfare. "Anyone mention a Heide van den Akker during any of your questioning?"

"Not that I recall. Who is she? And don't you dare shovel any more BS my way."

"Heide van den Akker is or was Buck Goodwin's girlfriend. Eric is her eldest son. He's the one we think we saw coming out of Busy Boxes this morning just before it opened. He was dressed in a dark hoodie and wearing gloves. And I think either he or his brother, Paul, is Bob Y, the reviewer with a hatred for secondhand stores and a love for food trucks. Paul used to work for Buck."

"And which one is with you now?"

I glanced over at Comfort Foodies. The lunch crowd was starting to swell. "Eric. His mother owns and operates a food truck called Comfort Foodies. They're parked at Cal State Fullerton right now, feeding hordes of college kids. And Buck Goodwin is with them."

"We're on our way," she told me.

I looked at my husband. He was scarfing down a sandwich with gusto, looking at me long enough to give a thumbs up with the hand not clutching the yummy-looking concoction.

My attention turned from my stomach back to the call. "I thought you were going to Busy Boxes."

"I'll send Leon to Bellflower. I'm coming to Fullerton. Do me a favor: if they try to leave, delay them."

"But I thought you didn't want us involved."

Another pause. I could almost see her aiming her gun at the phone. "I know you'll ignore any orders to stay away, so you might as well make yourselves useful and keep an eye on them for me . . . from a distance. You understand?"

"Greg wants to know if you arrest me, will I be able to have conjugal visits?"

Greg nearly sprayed food across the table.

"Laugh all you want, funny girl," Fehring said without a smidgen of humor. "But one day you'll get into something you won't be able to wiggle your smart ass out of."

Now it was my turn to pause for thought. I was being brazen toward Fehring. No doubt I was overcompensating for the heavy grief of losing Seamus. Dev hounded me all the time about how one day my luck would run out. Maybe losing Seamus was just the beginning — a prelude to tragedy, a trailer for coming attractions.

"We'll keep an eye out on them for you," I agreed. "They're supposed to be here until two o'clock."

"Good. I'm on my way, but in the meantime, do not engage them. You got that?"

I was about to say something snappy about already being married but wisely held my tongue. When the call was over, I dug into the food Greg had put on the table. In addition to the fries, he'd bought a pot roast sandwich and something called a chicken pot pie wrap. He'd divvied them up so we could try half of each and had already ploughed through his half of the pot roast. He was about to start on the chicken pot pie wrap.

"Oh my gawd," Greg said, wiping his mouth with a napkin, "this food is even better than you and Grace said."

I took a long drink from the tea bottle and contemplated which treat to dig into first. I picked up the pot roast. "Fehring wants us to watch the truck and make sure they don't leave before she gets here." I took a bite and understood instantly why Greg had eaten his like a starving fugitive.

Greg glanced over at the truck. "I doubt they'll be going anywhere with that crowd building like it is."

I stuck a fry into my mouth and nodded. "I agree," I mumbled through the goodness.

While we ate, we sent the photos and video to Fehring's cell phone.

We were almost done eating when someone popped out of the back of the truck. It was Buck Goodwin, toting a plastic trash bag. He went to the trash can nearest the truck and started shoving the bag into it.

Greg gathered some of our trash and started toward Buck. "What are you doing?" I asked.

"Going to see if he'll talk to us a minute."

"If he sees you, he might bolt."

"True, but even if he does, he won't get far on foot, providing he didn't drive his own car here, which I doubt since the cops are on the lookout for it."

I looked at the food truck. There was no way they could shut it down and make a dash for it in short order with that lumbering vehicle.

"Just don't tell him the police are on their way," I said in a hushed voice.

"And why would I do that?"

Greg rolled in the direction of Buck, who was occupied pushing his trash bag as deep into the receptacle as possible. When Greg reached him, Buck graciously stepped aside, inviting Greg to dump his trash. Then Buck recognized him, and his casual stance turned into one of indecision and defense. I half expected him to hit or shove Greg and take off. Greg was talking to him, saying things I couldn't hear. I watched Buck's shoulders sag and a sad frown cross his face as he looked over in my direction. I gave him a small wave and smile of encouragement. After more discussion, the two men moved in my direction.

"Odelia," Buck greeted me.

"I told Buck how you and Grace were nearly killed in the blast at his store," Greg told me.

"I feel real bad about that," said Buck. "About everything."

"So you set the bomb?" I asked.

Buck shook his head with vigor. "No ma'am, I did not. I would never destroy my store." The conviction in his voice was unmistakable and sounded sincere. "And I would never harm people like that. Those other store owners are my friends. I've known many of them for years."

It was exactly what Tiffany had said about her father.

"Then why are you in hiding?"

"I'm not in hiding." He stuck out his square chin to make his point. "If I were, we wouldn't be standing here talking. I'm just not making myself available until I sort things out."

"But what about your store?" I asked. "Are you just abandoning it, leaving the mess?"

"Since you're so interested, I've already called the insurance company. But until the investigation is over, they can't do anything."

"The police know you took off shortly before the bomb went off."

Buck fiddled with the front of the long apron he was wearing over a black tee shirt and jeans. In spite of the cool day, he was sweating. "After seeing poor Ina at the hearing, I couldn't work, so I grabbed a sandwich and took off for a drive up the coast to think this mess through. I do that sometimes to clear my head. I was on my way back when I heard about the bomb and about Red. That's when I decided to stay low but close. Heide's a good friend. She's been helping me."

So that was why Buck hadn't pulled and locked the security gate across the front of his store as Bill said he usually did — he was planning on returning to the store that day. If he hadn't left to drive up the coast, he would have probably died in the blast, and us with him since Mom and I probably would have been inside, questioning him. I shuddered.

"Do you know who did set the bomb and who killed Redmond Stokes?" Greg asked.

"I have my suspicions." Buck looked off, his eyes scanning the crowd. "I'm pretty sure it's the same people."

I reached out and put a hand on Buck's arm. He didn't pull away. "Then go to the police."

"I can't." He turned his face to me, and I saw anguish in his eyes. "At least not until I can protect Tiffany." He glanced over at the truck. "And Heide and her boys."

"Let the police help you do that," I urged.

"They can't, not like I can."

"What do the van den Akkers have to do with this, outside of helping you?" Greg asked. Seeing Greg wasn't playing the Eric card up front, I decided to follow suit.

"Nothing," Buck replied, a little too quickly to be convincing.

I looked at Greg with raised eyebrows. Buck saw it.

"What?" Buck asked, his stance and voice turning defensive again. "You two know something."

Greg cleared his throat, and I knew he was going to open the box of snakes and see what crawled out. "We know a drug business is being funneled through the auctions."

"You know about that?" Buck took a step backward in surprise.

"Yes, and so do the police," I admitted. "They know drugs have been exchanged through specially marked units up for auction. Linda McIntyre is in jail right now." I let the idea of Linda spilling her guts to the cops hang in the air like a stench, even though we'd been told she wasn't saying anything to anyone, just like Ina.

Greg adjusted his wheelchair closer to Buck. "Were Ina and Tom mixed up in this drug business? Is that why Tom was murdered and Ina won't say anything?"

"Tom was," Buck said quickly, "but not Ina. It's what set off their more recent battles. Tom wanted to stock their store with the goods Linda was buying but couldn't store, but Ina refused, saying she wasn't about to get mixed up in it. But Tom started selling the merchandise anyway."

I started putting the pieces together, hoping Fehring wouldn't arrive before we heard more. "Then Linda and Tom hooked up, and Ina was out?"

"I know Tom started seeing Linda; whether it was before he got involved with

341

the drugs or after, I'm not sure."

"Is that why Mazie Moore decided not to go into business with Linda, because of the drug connection?"

Buck shrugged. "Could be. Or it could be Mazie was scared off by Tom's murder. Linda had been buying up a lot of units lately and needed places to unload the goods. Her people didn't want the merchandise, just the drugs hidden in them. She needed legitimate businesses to take the furniture and other stuff off her hands. It was a lucrative racket. Her people would front the money for the units, and she'd buy the ones they told her to buy. The goods would be moved to someone's store, the drugs passed off to the people pulling the strings. Linda and whoever she partnered with had no outlay but received tons of merchandise they could resell with no cost to themselves. It was pure profit, except for the cost of moving it to the store."

"But," I pointed out, "it wasn't directly tied to selling the drugs. The auctions were the mule, so to speak, moving the drugs from the exporter to the importer without suspicion."

Buck nodded.

Greg looked at me. "The money Ina took from their accounts is making sense. Tom was already making extra money from selling the merchandise."

I turned to Buck. "Did you know Ina had drained their bank accounts and was about to flee the country?"

Buck shook his head. "No, but it doesn't surprise me. Too bad she didn't hit the road before Tom was killed."

"Do you know why they killed him?"

"No, but I'm guessing it was a warning to the rest of us. Or maybe Tom did something really stupid and pissed them off. It would be like him."

The comment drew no argument from either Greg or me and only underlined Ina's "stupid bastard" remark.

"And Red Stokes?" asked Greg.

The question clearly made Buck uncomfortable. "I doubt Red was involved. I've known and worked with the guy for years. He was too much of a straight arrow to get mixed up in something like this. I'm thinking he found out about it and raised a fuss with someone or threatened to go to the police."

I hit Buck quick and head-on with another question. "Were you selling merchandise from these units? Or were you involved in buying marked units?"

"Absolutely not. Linda approached me,

343

but I told her to go to hell."

"Is that why your place was bombed?" Greg asked.

"Could be."

"Does Tiffany know about this?" I asked.

Buck's shoulders sagged. "No. At least I don't think so. I tried to tell her, but she wouldn't listen. She got the wrong idea."

The wrong idea. More puzzle pieces were coming together, or else I was trying to force them to fit. "Tiffany said you two had a falling out because she's a lesbian. Is that true?"

"No," Buck insisted. "Like most fathers, I just want my daughter to be happy. I don't care if she's gay or not as long as she's happy and safe."

"But," I continued, "she thinks you objected to it, especially when she moved in with Kim Pawlak."

At the mention of Kim's name, Buck visibly stiffened. Greg and I both caught the change and exchanged glances.

"It wasn't Tiffany's sexual orientation you objected to," Greg suggested, "it was her choice of partner, wasn't it?"

Buck remained silent for a minute, then said, "Red might not have been involved, but I believe Kim is, deeply. I need to get my daughter away from her. I couldn't do

344

that if I'm stuck talking to the police about the bombing. I'll talk to them when she's safe."

Greg didn't seem satisfied. "How did you find out Kim Pawlak was involved? Was it from Ina?"

"Tiffany told us," I added, "that one of the reasons Ina went to the auction that morning was to tell you something. In all the chaos of that day, did she manage to tell you something important, like maybe how Kim was involved?"

He looked surprised. "No, Ina didn't say anything to me about the drug business. I didn't see her before the auction, and after Tom was found, that's all the focus was on. But I don't think she knew about Kim."

"So who told you?" Greg pressed, unable to give up on that line of questioning. "Frankly, I think it was Red Stokes."

Buck looked up at the sky, then over toward the tables where students were enjoying their lunch. "Yes," he said, not looking at us. "It was Red. He came to me after Tiff got involved with Kim and said he was pretty sure Kim was involved in something illegal. He wasn't sure exactly what it was, just that he felt she was using Acme to cover her activities, and he was investigating it. He was warning me to get my daughter away from her so she wouldn't go down when Kim went down."

It was all starting to fall in place in my crammed head. "So Red was investigating Kim and told you, and on the same day he was killed, an attempt was also made on your life."

Buck nodded. "Kim must have found out he was watching her and had talked to me."

"Buck," someone called. We looked over at the truck to see Eric van den Akker sticking his head out the back door. "Come on, man. It's getting busy."

"I gotta get back. These college events mean big money for Heide, and she needs the extra hands."

"Where's Paul today?" I asked. "Is he off writing hateful reviews about resale shops or is he backing off now that yours burned to the ground?"

Buck looked surprised at the question, then wary, answering my question with some of his own. "How do you know so much, and how did you find me?"

"The important thing is," I pointed out, "if we could find you, so can the police."

"We think we saw Eric at Busy Boxes early this morning," Greg told him, finally throwing that information onto the fire.

Instead of speaking, Buck spread his thick

legs and planted himself like a tree, crossing his arms in front of his beefy chest. A snake tattoo on his right arm nearly came alive with the itch to strike.

Greg didn't back down. "He's mixed up in this mess too, isn't he?"

Buck stuck a meaty index finger in Greg's face. "Eric has nothing to do with this. Nothing! Is that clear?"

Buck's earlier passion was straying into anger, but I moved closer. "We think Eric was scraping a mark off a unit today. We think he was sending a warning to whoever was going to buy it not to do it. That means he's working with them."

"I'm telling you, Eric has nothing to do with this. He's a good kid — moody, but solid and dependable. Hell, he supported his mother and brother after his father was killed."

Greg pulled out his cell phone and showed Buck a photo taken in front of Busy Boxes.

Buck started to comment but instead took off for the truck. He climbed into it and closed the door behind him.

"Do you think he's going to make a run for it?" Greg asked.

"Maybe, but it will take a few minutes before they can close up and maneuver the truck out of that spot without running people over. Hopefully Fehring will get here by then."

A minute later, loud male voices boomed from the Comfort Foodies truck. Around us, people stopped eating and stared at the restaurant on wheels. Customers at the window backed up. Next, a female voice joined the argument. I scooted over near the back door, hoping to catch what the fight was about, but before I could hear anything of value, the back door flung open, nearly smacking me in the face. Out jumped Eric van den Akker. As soon as his feet hit the ground, he took off running toward the parking lot.

Greg motioned for me to get out of the way, which I did, joining him by the table again.

"I couldn't hear much except swearing," I reported.

Greg took me by the elbow. "Let's get out of here too, sweetheart."

"You don't want to wait for Detective Fehring and tell her what we found out?"

"We can tell her by phone. Right now I'd feel better if we helped Buck out by finding his daughter and getting her away from Kim. If Kim is mixed up in this, she may use Tiffany as leverage."

A shiver went down my spine. "Meaning

she could be the third victim?"

"Exactly. The police can handle this and find Eric."

It was then we noticed campus security had moved in and posted themselves near the truck. In their hands were radios, which they were actively using. As Greg and I started toward the parking lot, taking the same path as Eric, we saw police cars edging their way down the paved walkways, being careful of the people milling about. They made their way toward the food truck — a pack of wolves moving in for the kill. No doubt Fehring was in one of the lead cars, and she'd brought reinforcements from the local cops. I started moving faster, with Greg keeping pace alongside me. We had to get out of there or we'd be caught up in questioning hell for hours.

TWENTY-THREE

With the police shutting down the Santa Ana auction, I wasn't quite sure where we might find Kim and Tiffany — or, more importantly, just Tiffany. I wanted to find out if she was involved in this or how much she knew. Was she blinded by love for Kim Pawlak or was paternal love blinding Buck Goodwin? It was difficult to say, but I felt confident that Buck believed with all his heart that Tiffany was not in the loop about the drug trafficking at the auctions. And who knew how much Kim Pawlak was involved. Was she a soldier or a general in the setup? Did she have Red killed and try to kill Buck or was someone else calling the shots?

Greg and I got our van out of the college parking garage as fast as possible just in case Fehring shut the place down in her hunt for Eric van den Akker. She would expect us near the Comfort Foodies truck and might be relieved to not find us, or she could worry that we were off pursuing another lead on our own. We drove several miles away from the campus before Greg pulled into a busy mall parking lot. Along the way, we'd discussed my thoughts and questions about Kim.

"I'm wondering," Greg said after pulling the van into a spot between two high-profile SUVs, using them for cover just in case Fehring had patrol cars on the lookout for us, "about the timing of Kim becoming a half owner in Acme Auctions."

"The woman who told me that said it was recent. Do you think Red would have sold it to her if she was mixed up in a drug trafficking business?"

"No, I don't. I'll bet he found out about the illegal stuff just after she became his partner."

Greg shifted in his seat. "Makes you wonder how many other auction houses might be involved or if it's just this one."

I nodded. Greg was right. It could be the drug traffickers had their fingers in several auction services, not just Acme. "Here's a thought. What if Red and Tom weren't murdered by the drug guys but by another auction house wanting in on the action?"

Greg blew out a gust of frustrated air at

the thought. "For now, let's just focus on who and what we know."

I nodded in agreement and kept the hamster wheel inside my head moving on our track.

Greg looked out the window, watching a young woman pushing a stroller from her car toward the mall entrance. "But if Kim is deeply involved in this mess, do you really think Tiffany would miss that?"

I shrugged. "In spite of her tough-girl appearance, Tiffany's pretty young and she's in love. Haven't you had relationships where you knew something was wrong but chose to ignore it?" I myself was remembering a man named Franklin Powers whom I almost married years before I met Greg. Franklin was a manic depressive given to bursts of violence. I ignored it in the name of love until I simply couldn't any longer and broke off the engagement two months before the wedding. "I know I have."

"Yes," Greg agreed, rubbing my arm with affection. I'd told him about Franklin when we started getting serious. "We all have."

"I think the question is how much does Tiffany know or suspect, and if she's involved herself."

"I hope for Buck's sake she's not involved at all." Greg started up the van. "So what's the plan?"

"Give me your phone." I held my hand out. "If I call and get the same woman, she might recognize the number and my voice."

Greg handed me his cell phone, and I placed a call to Acme Auctions. The same woman answered, and I tried to change my voice up a bit, which is another skill I lack.

"Hi," I said as soon as she answered. "Is Kim Pawlak in?"

"Why are you asking?" the grouchy woman asked.

Ah, geez, I really should have had a story ready. The Acme receptionist may not be Miss Congeniality, but she didn't strike me as stupid either. I decided to get snotty back and see if she'd back down. "I don't think that's any of your business." I paused and gave off a very audible and inpatient sigh. "Look," I said to the woman, "I'm a friend of Kim's and she told me to call her. Said it was very important. End of story. So is she there or not?" I held my breath, waiting to see if my plan worked.

"No, Ms. Pawlak is not in at the moment."

"How about her assistant? She said if she wasn't there, I should talk to her assistant. Oh gawd, what's her name? Tanya? Terri?"

"Tiffany."

"Yes. Tiffany. Sounds like some blond

bimbo from Beverly Hills. Kim always did have a secret fancy for girls like that."

"Ms. Goodwin is here," the woman said with a voice so sharp I got a paper cut in my ear, "but she's on the phone right now. May I take a message?"

"How about voice mail?"

Without another word, the woman slapped my call into voice mail. I heard Tiffany's recorded voice telling me to leave a message and phone number and she would return the call as soon as possible. I didn't leave a message.

"Tiffany is there," I said to Greg after I ended the call and handed him back his phone. "And Kim is not."

"Nice job, sweetheart," he said with a grin. "Now where to?"

I smiled at my husband and looked up Acme Auctions on my own phone. Even before I gave him the address, he was pulling out of the parking space.

Acme Auctions was located in Norwalk, back in the direction of Bellflower. We were certainly getting around today, but at least everything was fairly local and nothing was sending us off into Los Angeles proper, where the traffic would be worse.

The address brought us to a very small strip mall on the corner of Pioneer Boulevard and Lindale Street. There were only four businesses on the premises — Acme Auctions, a tax service, a liquor store, and a dry cleaners. Acme was sandwiched between the tax service and the dry cleaners. The parking lot for the businesses was tiny.

"Look for a back alley when I go around the corner," Greg told me.

"I don't see one."

"Good. That means she'll have to go in and out through the front. Too bad we don't know what Tiffany drives."

Greg went around the block. Once we were back at the small shopping plaza, he pulled into the lot by the dry cleaners and parked in a space on the end that gave us a good view of the front of Acme and an easy exit if we needed to pull out quickly.

I glanced at the clock on the van's dash. "It's only twelve thirty," I noted. "Feels like it should be two or later."

"That's because we ate lunch at eleven," Greg chuckled. "We're going to want dinner by four."

"Let's just hope she didn't leave for lunch while we were driving here. If she hasn't, we might be able to snag her on her way out."

"My guess," said Greg, "is that Acme doesn't get a lot of walk-in traffic or have a lot of employees. Might just be Tiffany and the receptionist in there. If no one comes or goes soon, we might want to go in."

A few minutes later, we saw the door to Acme open, and a woman with gray hair pulled back into a ponytail walked out. She had her purse hooked over one arm and was holding a small box. She headed straight for a dull brown sedan parked in front. A second later she was pulling out into traffic.

"I'll bet," Greg said, leaning toward me, "that's the receptionist, and she's heading somewhere for lunch."

I agreed.

"If we can't get anything out of Tiffany, we should try to crack that nut. Didn't you say she sounded very unhappy the first time you called?"

"More like she was disapproving of the new situation." I really didn't want to face the receptionist, especially now that I'd gotten a glimpse of her stony face. A bluff on the phone is one thing; in person, I doubted I could keep it up.

"Did you notice," I said, "that she didn't lock the door when she left? That means someone is still inside. Hopefully it's Tiffany and she's still alone."

As soon as the woman was gone, Greg and I left the van and made our way to Acme.

The décor inside was clean but sparse. The reception area also served as the main office area. A bank of old-fashioned, mismatched filing cabinets lined one wall. A big year-at-a-glance calendar was posted on another. Many of the date blocks were filled in with places and times. The front desk looked to be command central. I quietly moved around the desk to take a look. The bulletin board posted on the wall to the right of the desk was blank except for a few memos, but from the fading on the cork, it looked like until recently it had been covered with photos. There was a desktop computer, but it was old.

I heard someone talking. It was muffled but clearly a single voice. I looked to Greg, who pointed behind me. In the back were two closed doors leading to offices. The doors were wood inset with frosted glass. To the side was a solid door with a sign on it designating it as a unisex restroom. Next to the bathroom door was a counter with a copy machine and a coffeemaker. Under the counter was a small fridge.

I checked the phone on the front desk. There were several buttons evidencing several phone lines or extensions, but only one was lit. I looked from the phone back to the closed glass doors. The office on the left was dark, but lights were on in the one on the right. I started moving for it. Greg caught up to me. Since we didn't know for sure that Tiffany was behind the closed door or what her involvement was with the drug scheme, we approached carefully, standing to the side and not directly in front of the glass. The voice sounded normal and businesslike, and it was Tiffany. A second later, the call ended.

Greg and I looked at each other a moment, unsure of whether to knock or barge in. What we did know for sure was that the clock was ticking. The receptionist might be back soon and the police might show up anytime, especially since drugs were found in the Santa Ana facility this morning. No doubt they would be questioning everyone at Acme about it.

Our decision-making process came to an end when the door opened and Tiffany Goodwin popped out. We both let out a little yelp of fright at the unexpected surprise. Greg was the only one not shaken.

"What are you two doing here?" Tiffany asked, recovering first.

"We need to ask you some more questions," Greg told her. "It's important."

"To who?"

"To you," I answered. "And to Buck."

Tiffany's face melted from stern into worry. "Do you know where my dad is? Is he okay?"

"He was fine when we saw him about an hour ago," Greg told her. "But he's worried about you." I was relieved that Greg left out the part about Buck being surrounded by police last we saw him.

Hearing Buck was okay, Tiffany's face morphed back into defiance and her eyes rolled. "Did he send you here to make peace? If so, you can just leave."

"No," I told her. "He didn't, but he has good reason to be concerned about you." Before she could speak again, I quickly added, "He's not mad because you're gay. Really, he's not."

"Yeah, right." She put a hand on a slim hip. She was dressed all in black today — black jeans, black shirt, and black work boots, even thick black eye makeup. Only her spiky hair was light.

"It's true," Greg added, "he's concerned about Kim, about your relationship with her. He's afraid she's mixed up in something illegal and you'll get dragged into it."

"You mean the drug thing?" She voiced the question with casual indifference. "Go back and tell Dad to mind his own business. Kim is not involved in that. That was all Red's doing. That's why he was murdered."

I felt my face scrunch into curiosity. "Who told you that?"

"Kim. She found out about it shortly after she became his partner. She convinced him to pull out of it, but when he tried, they killed him."

"Did you tell the police that?"

"Kim did, or at least she's there now being questioned. They found drugs in one of the units up for auction today. She said it was time to stop trying to protect Red and clear the air. She's trying to save the business."

The words sounded good — too good and convenient. Buck had said he'd known Red for years and that the guy was a straight shooter. "Acme belongs totally to Kim now, right?"

"Yeah," Tiffany confirmed. "I think she owns it all now."

Greg swiveled his chair slightly. It was something he did when he was lost in thought, like running a hand through his hair. "Tiffany, your father does not believe Redmond Stokes was mixed up in any of this. He believes Kim is the one involved. That's why he was so upset when you moved in with her."

"He never said that to me. He just said he wouldn't let me move in with her. *Wouldn't let me!* I'm not a child anymore. I'm nineteen, almost twenty. He even threatened to lock me up to keep us apart."

Buck, Buck, Buck. It sounded exactly like something an upset and bull-headed parent might say.

"I think," I said to Tiffany, "that your dad might have put it badly in his desire to keep you away from Kim. He believes she's involved in the drug scheme, not Red, but he didn't want to tell you because knowing about it might put you in danger. He's really supportive of your coming out."

"He told us he just wants you to be happy and safe," Greg added. "Did you know already about the drugs?"

Tiffany was looking out the front window into the small parking lot but shook her head. "Not until today. I knew something really bad was going on because of Tom's and Red's murders and the blast at my dad's store, but I didn't know what it was. Kim said it had nothing to do with us — that they were all involved in something illegal."

"Even your dad?" I asked.

"She tried to tell me that, but it didn't sound like Dad at all. Then when his store was blown up, I started thinking she might be right."

Tiffany leaned against the wall and slid to the floor, covering her face with her hands. "I'm so confused, I don't know what to think."

"Didn't Ina try to tell you when she came by the night before Tom was found?"

She shook her head. "No. She just said she had something to tell my dad before she left town. Do you think she knew?"

I shook my head. "About Kim's possible involvement? I doubt it, or else she would have tried to get you away from her. Ina's your friend, isn't she?"

Tiffany nodded. "She's the one who encouraged me to come out, especially to Dad. She's always been there for me, like a big sister."

"Come on," Greg said, holding a hand out to the girl. "We need to get out of here, all of us."

"If what you say is true, where will I go?" She lifted her face to show tear tracks in her black eye makeup.

"You're coming with us," Greg told her. "Leave your car here."

"And your cell phone," I added. "We need to get you out of sight just in case the drug guys decide to pay a visit to this office."

"What about Kim?" Tiffany wiped her nose like a five-year-old. "I can't just leave her! She told me to stay here and wait for her. She said she would straighten everything out."

Greg shook his hand at her and this time she took it. "If Kim is innocent," he told her, helping her to her feet, "you'll be reunited, and I'll bet Buck will even give you his blessing this time. But if she's involved in this in any way, you need to stay away from her. She could be dangerous."

Tiffany looked torn by indecision, but in the end slipped back into the office and grabbed a black leather jacket. She shrugged into it and followed us out the door.

"What about the receptionist?" I asked as Tiffany locked the door of the office. "Do you think she knows about the drugs?"

"You mean Madeline? She just quit and left, like right before you guys showed up. I know the police questioned her about Red. She's worked for him for years, but if she knew anything about the drugs, she didn't let on to anyone."

On the way to the van, I said, "I got the feeling when I spoke to her on the phone that she wasn't too pleased with Kim owning part of the company."

"She and Kim never got along. Kim said

it's because Madeline is prejudiced against gays." Tiffany climbed into the van and buckled up. "But I've been working here a few weeks and Madeline has always been nice to me. In fact . . ." her voice drifted off.

Buckled up in my own seat, I turned to her. "In fact, what?"

"It's just something silly Madeline said to me one afternoon when we were alone. It was right before Red was killed."

Greg looked at Tiffany in the rear-view mirror. "What was it?"

"We were eating lunch together in the office, and Madeline, out of the blue, said I could do better than Kim. She said Kim wasn't a nice person and I shouldn't trust her." Tiffany thought about the words for a second, then added, "She didn't say I should find myself a nice boy, just that I could do better than Kim and shouldn't trust her. I thought she said it because she didn't like Kim. Now I'm wondering if it was a warning."

Greg and I exchanged looks as we pulled out of the lot.

We were heading back to our house. The plan was to stash Tiffany with my mother and decide what was next. After finding the drugs in the Santa Ana unit and probably in the Busy Boxes unit, the police of several jurisdictions would be busy rounding up witnesses and suspects. Greg and I didn't want to get in their way, but we also didn't want to stand around idle.

"That's funny," I said to Greg while we were on our way home. "I've called Mom on both our home phone and her cell, and there's no answer."

"Maybe she took Wainwright for a walk and forgot to take her phone."

"Maybe." But it still didn't feel right. Since coming to visit, I seldom saw Mom without her phone. She even told me she kept it close for emergencies in case she fell or felt ill. I put a hand on Greg's arm. "Honey, can you drive faster? I'm a little worried. She might have fallen or something." After what happened to Seamus and how sad it made Mom, I didn't want to take any chances.

In response, Greg increased the van's speed and did some fancy maneuvering in and out of traffic. For a man who couldn't move his lower limbs, Greg definitely had a lead foot when it came to driving.

Before Greg brought the van to a complete stop in our driveway, I jumped out and went through the back gate. Wainwright wiggled out his doggie door and made a beeline for me, his tail wagging in joy. He didn't seem distressed at all, which was a very good sign.

"Mom?" I called as I entered through the back door. "You here?" When I got no response, I headed for her room. It was empty. I checked the bathroom, then went to the other side of the house and checked the master suite just in case — nothing.

Greg and Tiffany were coming into the kitchen when I returned to the main part of the house. "She's not here, and her purse is gone," I told Greg.

"I'll bet she went someplace with my mom."

"Of course," I said with relief. I punched the speed dial for Renee's cell phone. She answered on the third ring. "Is my mother with you?" I asked.

"Why, no," my mother-in-law answered. "I called Grace to see if she wanted to go looking at more retirement places, but she said she had plans."

"Plans? My mother had plans?"

"Yes, with some gentleman she met."

I squeezed my eyes tight and tried not to groan. "Was his name Bill Baxter?"

"Yes, I believe his name was Bill. Grace sounded excited."

Before I could say anything more, Greg held up a note. "This was left on the kitchen table. I think it says she went out with Bill."

"Renee, Greg just found a note from Mom. Sorry to have bothered you."

"No bother at all, Odelia. I think it's lovely that your mother is already making friends. She'll enjoy living here and being close to you."

After hanging up, I scanned the piece of paper, taking in the short message in my mother's shaky scrawl. It did say she was out with Bill. But it also said something else — something about a lead. At least I think that's what it said.

"I wish Mom would learn to text," I said to Greg. "Her handwriting is atrocious." I showed the note to Greg and pointed to the sentence I was becoming more alarmed about by the second. "Does that say *lead*?"

Greg put on his reading glasses and took the note from me. "Yeah, I think it does. Something about them checking out a *hot lead.*"

I looked at the note again. "That word is *hot*? I thought it said *bat* or *love.*"

Greg read the note out loud in a halting voice as he sounded out Mom's hieroglyphics. *"Gone with Bill. Got hot lead.* Or it could be, *Good with Bill. Got hot bed."*

I tore the note out of my grinning husband's hands. "Funny." I looked at the note again. "Are you sure that word isn't *lunch* instead of *lead*?"

"Looks more like *lead* to me."

This time I did groan out loud. "Who knows what those two are getting themselves into?" I looked at Greg. "We have to find them somehow."

Tiffany seemed surprised by the conversation. "Are you talking about Bill Baxter, the locksmith?"

"That's the one. They met the day of the blast," I explained. "We'd stopped by the store to talk to your dad, but he was gone."

Tiffany shivered. "Bill's a creepy garden gnome. Even Ina thinks so." She laughed. "One time Ina was at Dad's store and Bill was standing by her car when she tried to leave. She threatened to turn him into road-kill if he didn't leave her alone."

Greg grinned. "Sounds like our Ina."

I looked at Tiffany with raised brows. "I thought Bill and your father were friends. He told us he kept an eye out for Buck's store when Buck wasn't around."

"More like he spies on Dad and the store — on all the people at that mall. He's always sneaking around and asking questions." She shifted from one foot to the other. "Most people there just tolerate him. Dad more than anyone else."

Something still didn't sit right. "When I spoke to Bill Baxter," I said, looking straight at Tiffany, "he seemed to know a lot of personal things about you, including about your mom and dad and how they met."

Tiffany shuffled from foot to foot. "When I first came to live with my dad, Bill was very nice to me, like a grandfather. I was lonely and mad about my mother. Dad and I were going through a lot of problems. I guess I told Bill a lot of personal stuff I shouldn't have." She stopped fidgeting. "It didn't take me long to catch on that he was just a nosy creep."

I stepped forward with concern. "Did he do or say anything to hurt you?"

"Oh no, nothing like *that*. Dad told me Bill was a lonely old man and to stay away from him if he made me uncomfortable." She looked around. "Hey, can I use your bathroom?"

I directed her down the hall to the guest bath. When she was gone, I said to Greg, "I don't like this at all. Bill Baxter might not be the harmless old coot I thought he was."

"Maybe he's just too nosy for his own good."

"And maybe it was Bill who planted the bomb at Buck's store," I suggested. "He would know when the store was empty. No one would think twice about him poking around in the back alley. That's where the trash containers are kept. He probably put his trash back there."

"And he's a locksmith," Greg pointed out, getting on board with my idea. "He could probably get into Buck's store to plant a bomb with no trouble."

I sat down in a kitchen chair with a heavy thud. "But why would he want to get involved with Mom if he was the one with the bomb?"

"To see how much she knows," Greg suggested. "To see how much the police might have told the two of you?"

"But what about the lead bit?" I put my head in my hands. "Oh my gawd, where could they have gone?"

I didn't wallow long. As Tiffany was coming out of the hallway, I was going down it, heading for Mom's room and her iPad, hoping she didn't have it secured with a password. I also hoped she'd been doing some research before she'd left with Bill. If so, it might give me a clue as to where they were headed. While I did that, Greg tried her cell phone again.

Mom's iPad was sitting on the nightstand. I opened the cover and turned it on. It prompted me to provide a four-numeral password, just like my iPhone did. *Good gawd!* It could be anything. After a little calculation, I tried my mother's year of birth. It wasn't that. I tried Clark's year of birth. Nada. Not knowing how many tries I got before the thing locked or melted into toxic goo, I stopped and thought about what those four numbers could be. It was then I spied a postcard from Marie, Clark's eldest daughter. It was tucked inside a front pocket of the cover. On the front was a photo of a lovely beach in the Bahamas. It appeared to have been mailed in early spring and was addressed to Mom at the retirement home in New Hampshire. My eye caught on the address: 1716 Chestnut Lane.

Not having better prospects, I plugged 1-7-1-6 into the password blocks. The iPad came to life. I went immediately to the web browser and checked for recent searches, praying it didn't clear automatically. It looked like Mom had looked up Otra Vez, the store owned by the Vasquez family. I hit the back button a few times and saw that she'd been searching for information on Mazie Moore. Mazie had two stores. Combined with the location for Otra Vez, it meant Mom and Bill might be heading in any of three directions.

I brought the iPad out to show Greg.

"What do you think?"

He pulled out his phone. "What's the phone number for Otra Vez?"

Going back to that page, I read off the phone number for the store. Greg punched in each number as I said it. "Hi," he said as soon as the call was answered. "My name is Greg Stevens. I think my mother-in-law is on her way to your store, and I need to reach her."

He listened for a moment, then added, "Her name is Grace. She's about eighty, short gray hair, and might be with" — Greg's voice halted as I pantomimed short and stocky — "she might be with a short elderly man." He listened again while I stood on shaky legs. Tiffany stroked Wainwright while she waited with me for news.

"Uh-huh," Greg finally said. "Well, if you do see them, could you ask Grace to call me or her daughter? It's a family emergency." He listened again before adding, "Thanks. Appreciate it."

"No luck there?" I asked as he closed his phone.

"They haven't seen them."

"Mazie has two stores," I said, looking at her website. "One in Pico Rivera and one in Inglewood."

"Pico Rivera is closer," Greg noted. I gave

him the phone number and he called it, giving the person who answered the same spiel as he'd given before. They also had not seen Mom.

Before he hung up, I whispered, "Ask them if Mazie's there."

He did, then listened to the reply. "How long has she been gone?" he asked. When he ended the call, he said to me, "The woman on the phone said Mazie went on an extended vacation out of the country. She left Tuesday, and they don't know when she'll be back."

"If it's the truth, then Mazie left the country the day after the auction. I'm guessing she's involved. She and Linda were arguing right before Linda took off on Monday." My brain went into overdrive. "Could be she was already selling the goods Linda was buying, and once she saw Tom's fate, she was worried the same might happen to her, so she left until things cooled down."

"Or," Greg added, "the woman on the phone lied to me, and Mazie hasn't left the country."

"Either way, Mazie isn't around where people can find her."

Greg called Mazie's Inglewood store and asked the same questions. They also hadn't seen Mom and Bill and gave him the same story about Mazie's whereabouts.

Three strikes; we were out.

I checked back as far as I could on the iPad but didn't see anything else worth pursuing.

"Maybe they did just go to lunch," Greg suggested.

TWENTY-FOUR

When I waltzed into the T&T office with Tiffany Goodwin in tow, Jill Bernelli was the picture of surprise. "I thought you were out all this week."

"I am, but I need a favor."

"From me or the boss?"

"From you." I indicated for Tiffany to take a seat in a chair by Jill's desk while Jill and I retreated to my office. "That's Tiffany Goodwin. Can I park her here with you for a few hours?"

Jill gave me an odd look. "She's a little old to need a babysitter, isn't she?"

I gave Jill a quick rundown of the situation. "If you don't want to get involved, I'd certainly understand."

She gave it some thought, then answered. "Tell you what, how about you and Greg run along and do whatever you need to do. It's Friday and quiet around here."

"We'll be back as soon as possible, I promise."

Jill put an affectionate hand on my arm. "Go look for your mother, Odelia, and don't worry about hurrying back. I'll take Tiffany home with me tonight. Might do the girl good to see a stodgy lesbian couple in their natural habitat."

"I can't impose on you and Sally like that."

"Sure you can," Jill insisted. "No one would look for the girl at our place, and you can put your mind at ease about her. In fact, let's just plan on her spending the night with us. We have no plans this weekend, and I'm sure we can rustle up some fresh clothes for her."

I wrapped my arms around Jill, giving her a warm hug. "Thanks, Jill. I owe you."

She hugged me back, then said, "Now get out of here before Steele sees you. He's on a conference call right now." I love Jill. She decent, kind, and practical, and dead right about me skedaddling before Steele got off his call.

Unfortunately, when we opened the door to my office to leave, Steele was standing by Jill's desk, chatting up Tiffany Goodwin. When he saw me, Steele started for his office, indicating for me to follow him.

"Can we do this next week, Steele? Greg's

downstairs waiting for me."

"Now, Grey." He stood by his doorway, waiting for me to enter the lion's den. When I did, he followed me in and closed the door.

"Who's your little goth friend?" he asked as soon as we were alone.

"Down, Steele. She's only nineteen and she's gay. I brought her by to meet Jill. You know, for some mentoring."

"Right." He nodded in understanding, but his tone was that of an unbeliever. "And who is she really? And what happened to your face? It's bruised."

"By the way, Seamus died yesterday." I threw out the information hoping to deflect Steele's attention away from Tiffany and my injury and sent up a prayer to animal heaven for Seamus to forgive me.

"What?" Steele leaned back against his desk, his face crestfallen. "Seriously?"

"Yes, seriously." Even though I was using the death of my cat to cover up my current activities, I barely got the words out without choking. "He had a stroke."

"I'm terribly sorry, Grey." From the tone and look on Steele's face, I knew his condolences were genuine. "I know how much that animal meant to you. And to Greg."

I nodded, fighting back tears. My lower lip trembled. Steele stepped forward and gave me a hug, holding me in his embrace almost a full minute. It was the first time he'd ever done that, and I hugged him back, grateful for the sympathy. Steele was the first person outside the family I'd told about Seamus, and saying the words had opened the wound like a yanked scab loosens blood.

When he stepped back, Steele said, "Forget the work I brought you. It can be done later. Just relax and be with Greg and your mother."

As soon as he said "mother," I started weeping. Steele placed a comforting hand on my shoulder. "It's okay, Grey. You took that raggedy old cat in and gave him a loving home. His life was better because of you."

I sniffed back the tears. "It's not Seamus — not entirely. Mom's missing."

"What?" Steele removed his hand and fell back again against the edge of his desk. "Grace is missing? Did she wander off and get lost? Did you call the police?"

I gave Steele a quick rundown of what had happened since I last saw him. When I was almost done, he stopped me by holding up a hand.

"Are you telling me that you and Grace were in front of that store in Torrance when it was turned into a war zone?" His face was tight. Lasers of intensity shot from his eyes. "And now you're running down leads on drug traffickers?"

"No, Steele." I reached into my bag, grabbed a purse pack of tissues, and started dabbing my face. "We were safely down the street when the bomb went off." From his reaction, there was no way I was going to mention that I had been poking around behind the store just yards from the bomb or that I initially thought my mother had had a heart attack from the blast. "And right now, we're looking for my mother, not drug traffickers."

Before either of us could say more, my cell phone gave off Greg's assigned tone. I dug it out of my purse and answered. "I'll be down in a minute, honey," I said into the phone.

Steele snatched the phone from my hand. "Greg, this is Steele. I'm coming down with her. I want to help." He looked at me, the phone still pressed against his ear while he listened. "She just told me about the cat." Pause. "Yeah, she's a mess."

I stuck out my chin in protest, but my defiance was cut short by the need to blow my nose.

"I think we need to come up with a solid plan," Steele said into the phone. He listened again. "Great." With that, he shut the phone and handed it back to me.

"We need to get going," I said, wiping my nose and standing. "And I mean Greg and me, not you, Greg, and me."

"What, Grey, you're not into *ménage à trois*?"

Without waiting for a response, Steele started closing down his computer and putting away his work with quick, efficient movements. Steele never left his desk a mess when he left for the day. "Quick, now: bring me up to speed with the rest."

I shrugged, giving in. "Mom was researching three secondhand shops before she left the house with Bill Baxter. She could be headed to any of them, or even to none of them." I took a deep breath to fight off fresh tears. "Or she could be having a nice lunch with a creepy old guy who looks like Bilbo Baggins. Who knows? We've left word at all three of the stores for her to call us if she shows up."

Steele picked up a legal pad and a pen from his desk. "Do you have the addresses of those places?"

"Yes." I dug around in my purse, then stopped. "I forgot. I left the list in the car with Greg."

"Maybe I could go to at least one of them

and see if they show up, and you and Greg go to the others."

"You in Inglewood?" I almost laughed but felt too miserable.

"You'd be surprised where I've been in my life, Grey."

I had to admit, Steele was always full of surprises. I gave him a quick update on as much as I could, including Tiffany's part in it.

"You were right to bring that girl to Jill." He buzzed Jill from his desk phone and asked her to come in.

When Jill entered Steele's office, he said to her, "Stick to that girl like glue, Jill."

She gave him a two-fingered salute. "That's the plan, Stan."

"Is that work I gave you finished?"

Jill nodded. "Yep and already in the mail-room."

Steele retrieved his suit jacket from the hanger behind his door. "Good, then take off for the day, but stay close to your phone."

"But I have work to do for Jolene," Jill protested.

Steele fixed his eyes on her. "But mine's caught up?"

"Yes."

He slipped into his jacket and loosened

his tie. "Then that's all I care about."

I rolled my eyes in spite of the grave situation. Typical Steele. He'll gladly wear a white hat as long as his work is done first.

"Now take the girl and go," Steele told Jill. "Tell Jolene you're doing something special for me out of the office. If her work has to go out today, she can have someone else take care of it. If she balks, have her call me."

Jill gave Steele another salute before leaving. I could have sworn this one only contained one finger — the middle one.

Before I could stop him, Steele had stuffed his cell phone into a pocket and was heading for the elevator. "You really don't need to do this, Steele," I said as I scampered to keep up.

"I know, Grey," he said, holding the elevator door for me. "I want to."

When we reached the van, which was parked on the street level of the parking garage in a disabled parking spot, Greg and Steele acted like two generals planning an attack.

"Don't you think we should get the police involved?" asked Steele.

"Not yet, Mike," Greg answered. "We don't know for sure what's happened to Grace."

"Grey just filled me in. I would think her mother missing would rate a call to the police — at least to Dev Frye."

"No, Steele," I said, backing up Greg. "We don't know if she's been taken by bad guys or simply running around playing geriatric detective with a nosy old guy. The police have their hands full right now with the drugs and piecing together the whos and whys of the murders."

"If we find out Grace is in danger," Greg added, "then for sure we'll call the police, and pronto."

"Then let's hit the road," Steele said. "You have that list of addresses?"

Greg handed the list I'd made to Steele. "Here — take this. I've already plugged all three into my GPS."

Steele scanned the addresses. "How about I take Inglewood for starters and you guys take Pico Rivera. Lynwood is sort of in the middle. We can meet up there."

"Sounds good," Greg agreed.

"Bill's car is a tan Honda Element with his locksmith business logo on the side," I told Steele. "And thanks, truly, for helping."

With a salute containing all fingers, not just a single digit, Steele took off at a run for his car.

We were almost to Pico Rivera when my

phone rang. It was Mom. I almost dropped it in my haste to answer the call. "Mom, where are you?" I looked over at Greg. Relief was written all over his face.

"I'm with Bill Baxter," she told me, sounding annoyed. "I left you a note. Didn't you see it?"

"Yes, we saw the note, but it was difficult to read. Are you at lunch or following a lead? We weren't sure."

"Both. Bill took me for a lovely lunch, then we decided to check out some of the secondhand stores you and I didn't have time to get to. We started with Otra Vez. When we got here, the man at the counter said to call you. What's the emergency?" There was a short silence followed by a choked, "Please tell me the other animals are okay."

"They're fine, Mom. We tried calling you several times."

"Somehow I managed to shut off the ringer on my phone. Didn't notice that until I called you. I see you and Greg left messages."

My body sagged with relief. "We were worried about you."

"Why?"

Not knowing where Bill was at the moment, I was concerned about saying something to Mom that might trigger a response from her to put him on his guard. I started rocking in my seat, worried about what to say to her. Greg reached out a hand and steadied me. "Mom, don't say anything, just listen."

"Okay," came a tentative voice from the phone.

"We're not sure how much Bill Baxter is involved. It could be that he was the one who planted the bomb."

"Do you know that for sure?" she whispered.

"No, we don't, but don't you think it's odd he called you about lunch so soon with everything going on?"

"Actually, I called him."

"You did?" The surprise in my voice only made Greg more concerned.

"Yes," Mom answered. "Since he knows so much about Buck and is as curious as we are, I thought he might be interested in giving me a lift to the other secondhand stores. Didn't seem like he was all that busy at his shop. Lunch was his idea."

"Oh, Mom. Why couldn't you just stay out of it?"

"If you're going to talk like that, I'm going to hang up."

I gritted my teeth. "Mom, a lot has happened today that you don't know about. Bill might not be the harmless old man we thought he was, and Heide's son Eric and Kim Pawlak might be involved. We know for sure Kim is up to her neck in this. Who knows who else? Mazie Moore has taken off. And the police found drugs in at least one of the auction units today." When Mom didn't say anything, I added, "Why don't you sit still and we'll come get you? I need to know you're safe, and I won't feel that way if you're with Bill Baxter."

More silence, then a whisper, "But what do I say to him?"

"Geez, Mom, you're supposed to be the ace liar in the family." I paused, trying to think of something. "I know, tell him Clark's been hurt. There's no way he can check up on that. Tell him Greg and I will pick you up so he doesn't have to come all the way back to Seal Beach."

"But I told him Clark was out of town."

"Then tell him Greg's dad was hurt and we're all going over there to make sure he's okay." I looked at Greg, who was staring at me in disbelief. "Whatever you do, stay at Otra Vez and don't go off with Bill."

Without being told exactly what was going on, Greg took an off-ramp and turned left at the bottom of it. He was making a wide U-turn, getting back on the 605 heading south to head for the 105 Freeway, which led to Lynwood.

"Okay, I'll think of something," Mom told me with a sigh. "You going to be here soon? I don't want to wait around all day."

"We'll be there soon," I assured her. Greg flashed five fingers three times at me. "Greg says fifteen minutes."

I closed the phone and turned to Greg. "Really? Only fifteen minutes?" I was nervous and wouldn't relax until Mom was in my sights.

"Twenty tops. We weren't far from the turnoff."

I filled him in on what Mom had just told me. "Mom's pretty sure Bill is just a busybody. In fact, *she* called *him* to go out snooping — he didn't call her."

I dialed Steele. "The Mom has landed, Steele. She's at Otra Vez in Lynwood. We're on our way there now to pick her up."

"You want me to head there too?"

"Nah, we've got this, but thanks for everything."

"Let me know if there is anything else I can do for you," Steele said. "Seriously, just call."

Twenty-Five

Ten minutes later, Mom called again. "Where are you?" she whispered.

"Almost there," I told her. I looked to Greg and he nodded to confirm it.

"Don't," Mom said. "Stay away."

"What?"

"I said don't come here. Call the police instead."

"Mom, can you speak up?"

"No, I can't."

"Why's that?"

"Something funny is going on."

"Where are you?"

"I'm in the restroom. Something's wrong. A man showed up here with a gun."

"Is the place being robbed?"

"I don't know," she whispered as I strained to hear. "He's arguing with Roberto over something, so maybe not. He's in one of those sweatshirts with a hood. Like the kids wear."

A hoodie. Was it Eric? Was Roberto Vasquez mixed up in this nasty business, too? Or was he one of the holdouts being taught a lesson?

"Mom, is the hoodie the guy's wearing navy blue? Is the guy Eric van den Akker — you know, Heide's older son?"

"Yes, it's blue, but the hood is pulled down over his face, so I can't tell who he is."

I turned to Greg. "Call Fehring. Tell her to get to Otra Vez immediately. There's a gunman there, and I think it's Eric van den Akker."

Greg pulled out his phone and started pushing buttons. "Good thing I put her on speed dial just in case."

While Greg tried to reach Fehring, I talked to Mom. "Stay on the line, Mom, but try to stay quiet. Greg is calling Detective Fehring. Is Bill still there?"

"No, it took some doing, but I finally convinced him to leave. He wanted to stay until you arrived. He's such a gentleman. I really don't think he's the bomber."

"Is anyone else in the store?"

"Just Roberto and me. His wife was here but left. They're very nice people, Odelia. His wife gave me coffee while I waited for you. I hope nothing happens to them."

"Me, too, Mom. Me, too."

My insides were turning to jelly. My mother was stuck in a bathroom with a gunman just feet from her. I wanted to warn her not to talk so much, but I needed to hear her voice to know she was okay, and I got the feeling she needed to talk to me to keep calm. Still, one overheard word could set off the guy with the gun.

"Shh, Mom. Don't talk unless you need to. We don't want that guy to know you're there."

"Fehring's on her way," Greg told me. "But she said it can't be Eric van den Akker."

I turned to him in surprise. "Why not?"

"He's at the Long Beach police station right now being questioned."

"So who is this guy?" I looked at the phone in my hand as if his picture would magically show up.

"Fehring is also calling the sheriff's department," Greg added. "They service Lynwood and should get there faster."

I put my phone on speaker. "Mom, the police are on their way. Hold tight and don't leave that bathroom."

"I've turned off the light, but if he comes in here, I'm a sitting duck."

"You cannot outrun a bullet, Mom. Trust

me, I've tried."

"There's a small window I might be able to squeeze through, but it looks like it has bars across it."

"Don't squeeze through anything," I told her. "Help's on the way."

Greg slowed the van and pulled over to the curb. I wondered why until I saw we were across from Otra Vez.

The store was right on the street, flush with a uneven sidewalk. Two front windows were crammed with merchandise, blocking any view directly into the store. A sign in one of the windows announced parking behind the store.

"Uh-oh," I heard my mother say.

"What the matter?" I asked her.

"Sounds like they're having a big fight."

"Sit tight, Mom."

Greg pointed at the front door. "I'll bet whoever is in there entered from the back. This entrance doesn't look very used even though it's in front, and he wouldn't have wanted to be seen."

"I think you're right." I opened the van door.

"Where do you think you're going?" Greg asked.

"To get my mother."

"Odelia," he started, then stopped. After a

big sigh, he shut down the engine and opened his door. "We'll both go."

"You can't, honey. If the gunman sees you, you'll be a sitting duck." It was the same phrase my mother used — sitting duck. Two people I loved could be used for target practice by some thug. I wanted to scream. "And we don't even know if this is related to Tom's murder."

"Doesn't matter. My mother-in-law is in trouble. You'd do the same for my mother."

When I continued my protest, he fixed his eyes on me. "Try to stop me, Odelia."

Without another word, I got out of the van and crossed the street. In no time Greg had retrieved his wheelchair and caught up with me.

"They're arguing about a deal that didn't happen," Mom reported.

A deal. Maybe like Linda, Roberto was supposed to buy units and turn the drugs over to the gangs or whoever ordered them.

"Help's on the way, Mom."

I edged closer to the store. It stood alone in its own building located on a corner. The building next to it appeared to be an empty storefront. Between the two was a narrow alley. Greg might make it through, but it would be rough going. The only other way to reach the back would be to go all the way around the front of the building to the other side that bordered the side street and down that sidewalk. Traffic on the street was light, since there appeared to be more empty stores than open ones in the neighborhood. Overhead the afternoon sky grew dark with the incoming storm.

"I'll go through here to the back," I told Greg. "Why don't you watch the front door and flag down the police?"

He nodded. "Sounds good, but I wish we had weapons of some sort."

I looked around on the ground and spotted some loose bricks. I picked one up and handed it to Greg. "Here, take this. I'll take one too. It's better than nothing."

"Not much," he groused. "Maybe we should buy a gun when this is all over."

I shot Greg a nasty look that conveyed my feelings on the subject loud and clear.

Clutching my phone in one hand and the heavy brick in the other, I scooted down the narrow alley and poked out the other end. Behind the store was a wider service alley and parking for about a half dozen cars. There were two cars parked there already. I also saw two back doors into the store. One was glass and had an Open sign on it, and a roll-up door similar to the one at the back of Buck's store but smaller. I looked for the small window Mom had mentioned but didn't see it.

"Mom," I whispered into the phone, "you still there?"

"Yes," came a whisper back.

"Where's that window you talked about? I'm in back of the store and can't see it."

"I think it's on the side. It looks out on another building."

That meant it had to be on the alley side, not the side facing the small side street. I had passed right by it. Turning back to the alley, I scanned the wall. Sure enough, not far from the back corner there was a small window, and across it was a metal grid. The room on the other side was dark, and the narrow space and gloomy sky allowed little light into the alley. The window wasn't too high, and it looked wide enough for a person to squeeze through, providing that person wasn't too bulky. Mom could certainly fit, but could she reach it? And even if she could, she was in her eighties. Would she be able to contort herself through it? I pulled on the security bars and found them to be rusty and loose. If I weren't afraid of making too much noise, I'd try yanking them off.

"Mom, I'm under the window now," I said into the phone.

In answer, Mom quietly scooted the sliding window aside and presented her face in the window. I reached through the bars and touched her face through the screen.

"Thank goodness, Odelia," she said through the open window in a voice barely above a whisper. "Where are the police?"

"They're coming, Mom." I ended my phone connection and called Greg.

"Found Mom," I told him in a whisper. "I think I can get her out the side window."

"Be careful."

After pocketing my cell phone and putting down the brick, my fingers got to work on the loose screws holding the metal grid in place. "If enough of these screws are loose," I said to Mom, "I might be able to work the grid off without too much noise." One corner screw started coming undone, but it was taking forever and destroying my manicure. "Can you remove the screen from the inside?"

Mom tugged on the screen, and it popped out without too much effort.

"Right about now I'd trade my car for a screwdriver," I said under my breath.

A moment later, a thin hand poked through the bars. Clasped between two fingers was a small Swiss Army knife. "Will this help?" Mom asked.

I took the knife. "Did you find this?"

"No, I always carry it," she whispered. "Clark's dad insisted we all have one. Can't tell you how often it's come in handy."

Using the screwdriver attachment, I worked the second lower screw. It turned without much trouble. Reaching up, I started on the higher screws. They were tougher and the angle awkward, but the screws were moving.

From the open window I heard muffled shouting and what sounded like a struggle. I had to get my mother out of there *now.*

"Mom, is there something for you to step on to get to the window?"

"Yes, it's directly over the commode. If I put the seat down, I might be able to get a leg through it. I just wish I hadn't worn a dress today."

Geez, it was bad enough my aged mother was going to squeeze herself through a window, but now she was going to try it in a dress? My mind was about to explode with worry, but I shoved it aside and got down to business.

"Instead of going leg-first," I told her in a hurried voice, "come though it arms- and head-first."

"And land on my head on the pavement? Really, Odelia."

"Mom, don't worry. I'll have a hold on you and help you through. If you fall, you'll fall on me. I have enough padding to break the impact."

After a few seconds of consideration, Mom said, "Guess I'll have to go head-first after all. I can't seem to get a leg up that high without going off-balance, not even with my dress hiked up. It's a bitch getting old. Time was I could lift my legs high with no problem."

I didn't even want to think about what Mom looked like from behind at this moment. "Come on, Mom, hurry — before he realizes someone is in the bathroom."

The voices from inside the store rose and ebbed in argument as Mom readied to shimmy out of the window. She handed her purse out to me. I took it and placed it on the ground. Next came her arms and her head. When they appeared, I grasped her shoulders and eased her out inch by careful inch like I was easing a baby pushed from a womb.

"Wait a minute," she said, "my jacket's caught." I stopped pulling. She reached a hand back in and freed up her jacket, then we started again.

Mom was halfway out. I had my arms wound tightly around the top of her torso.

She had her arms wrapped around my neck and her face was cupped between my shoulder and ear. I could hear her holding back groans and grunts as I pulled. Working together, we eased her out as quickly and carefully as possible. As her body inched out, I supported it with mine, like we were lovers dancing cheek to cheek to a slow, sultry tune but only with the top half of our bodies. The last thing we needed was for her to fall and break brittle bones.

Her hips had just passed the window ledge when I heard a sound that nearly sent urine down my leg. It was a gunshot — loud and clear — that halted the argument inside the store.

"That was a gunshot, Mom. We gotta move."

"Let me get both my feet on top of the tank. Then I think I can just pop out." She stopped moving to adjust her feet. "Oh!" She slid back a few inches.

"What's the matter, Mom?"

"My foot slipped. Let me try again."

I waited until Mom gave me the signal she was ready. "Okay, here goes. One. Two." Before I could get to three, the sound of another shot filled the air. I leaned back and pulled Mom the rest of the way out in one big yank, using my own body as a ledge for her body's support. She cried out. As soon as she was free, I fell backward and would have landed on my back if the alley had not been so narrow. Instead, I landed hard against the brick wall of the vacant store. My legs wanted to buckle but I held on, clutching my mother to me like a new babe, using the wall as support for the two of us.

"Are you hurt?" I asked her.

"My legs scraped on the windowsill on that last pull, but other than that I'm okay." She tried to stand on her own but was wobbly. I looked down and saw the scrape on one leg was oozing blood.

"We have to get out of here." I put an arm around her waist and her arm around my shoulder and started for the street at the far end of the alley, toward the safety of our van. It was slow going.

"Halt," said a man's voice behind us.

We froze where we stood. As a single unit, Mom and I pivoted slowly around to face a man holding a gun.

It was Detective Leon Whitman. I breathed deeply and relaxed, thankful to see him.

"It's us, Detective, Odelia Grey and Grace Littlejohn. We're so glad to see you."

"I didn't hear any sirens," Mom noted.

"We don't use them when we're trying to

sneak up on the bad guys." He smiled but continued to hold his gun. "What were you two doing?"

"Mom was in the store," I explained, "and when the gunman came in, she hid in the bathroom."

"Did you see anything, Mrs. Littlejohn?"

"Not a thing," Mom answered in a halting voice.

"You sure? It could be helpful," Whitman prodded.

"She saw a man in a blue hoodie," I answered. "He was holding a gun on Roberto Vasquez and arguing with him."

"Don't worry, ladies," Whitman told us. "The guy with the hoodie is dead. He shot Vasquez just as I got here. I took down the gunman."

"Is Mr. Vasquez dead too?" I asked.

"I'm afraid so."

Something was bothering me, a harsh itching in the back of my brain like poison ivy, but I couldn't put my finger on it. Mom's foot was tapping on mine, which wasn't helping my concentration. Thinking she was wobbling again, I tightened my grip to support her better. "My mother has been through a lot, Detective. I need to get her where she can sit down."

"Of course." Whitman backed out of the

alley. "My car's back here. She can sit there until we sort this all out."

Mom's foot continued to step on mine, but now with more urgency. She wasn't wobbling, she was trying to tell me something, just as my brain was also trying to send me a message. Something wasn't right.

"Where's your husband, Odelia?" Whitman asked. "Did he come with you?"

I'm not sure why, but my gut told me to lie. "No, he didn't." Had Whitman not seen Greg in the front when he first arrived?

Mom continued to tap-dance on my foot as my brain multitasked, thinking about the puzzle pieces that weren't fitting while I worried about getting Mom to safety and comfortable. Mom was slightly taller than me and leaned her head down as if she was fading fast into a collapse.

"He was in the store," she whispered in a voice barely louder than breathing. "I heard him."

Then I knew what she was trying to say with her foot. She might have seen a hooded gunman, but she'd heard Whitman's voice. I quickly wound my memory back a few minutes, trying to isolate the voices arguing in the background while I'd been pulling Mom from the window. Then it hit me: the cops weren't here yet or Greg would have found me or at least called. And the gunshots were too far apart to have been a quick exchange.

Greg had to have heard the shots. I didn't know where he was but prayed he wouldn't wheel into the alley and get mixed up in this mess. What I hoped is that he was on his phone to Fehring, demanding to know where the cops were and letting her know things had taken a turn for the worse.

"I really need to get some medical help for my mother," I told Whitman. "She's got a bad scrape on her leg." On cue, Mom's injured leg started to buckle and she let out a little cry of pain.

"I'm a diabetic," she said to Whitman. "It's important that I get bad injuries like this attended to immediately."

As far as I knew, Mom wasn't a diabetic, but I played along. "Let me take her to urgent care. As soon as she's patched up, we'll come back and answer all the questions the police want."

"That won't be necessary." Whitman waved the gun back toward the parking lot. "I have a first-aid kit in my car. We can have her fixed up in a jiffy."

"I don't know," I said, looking down at Mom's leg. "She's probably going to need a tetanus shot." I got a good grip on Mom and started for the street again.

"You're not going anywhere, ladies."

Ignoring him, I kept us moving. Cradled next to me, Mom was shaking but moving forward like a good soldier. The building wasn't deep. If Whitman wasn't the gunman, he'd let us continue; if he was the killer, our lives could be measured in seconds.

"Stop or I'll shoot." It was Whitman, letting me know for sure he wasn't wearing a white hat.

Mom and I turned slowly around but didn't move toward him. I wanted to tell him the police were on their way but was afraid it might expedite his plans for us. I only hoped Mom kept mum about it.

Again, he waved the gun toward the back. "Come on, you two. I haven't got all day."

"What are you going to do with us?" Mom asked.

"You're my insurance. If I have you and run into trouble, you could be useful. Or I could just shoot you and leave you here. I haven't made up my mind yet."

"You're the reason Ina and Linda McIntyre won't talk, aren't you?" I said. "They both know you were involved with the drugs and are afraid. It's kind of tough to get help when the police are the bad guys."

"Ina's a good girl and smart. When she saw me handling the investigation, she knew to keep her mouth shut or other people close to her might die." As he said the words, he raised his gun at us. "She seems particularly fond of that husband of yours."

I wanted to vomit. *Please, Greg, do not come around that corner.*

"It was you who went to Busy Boxes this morning and scraped off the mark on the unit up for auction, wasn't it?"

"You know entirely too much, Odelia, but not everything. The kid in the hoodie you saw is the same one dead on the floor in there." He waved his gun at the building. "Young van den Akker."

"So it was Paul who was working for you, not Eric. Was it Paul who bombed Buck's store?"

In answer, Whitman smiled the slick smile of a snake. "Fehring told me not to underestimate you, but I didn't believe her. Seems I should have."

My eyes popped open. "Andrea Fehring is involved in this?"

"Of course not." Whitman laughed. "Fehring's totally by the book — one of those career cops who bleeds public service and believes in fighting evil for low wages. She told me you were smart and could be useful to our investigation if you didn't get in the way. I simply thought you were a harmless busybody." He laughed again. "Busybody you are; harmless — not so much."

I wanted to know more, and I wanted to stall him until the police arrived. "So you killed Tom Bruce and Redmond Stokes." It was a statement, not a question.

"Tom got greedy," Whitman explained. "He wasn't happy with his part. He had big plans — plans me and my partners had no interest in. We had to send a message in case others also had grand ideas of moving up. As for Linda, she's an old mule who follows orders. If she had any ideas of going big-time like Tom, his death put her back in harness. She's smart enough to understand she's better off in jail than crossing us. Ina understands that, too."

"And did Red have big plans?"

"No. Red was one of the good guys, just like Ina's pal Buck. Once he learned what was going on and how his company was being used to facilitate things, he went to the police." He grinned. "As it so happens, because of the location of Elite, he called the Long Beach PD, and I took his call."

"Poor guy," Mom piped up. "He stumbled right into the snake's nest, and you killed him."

"I didn't kill Redmond Stokes. We contracted that job out."

Feeling Mom's strength fading, I tightened my grip on her. "Red didn't know you were involved, but he'd figured out Kim was up to something."

"Kim's an ambitious girl. Convincing Red to sell her half of Acme only made it easier. He totally trusted her until it was too late. Kim's doing damage control right now with Fehring. Hopefully that innocent, boyish face of hers will convince them Red was the drug contact."

"What about Tiffany?" Mom asked. "Did Kim play her for a fool?"

"Tiffany's an innocent — a cute, young innocent who thinks she's a tough girl. She was also insurance to use against Buck in case the bomb didn't send a big enough message. She might still be useful."

The filthy smirk on Whitman's face made me want to spit nails. I was so glad Tiffany was safe and out of their clutches. Whitman obviously did not know that yet.

The more he told us, the more I knew he wasn't going to let Mom and me go. Knowledge is usually power; in this case, it was a death sentence. Where were the damn police Fehring sent?

Whitman continued to stand near the

back end of the narrow alley and motioned for us to move forward. Urging Mom along, we took a tenuous step in his direction. He must still be thinking about using us as hostages or he would have shot and left us in the alley by now. I had no doubt ultimately killing us was still on his mind, but stalling that action could buy us precious time.

"Come on, Mom," I said, tightening my grip on her waist. "Let's do as he says."

Mom nodded, keeping quiet and letting me handle the situation. Together we took a few more steps. Whitman backed up a little more as we got closer. Beside me Mom was stiff, catching her breath with each step. I looked down and saw that her leg was looking nasty.

We were near the window again, getting close to the end of the alley. Whitman took another step back, keeping close watch in case of any Hail Mary–play on our part. He cleared the shadowy alley, standing halfway in the gloomy daylight. Overhead, the clouds thickened and a light rain started. Ignoring the weather, Whitman waited for us to finish our slow walk.

And then he was on his back.

It happened so fast, I stood rooted to the ground, clutching my mother. Whitman moaned and stirred but did not get up.

"Get his gun, Odelia. Quick!" yelled a familiar voice — a voice that meant love and security. It shook me out of my stupor. I let go of Mom. She crumpled to the ground with a short cry as I ran to Whitman. The gun had fallen from his hand. He rolled to his side and tried to reach for it. I kicked the gun out of his reach. It skittered several yards across the blacktop with a raspy metal sound. Whitman's temple had a bloody gash. When he tried to get up, I kicked his head as I had the gun. He fell onto his back and didn't move.

I looked up from Whitman to Greg. He was near the end of the alley up close to the building, using it as cover as best he could. "You were right, Odelia," he said, wheeling close. "That brick was better than nothing. And it's a good thing I have an accurate free-throw arm."

I threw my arms around my husband and kissed him hard on the mouth, then dashed to Mom and got her to her feet. We'd moved forward just a few steps when we heard sirens. The cavalry had finally arrived.

TWENTY-SIX

It looked like the off-and-on drizzle had finally moved on, leaving us with the first full sunny California weekend since Thanksgiving. A week had passed since the event at Otra Vez, and Greg and I had decided it was time to formally say goodbye to our beloved Seamus.

At first we were going to privately put him to rest, but with the events of the past few weeks and our thankfulness that we were all okay, we decided to make a party out of it. Greg fired up the grill and was cooking up steaks, chicken, and salmon. Mom and I had whipped up salads, veggies, and other side dishes. Cruz and her husband had arrived with her award-winning homemade tamales. Seth and Zee were back in town, and Zee contributed some of her best desserts.

We'd even invited Heide and Buck, but understandably Heide van den Akker wasn't in much of a partying mood. Criminal or not, Paul was her son, and he was dead. He had been recruited by Kim Pawlak while working with Buck. When Paul tried to convince Buck it was a good setup, Buck fired him. That's when Paul took his revenge — not only on Buck's store with his ugly reviews as Bob Y but on the resale business as a whole. When he wasn't working the truck with his mother and brother, Paul was working for Whitman and his associates doing odd jobs and spying.

The good news was that Roberto Vasquez hadn't been killed, only seriously wounded by Paul. He'd recently been released from the hospital and was quickly mending. He hadn't been involved with the drugs but had been approached. As payback for turning down the scheme, Whitman had nailed his nephew Guillermo for being an illegal. He and Paul were at Otra Vez that Friday to use freeing the cousin as leverage to pull Roberto into the drug trafficking. That was the deal Mom had overheard them arguing about — Roberto's nephew in return for helping with the drugs. When the arguing escalated, Roberto pulled a gun he kept behind the counter, but Paul shot first. Thinking the storeowner was dead, Whitman had killed Paul, planning to pass it off as a shooting in the line of duty, but in reality getting rid of a liability and giving him a fall guy. Had Mom and I not been there, he might have gotten away with it. Steele is currently calling in some favors with an immigration attorney he knows to see if he can get Guillermo freed.

I carried a salad bowl to our kitchen table, which had been set up as an extra buffet. As I set it down, I heard Tiffany laughing. It was light and carefree, as a nineteen-year-old's laugh should be. I looked out the patio door to see her with her head close to Ina's, sharing something fun. Muffin was curled up in Ina's lap. In light of everything, the judge had decided not to charge Ina with a felony but released her with only a five-hundred-dollar fine. Both young women seemed to be weathering the horrible situation with the resiliency of youth. Buck hadn't come, choosing instead to stay with Heide and give her comfort.

Sally Kipman and Jill Bernelli stood with their arms wrapped lovingly around each other, talking with my in-laws. Sally looked up, caught my eye, and winked. They were doing a great job of mentoring Tiffany, and I knew they would remain close to the girl. Tiffany had moved from Kim's and was staying with Ina for the time being.

With Whitman behind bars, Ina's tongue had loosened and she told the police how Whitman had come to the store and threatened them when Tom started talking about wanting a bigger piece of the action. Tom, not ever having been that smart, had gotten blustery back at Whitman. It was then Ina decided to leave Tom once and for all and get out of town. The money she'd taken from their accounts had been stashed in a motel room she'd rented near the airport and where she intended to hide out until her plane for France left. She'd gone to Elite the day of the auction to say goodbye to Buck and to let him know that Leon Whitman was calling the shots on the smuggling scheme. Buck only knew about Kim's part, just as Ina did not realize Kim was involved. Whitman had planted the idea with Ina and Tom that Red was the connection at Acme. Had Buck and Ina been able to connect their individual information, they would have sorted it out on their own, but that would have only put them in more danger.

Kim Pawlak, Leon Whitman, and Linda McIntyre remain in jail. Kim and Whitman are charged with murdering Tom Bruce and Redmond Stokes, and Whitman also with the murder of Paul van den Akker. Linda has been charged as an accessory and for drug smuggling. According to Detective Fehring, the police would be unraveling the drug trafficking scheme, including rounding up all the players, for a long time.

"Sis, you okay?" It was Clark. He'd returned to town just the day before. I wrapped my arms around him and gave him a hug. He returned it and held tight.

"Yeah, I'm fine, just happy everything turned out okay."

"If I'd known what you and Mom were into, I'd have sent a battalion in."

"To help us?"

"Hell no. To kidnap you until it was over." He hugged me tighter. "But except for the memorial to your cat, Mom's blog was all hearts and flowers and sightseeing. Not a peep about trouble after the post about finding Tom's body. I should have realized all that fun stuff was a sign of trouble brewing behind the scenes."

I glanced out the patio door again to see Mom sitting like a reigning queen, Bill Baxter by her side. We'd been wrong about Bill. He was just a lonely old man with too much time on his hands. Mom was holding court, telling everyone how she freed herself by jumping out a window. To hear her talk, it was two stories up and shots were being fired at her at the time.

"Mom says she's moving here," Clark said. "That true?"

"Yes, I think so." I looked up at my older half brother. "You'd think with everything that has happened, she'd run back to New Hampshire as fast as her spindly legs could carry her, but no."

Clark laughed. "Not now. Not when she's gotten a taste of excitement and bonded with her favorite daughter."

"I'm her *only* daughter."

"Ah, yes, but still her favorite." He turned serious. "I'm really happy you and Mom seem to have settled your differences. She can be a real pain in the ass, but she loves you and would die for you."

"I know." I glanced out the door again. "Really. I know that now."

"And how about that Bill guy? You think he'll end up being our stepfather?"

I shook my head and grinned. "No. Something tells me Mom will tire of him quickly. He's too needy for her. She's already told me she wants to keep her options open."

Clark laughed. "Jesus, but she's a pistol."

The front door opened, and Wainwright charged for it. I handed my brother a bottle of wine and asked him to go around and replenish people's glasses while I greeted the new guest. This time it was Dev Frye.

414

He was alone. I gave him a warm hug. "I'm so glad you're here. On the phone you sounded doubtful. Where's Beverly?"

"Odelia, Bev and I broke up." He said it with the same bluntness reserved for interrogations. I know because he's had to interrogate me on more than one occasion. "Our trouble started around Halloween and finally collapsed just before Thanksgiving."

I took a step back and studied his face. He looked tired, like he needed a two-day nap. "I'm so very sorry, Dev. What happened? I thought you two were happy."

He shook his head like a dejected old bull. "Bev didn't want me to return to the job after my heart attack. She hated my being a cop. That was the beginning. Then she got a great job offer in Seattle and asked me to retire and go with her. For the past few weeks I've actually been weighing that option."

"That's why you haven't been yourself lately." I took his beefy hands between mine. "So you decided to stay, and that ended it?"

"Yep." His head bobbed in confirmation. "I didn't want to leave my daughter and her family. I didn't want to start over and make new friends. And I love being a cop. It's who I am. It's all I know." He squeezed my hands. "I owe both you and Greg an apology for that night. I was really out of line with that BS about Willie."

"Not at all, Dev." I gave him another quick hug. "I'm so sorry about Bev but so glad you're staying."

"I have to stay. I have to keep you and Greg in line. Andrea can't do it all by herself."

I laughed and started directing Dev through the house to the back. "Speaking of Andrea" — I pointed to where the detective stood — "She's right there, talking with Clark. Go be amongst your own kind."

Dev's eyes moved from Andrea to my mother. "I hear Grace is staying on in Cali."

"You heard right."

"Good thing, then, that I'm staying put. Now there's three of you snoops to keep track of." He bent, kissed my cheek, and took off in the direction of Andrea and Clark.

It was almost time to eat when Zee came into the kitchen. She gave me a long, warm hug. Gawd, how I miss her when she and Seth travel.

She ended the hug and said in a soft voice, "Greg says it's time, Odelia."

I nodded, picked up a plain box from the edge of the kitchen counter, and followed Zee outside.

Greg handed the grill tongs off to Seth and joined me in front of the bougainvillea. He put his hand on the small of my back. From it I absorbed warmth and strength. Everyone stood. Greg called Wainwright to his side. Ina brought Muffin over and put her in Greg's lap.

"We have a lot to celebrate today," Greg began, "and are so happy you, our family and our friends, both new and old, are here with us today. Ina is free." He nodded to his cousin. "Grace is coming to live here." We both smiled at Mom. She was standing in front of the crowd, staring at the box and dabbing at tears with one of her linen hankies. Clark was beside her, one of his strong arms tucking her close.

"We are also gathered here today," Greg continued, "to say goodbye to Seamus, a beloved and faithful companion. I remember when Odelia and I first started dating. Wainwright wanted to be friends with Seamus, and the cranky old cat wanted none of it. You've never seen such fussing, hissing, and scratching. And that was from Odelia."

Everyone laughed, even those who were crying. I whacked my husband's shoulder with my elbow and everyone laughed again.

"But in time," he continued, "we became

a family. Seamus and Wainwright became good friends and even welcomed Muffin when she came on board. Odelia and I have been blessed with loving families, loyal friends, and the best four-legged companions anyone could hope for. But today we lay one of our fur kids to rest, thankful that for a while he was a wonderful part of our lives." Finished, Greg turned to me.

I had something prepared to say about how Seamus came to live with me all those years ago, but I couldn't make it through the words. I clutched the box to my breast and felt hot tears run down my face. Greg's wonderful words would have to serve as Seamus's only eulogy.

I opened the box, knelt in front of the bougainvillea, and scattered the cat's ashes around the base of the plant he had loved so much.

I swallowed and sniffed. From over my shoulder a white cloth appeared. It was one of Mom's linen handkerchiefs, one of the ones we had bought her. She had stepped forward and was offering it to me — an olive branch of peace and shared grief. I took it and wiped my eyes and stared at the base of the bush where soon the gray ashes would mingle with the ground moisture to be absorbed into the earth. Ashes to ashes, dust to dust. But nothing would ever dilute my memory of the cat who came to me dyed green and in need of help and stayed to steal my heart.

I touched the damp ground under the bush. "Goodbye, dear friend. Thank you."

ABOUT THE AUTHOR

Like the character Odelia Grey, **Sue Ann Jaffarian** is a middle-aged, plus-size paralegal. In addition to the Odelia Grey mystery series, she is the author of the paranormal Ghost of Granny Apples mystery series and the Madison Rose Vampire mystery series. Sue Ann is also nationally sought after as a motivational and humorous speaker. She lives and works in Los Angeles, California.

Other titles in the Odelia Grey series include *Too Big to Miss* (2006), *The Curse of the Holy Pail* (2007), *Thugs and Kisses* (2008), *Booby Trap* (2009), *Corpse on the Cob* (2010), *Twice As Dead* (2011), and *Hide & Snoop* (2012).

Visit Sue Ann on the Internet at
WWW.SUEANNJAFFARIAN.COM
and
WWW.SUEANNJAFFARIAN.BLOGSPOT.COM

The employees of Thorndike Press hope you have enjoyed this Large Print book. All our Thorndike, Wheeler, and Kennebec Large Print titles are designed for easy reading, and all our books are made to last. Other Thorndike Press Large Print books are available at your library, through selected bookstores, or directly from us.

For information about titles, please call:
  (800) 223-1244

or visit our Web site at:
  http://gale.cengage.com/thorndike

To share your comments, please write:
  Publisher
  Thorndike Press
  10 Water St., Suite 310
  Waterville, ME 04901